"STUNNING ...

Updike is clearly having a wonderful time with this romance."

—USA Today

"Thrilling ... BRAZIL is a richly patterned metaphysical cliffhanger. It's also a dark, disquieting meditation on what it is to be male and female, black and white, rich and poor, at one with the world and at odds with every man."

—The New Criterion

"Mythic ... [A] depiction of a dauntless love that transcends mere passion."

—The Washington Post Book World

Also by John Updike
Published by Fawcett Books:

THE POORHOUSE FAIR
RABBIT, RUN
PIGEON FEATHERS
THE CENTAUR
OF THE FARM
COUPLES
RABBIT REDUX
A MONTH OF SUNDAYS
PICKED-UP PIECES
MARRY ME
THE COUP
TOO FAR TO GO
PROBLEMS
RABBIT IS RICH
BECH IS BACK
THE WITCHES OF EASTWICK
ROGER'S VERSION
TRUST ME
S.
SELF-CONSCIOUSNESS
RABBIT AT REST
MEMORIES OF THE FORD ADMINISTRATION

BRAZIL

John Updike

FAWCETT CREST • NEW YORK

A Fawcett Crest Book
Published by Ballantine Books
Copyright © 1994 by John Updike

All rights reserved under International and Pan-American Copyright Conventions. Published in the United States of America by Ballantine Books, a division of Random House, Inc., New York, and simultaneously in Canada by Random House of Canada Limited, Toronto.

Library of Congress Catalog Card Number: 93-28632

ISBN 0-449-22313-2

This edition published by arrangement with Alfred A. Knopf, Inc.

Manufactured in the United States of America

First International Ballantine Books Edition: October 1994
First Domestic Edition: February 1995

10 9 8 7 6 5 4 3 2 1

Thou know'st 'tis common; all that live must die,
Passing through nature to eternity.
                                        —THE QUEEN, in *Hamlet*

Welcome, Brazilian brother—thy ample place is ready;
A loving hand—a smile from the north—a sunny instant
        hail!
                                        —WALT WHITMAN, "A Christmas Greeting"

i. *The Beach*

BLACK is a shade of brown. So is white, if you look. On Copacabana, the most democratic, crowded, and dangerous of Rio de Janeiro's beaches, all colors merge into one joyous, sun-stunned flesh-color, coating the sand with a second, living skin.

One day not long after Christmas Day years ago, when the military was in power in far-off Brasília, the beach felt blinding, what with the noon glare, the teeming bodies, and the salt that Tristão brought back in his eyes from the breakers beyond the sandbar. So strongly did the December sun strike down that small circular rainbows had kept appearing in the spray of the breakers, out there beyond the bar, all about the boy's sparkling head, like spirits. Nevertheless, returning to the threadbare T-shirt that served him also for a towel, he spotted the pale girl in a pale two-piece bathing suit, standing erect back where the crowd thinned. Beyond her were the open spaces for volleyball and the sidewalk of the Avenida Atlântica, with its undulating tessellated stripes.

She was with another girl, shorter and darker, who was anointing her back with lotion; the cool touches made the first, pale girl arch her spine inward, thrusting her breasts one direction and in the other the sleek semi-circles of her already greased hips. It was not so much the pallor of her skin that had drawn Tristão's stinging eyes. Very white foreign women, Canadians and Danes, came to this celebrated beach, and German and Polish Brazilians from São Paulo and the South. It was not her whiteness but the challenging effect of her little suit's blending with her skin in an impression of total public nudity.

Not total: she wore a black straw hat, with a flat crown, rolled-up brim, and glossy dark ribbon. The sort of hat, Tristão thought, an upper-class girl from Leblon would wear to the funeral of her father.

"An angel or a whore?" he inquired of his half-brother Euclides.

Euclides was shortsighted and where he could not see he hid his confusion behind philosophical questions. "Why cannot a girl be both?" he asked.

"This dolly, I think she was made for me," said Tristão, impulsively, out of those inner depths where his fate was being fashioned in sudden clumsy strokes that carried away, all at once, whole pieces of his life. He believed in spirits, and in fate. He was nineteen, and not an *abandonado*, for he had a mother, but his mother was a whore, and even worse than a whore, for she drunkenly slept with men without money, and bred tadpole children like a human swamp of forgetfulness and casual desire. He and Euclides had been born a year apart; neither knew any more about their fathers than the disparate genetic evidence on their faces. They had spent enough time in school to learn to read street signs and advertisements and no more; they worked as a team, stealing and robbing when their hunger became great, and were as afraid of the gangs that wished to absorb them as of the military police. These gangs were children, as merciless and innocent as packs of wolves. Rio in those years had less traffic and violence and poverty and crime than now, but to those alive then it seemed noisy and violent and poor and criminal enough. For some time Tristão had been feeling he had outgrown crime and must seek a way into the upper world from which advertisements and television and airplanes come. This distant pale girl, the spirits now assured him, was the appointed way.

His wet and sandy T-shirt in his hand, he picked his way through the other near-naked bodies toward hers, which she held more stiffly, in the knowledge that she was being hunted. His T-shirt, a sun-faded orange, said LONE STAR, advertising a restaurant in Leblon for gringos. Within his black swimming trunks, so tight they showed the compacted bulk of his genitals, he carried, in the little pocket for change or a key, a single-edged razor blade called Gem, sheathed in a scrap of thick leather he had carefully slit. His blue rubber sandals from Taiwan he had tucked beneath a clump of beach-pea at the edge of the sidewalk.

And, he thought, he had yet another possession: a

ring yanked from the finger of an elderly tourist gringa, a ring brassy in color, with the letters DAR on a small oval seal, letters that seemed endlessly curious to him because they meant "to give." Now he thought to give this ring to the pale beauty, who proudly radiated fear and defiance from her skin as he drew near. Though she seemed tall from afar, Tristão was a hand's breadth taller. A smell from her skin—sun lotion or a secretion sprung by her surprise and fear—brought back to him an odor from the swamp of his mother, a soft mild medicinal smell dating from a time when he had been sick with fever or worms, before drink had so thoroughly rotted her system, so that she still functioned, in the windowless dark of their *favela* shanty, as a source of mercy, a coherent pressure of concern. She must have begged the medicine from the mission doctor at the base of the hill, where the rich people's homes began on the other side of the trolley tracks. His mother would then have been nearly a girl herself, almost as firm in body as this one, though without such slender bones, and he, he would have been a miniature of himself, his feet and hands fat on their backs like small loaves of bread rising, and eyes bursting like black bubbles from his skull, but it was beyond memory, the moment that had planted this delicate mild smell, which felt stretched within him like a sleepy cry; he was awakening, here in this sunny salt atmosphere, windward from the fair dolly's body.

Against some resistance of his sea-wrinkled wet skin, he pulled the ring from his little finger, where it fit tightly. The old gringa, with curly blue hair, had worn it where a wedding band would go, on the opposing hand. He had caught her beneath a broken streetlight in Cinelândia while her husband was engrossed in the advertisements for a nightclub show around the corner, photographs of mulatta showgirls. When he held his razor blade against her cheek she went limp as a whore herself, the old blue-haired gringa, a few years from the grave yet terrified of a scratch on her wrinkled face. While Euclides slit the straps on her purse Tristão pulled off her brassy ring, their hands entwined for a moment like those of lovers. Now he held out the ring to the strange girl. Her face in the shade of the black hat had a monkeyish look, an outward curve of the face over the strong teeth that seemed a smile even when her lips were, as now, unsmiling. Her lips were full, the upper especially.

"May I make you this trivial present, *senhorita*?"

"Why would you do that, *senhor*?" This courtliness of address, too, felt like a smile, though the moment was tense and her squat companion looked alarmed, putting a hand across her breasts in their bathing-suit bra as if they were treasures that might be stolen. But they were brown bags of fat, of no value above the common value, not worth the smallest deviation of Tristão's steady gaze.

"Because you are beautiful and, what is rarer, not ashamed of your beauty."

"It is not the modern style, to be ashamed."

"Yet many of your sex still are. Like your friend

5

here, who covers her heavy jugs." The lesser girl's eyes flashed, but, with a glance toward Euclides, her indignation collapsed, and she giggled. Tristão felt a slight squirm of disgust at the complicitous, surrendering sound. The female need to surrender always troubled his warrior spirit. Euclides moved a half-step closer on the sand, accepting the space surrendered. He had a frowning broad face, relentless and puzzled and clay-colored. His father must have been part Indian, whereas Tristão's had boasted pure African blood, as pure as blood can be in Brazil.

The shining white girl kept her chin high, stating to Tristão, "It is dangerous to be beautiful—that is how women have learned shame."

"You are in no danger from me, I swear. I will do you no harm." The pledge sounded solemn, the boy's voice experimentally dipping into a manly timbre. Now she studied his face: the full Negro features were carved on a frame that had never known gluttony, with a childish shine to the prominent eyes, a rampartlike erectness to the bony brow, and a coppery tinge to his crown of tightly kinked hair, the merest dusting, that yet made some filaments burn red in the sun's white fire. There was a fanaticism in the face, and distance, but toward her no harm, as he said.

Lightly she reached out to touch the ring. "To give," she read, and playfully stiffened her pale hand so he could place it on a finger. The third finger, where the gringa had worn it, was too slender; only the biggest, the central finger, offered the necessary resistance. She held it out in the sun, so its oval face flashed, toward her companion. "You like it, Eudóxia?"

Eudóxia was horrified by the contact. "Give it back, Isabel! These are bad boys, street boys. No doubt it was stolen."

Euclides squinted at Eudóxia, as if straining to see her bunched, voluble features and her middling color, which was close to his own, a terra-cotta, and said, "The world itself is stolen goods. All property is theft, and those who have stolen most of it make the laws for the rest of us."

"These are good boys," Isabel reassured her companion. "How can it harm us if we let them lie with us while we sun and talk? We are bored with ourselves, you and I. We have nothing they can steal, but our towels and our clothes. They can tell us of their lives. Or they can tell us lies—it will be equally amusing."

As it evolved, Tristão and Euclides told almost nothing of their lives, of which they were ashamed: a mother who was not a mother, a home that was not a home. They had no lives, just a constant scurry and hustle, propelled by their empty stomachs. Instead, the girls, talking as if only to each other, displayed their luxurious, lightweight lives as if revealing silken underwear. They described the nuns at the school they attended together—those who were so like men as to have mustaches, those who were thought to be lesbians enjoying a mock marriage, those who were "cocks" and those who were "chickens," those who sought to seduce their pupils, those who were love-slaves to priests, those who paid the gardeners to fuck them, those who covered the walls of their cells with pictures of the Pope and masturbated with his sour-mouthed, worried image in their eyes. It was all as in a book, a book of sex, verbal embroidery wrought with the nimble fingers of girls in a sewing circle, their giggling glinting through their embroidery like a silver thread. Tristão and Euclides, who lived in a world where sex was a common staple, like red beans or *farinha*, worth no more than a few tattered cruzeiros tossed on a wine-stained wooden table, and who had lost their virginities when not yet in their teens, were thick-tongued but enchanted as the girls spun their fantastic suppositions, amusing each other to the point of tears.

In evoking the cloistered school they had mentioned an illegal radio one of the nuns had confiscated, and this gave Tristão the opportunity to interpose his knowledge of samba and choro, forró and bossa nova, and the stars—Caetano, Gil, and Chico—each form of music generated; the entire electronic heaven above them, wherein singers and soap-opera actors, soccer stars and the superrich floated like spangled angels, descended and became a common ground. Sparks of love and hate, emphatic adolescent opinions, flew rapidly among the four of them, equal in their infinite distance from this world, as they were equal in having bodies—four limbs, two eyes, one continuous skin. Like pious peasants of the Old World, they believed that this heaven, which sent them its news on invisible waves, directed its smiling, soulful face toward them personally, just as the impalpable dome of blue sky above is centered precisely upon each upward gazer.

The heat of the beach baked them from beneath; a potent lassitude slowly extinguished their conversation. When Euclides and Eudóxia, rising in hesitant unison, went down to the water to swim, a taut silence reigned between the other two. Isabel reached toward his palm, the color of silver polish, with the hand that glinted with the stolen oval ring. "Would you like to come with me?"

"Yes, always," Tristão said.

"Then do."

"Now?"

"Now is the time," she said, her blue-gray eyes gazing into his, her plump upper lip puckered in solemn thought, "for us."

ii. *The Apartment*

ISABEL carried a gauzy beach dress, the orange-yellow of a *maracujá*, but chose to leave the beach not wearing it, slipping on only sandals of thin white leather to walk along the famous sidewalk of sinuous black-and-white stripes beside the Avenida Atlântica. She cradled her dress and her towel crumpled in her crooked left arm, so that at least one passerby glanced down expecting to see a brightly swaddled baby. Her dark straw hat, dyed as if with the juice of *genipapo* berries, floated ahead of Tristão like a flying saucer, the trailing ends of its black ribbon fluttering. She moved more swiftly, with a more athletic gait, than he had expected, causing him to stumble and skip-step at her side, catching up. His own sense of decorum had led him to slip on the sandy shirt saying LONE STAR; his tattered blue rubber sandals, retrieved from the struggling little bush, flopped loosely.

The pale girl, appearing all the taller for the length of bare legs, strode as if with a sleepwalker's blind determination, or as if one hesitation might undo her resolve;

she walked south, toward the fort, and then turned right on a street that led over to Ipanema—Avenida Rainha Elisabete or Rua Joaquim Nabuco, he was too distracted and fearful to notice. There, in the shadows of the buildings and trees, among the shops and restaurants and the glass-and-aluminum fronts of banks, with doormen and security guards standing erect in uniform, her near-nudity glowed eerily, and drew more glances. Tristão drew protectively closer, although her betranced imperviousness, which had turned her hand icy to his touch, made him feel clumsy and extraneous. In this world of apartment houses and guarded streets she was his leader; she turned at a numbered maroon canopy into a dark foyer, where a Japanese behind a tall desk of black marble veined with green blinked to show surprise but gave her a small key and buzzed a button that caused an inner glass door to slide open. Passing through this doorway, Tristão felt himself X-rayed, the razor blade in his narrow damp black trunks tingling, and also his penis, its shrunken curve like that of a cashew.

The elevator, faced with doors of a silvery metal patterned like cloth in triangles, slid upward: a knife slithering from its sheath. There was a brief corridor, its striped walls a subdued version of the fruity golden color of her crumpled beach dress. A door of red brazilwood, waxed to a shine, of many raised panels yielded to her little key, no bigger than his razor blade. Inside, there reigned a silence of expensive surfaces—vases and carpets and fringed pillows and the gilded leather backs of books. He had never been in such a space; he felt his breath and freedom of movement taken from him. "Whose home is this?"

"My uncle Donaciano's," the girl said. "Don't worry, you won't have to meet him. He works all day, in the Centro. Or else he plays golf and has drinks with his business friends. Drinking with his friends is in fact his work. I will tell the servant to bring us something to drink, too. Or perhaps you would like something to eat."

"Oh, no, *senhorita*; I am not hungry. A glass of water or a little *suco* is all I need." His mouth had gone very dry, as he looked around. So much here to steal! He and Euclides could live for a month on one silver cigarette box, on two crystal candlesticks. The paintings, of squares and circles and furious slashes, could not be worth much, except perhaps to the painter at the moment of painting, but the backs of the books held letters of gold. He marvelled at the height of the bookshelves, which ascended to the height of a palm tree. This room of the apartment had inner balconies on two walls and for a ceiling a domed rose of frosted glass petals, from whose center hung, on a chain as long as that of a holy light in a church, a chandelier with arms like brass S's. Indoors, to Tristão, meant the sunless cave of a shanty; here there was so much light he felt he was outdoors, only sheltered, so no wind blew, in a radiant stillness of which he was now part.

Isabel called in a flat voice, "Maria."

The thickset, youngish maid who came, in no great

hurry, as if from many rooms away, glanced at Tristão contemptuously, and with a little flare of terror in her sunken eyes. Her cheeks were puffy, with an Indian puffiness, or as if she had been beaten, and bore pockmarks. Her mix of blood had turned her skin a sullen snuff color. She would have read his thieving thoughts, and thought herself above them. As if living in the homes of the rich, and parading in the clean clothes they have provided, was not in itself a form of thievery.

"Maria," said Isabel, in a voice trying to be neither harsh nor timid, "two *vitaminas*, with banana or avocado if there is some. That will do me, but something for my friend, some of whatever you have made for your own lunch? This is my friend Tristão." To him she said, "A sandwich?"

"It is not at all necessary, I swear," the boy protested, with that gallantry presaged by the rampartlike quality of his brow, the prominent bright eyes, the distances behind his face.

Yet when the food came—warmed-up *acarajé*, with its fried balls of *vatapá*, shrimp, and peppers—he ate like a wolf. He had trained his hunger to lie low, but food maddened it, and he left nothing on his plate, not even a smear. She slid toward him on the low marquetry table her own half-eaten plate. He devoured this, too.

"Coffee?" Maria asked, when she came and cleared. She gave off less hatred, and a faint scent of conspiracy, like the *dendê* oil with which all cooking from the north is flavored. Perhaps this curious household, of a

13

girl and her uncle, already contained something amiss, of which the maid disapproved. She was open, as the lowly are, to mischief and change; the world does not exist for them like a precious relic under glass, to be preserved forever.

"Yes, and then leave us alone," Isabel said. She had removed her little hat, and her long blond glimmering hair heightened her nakedness and gave him back that feeling of blindness when he had just emerged dazzled from the sea.

"You like me?" she asked, averting her eyes and blushing.

"Yes. More than that."

"You think I am a flirt? A bad girl?"

"I think you are rich," he replied, looking around, "and being rich makes people strange. Rich people do what they want, and so they do not know the price of things."

"But I am *not* rich," Isabel said, with a new note of grievance and petulance. "My uncle is rich, and my father, too, off in Brasília, but I have nothing of my own—they hold me like a pampered slave, to be given when the nuns have graduated me to some boy who will grow into a man like them, sleek and polite and uncaring."

"Where is your mother? What does she say of your future?"

"My mother is dead. The baby brother she was making for me strangled on the cord on the way out and tore up her uterus in his dying fury. Or so I was told. I was four when it happened."

"How sad, Isabel." Though he had heard Eudóxia use her name in their chatter, he had not pronounced it before. "You have no mother, and I have no father."

"Where is your father?"

Tristão shrugged. "Dead, perhaps. Vanished, certainly. My mother has had many men and is not certain who he was. I am nineteen, it would be twenty years ago. She drinks much *cachaça* and cares about nothing." Still, once she had got him the medicine he needed. She had suckled him, and picked lice from his head, and inspected his turds for worms.

To call him back to her, Isabel announced, "I am eighteen, still."

He smiled and dared reach out and touch her luminous hair, full of many little lights like Rio at night seen from Sugar Loaf. "I am glad. I would not want you to be older as well as richer."

She accepted his touch without flinching but did not answer his smile with another. "This ring you gave me." She held up her hand with the brass oval upon the thickest finger. "I must give you something now."

"It is not necessary."

"The gift I have in mind would also be a gift to myself. It is time. It is the time in my life."

She stood and pushed upward at his lips with her own, less a kiss than an imitation of kisses seen in magazines or television. Her life up to now had been a matter of studying other people's stories; now she was creating her own story. She led him to a spiral staircase, of metal painted a dusty pink, that led to the second floor. Her body as it twistingly ascended above him was broken into many foreshortened slices, triangles of flesh flickering half-eclipsed among the triangles of the spiral stairs. Trailing a finger experimentally along the railing, as if across a surface of water, Isabel moved down the corridor suspended here at the height of the snaky-armed chandelier, and thence to a room that was hers, still full of girlhood's stuffed animals, with posters on the wall of long-haired singers from England. The pressure on Tristão's lungs here seemed less thunderous, as if between these childish walls the wind of money did not blow so fiercely. The little pale pieces of Isabel's bathing suit came off with a shrug and a squirm, a casual accustomed dance of her slender body, done with a half-defiant, half-questioning smirk on her brave monkey face. She appeared little more naked now than before. He had never before seen a pubic bush like hers, so transparent and uncurly. Her nipples, in disks of skin faint brown in color, were stiffened by their exposure to the air and to his seeing. "We must get clean," she told him, firmly.

The shower knobs within the marble cubicle were numerous, and produced various kinds of sprays—a bouquet of fine needles, or a battering of coarser strings of water in the rhythm of a rapid pulse. Standing with her in the warming waterfall, soaping her skin so its yielding silk was overlaid with a white grease, and then letting her soap him in turn, he felt his cashew become a banana, and then a rippled yam, bursting with weight. She soaped him there seriously, bending her oval head into the pounding water to see better the swollen veins, the purple-black skin, the violet heart-shaped one-eyed glans. As she inspected, the partings of her hair showed her scalp to be pink—not white, as he had expected. When the shower was over, she said, still looking, her fingers tracing one vein, "So that's what it is. I like it. It is ugly but innocent, like a toad."

"Never before?" he asked, embarrassed, grateful to be momentarily concealed in the powdery blanket of a vast white towel that she produced from a bathroom closet. In the mirrors everywhere in this room he saw himself cut into slices of white and black. His face seemed a stern warrior's, photographed simultaneously from many angles.

"No, never. Does that frighten you, Tristão?"

Yes, it did, for if she was a virgin, fucking her became religious, a kind of eternal incrimination. But his blood, helplessly pounding in the yam he carried before him, wrapped in his robelike towel, drew him after this apparition, who wore her own towel high, like a cape, exposing her lower portion, her tight seesawing buttocks. As she bent over at the bathroom's marble threshold to pick up his little black bathing suit for him, where he had dropped it, her white buttocks parted, showing a vertical brown lining between them, a permanent stain of skin around her anus, slightly disgusting him.

Then, as she shook and folded his bathing trunks, to

17

hang them neatly up, she exclaimed in surprise. The razor blade in its little pocket had slipped from its crude sheath and nicked her thumb. She showed him the white skin with its whorl of texture, the sluggish leak of jewel-bright red. This, too, frightened him, as a prophecy: he would bring her pain.

Yet, sucking her thumb with a hurt expression, blotting its wound on a corner of her vast towel, she continued her drift toward her girlhood bed, a narrow bed covered in a light quilt whose delicate shade of green Tristão had seen in the *favela* on china pitchers and chamber pots, a line of delicate scum below the rim. Above the brass rails of the headboard hung a little oily picture of the Virgin, wearing a halo like a sunhat tipped back, an unnaturally solemn and big baby in her lap, making an awkward gesture with its fat fingers. Isabel, her monkey face grave and determined, lifted the image off the wall and placed it under the bed. As she lay down naked on top of the quilt, some glass-eyed animals were displaced; she stuffed them into one of several shelves beside the bed, each shelf once painted a different color of the rainbow, to amuse a child. She did these things quickly, expertly, and flopped herself back strictly in the middle of her little bed, leaving nowhere for him to lie but on top of her. Yet when he obediently did she pressed his chest with her fingertips as if to hold him off, to stay this moment. Her eyes, their grayblue composed of hundreds of fragile threads, stared up into his almost with anger. "I had not thought it would be so big," she admitted.

"We need do nothing now. We can simply hold one another, and stroke one another, and tell of our histories. We can meet again tomorrow."

"No. If we wait, it will not happen. This is our time."

"We can meet again tomorrow, at the beach."

"We will lose courage. Other people will interfere."

Uncertainly, studying his face for direction, she spread her white legs.

She asked, "You have had many girls?"

He nodded, ashamed that not all had been girls, that in the beginning there had been women twice his age, old drunken women, friends of his mother's, throwing him this scrap of themselves like food to an amusing little pig.

"Then have you any advice for me?"

His glans, like a violet heart ripped from a creature the size of a rabbit, rested on the transparently furred curve of her mons veneris. Usually, the woman he was with took it in her hand and guided it in. This girl lifted her buttocks awkwardly, and looked into his eyes for guidance. She saw his dark irises melting into the black of his dilated pupils. He dipped his voice into the manly timbre again, saying, "My advice is to let yourself sink to the point where my pleasure and yours are the same. It will not be easy, the first time. It will hurt." His breath smelled of spicy *acarajé*.

With his own hand he explored below, found the place where her lips had begun stickily to part, and did the guiding. A little later, as if doubting his own advice, he asked, "Does it hurt?"

19

Isabel had stiffened beneath him in the effort of over-riding her flesh's instinctive rejection. A sudden warm sweat had arisen all across her pale skin. Her chin jerked back and forth as if no other part of her impaled body dared move. He, too, was sweating, with worry, at her virginal tightness; it was a burden, being a lover and not a pet pig gobbling a wet scrap. Yet beyond the dark wall they were facing was a paradise, he knew.

"Shall I stop? I could come out."

Furiously her chin now snapped back and forth, say-ing no. "For God's sake, *do* it," she said nevertheless.

He drove hard into the darkness, each thrust deepen-ing the shade of red behind his clamped eyelids. Within himself, in a place beyond the seat of hunger, a con-stricted passageway was trying to accommodate a rush of light, a choking, chilling, building pressure that made his heels dance as its verge was approached and, through an upward loop of world-blotting sensation, vaulted over. The convulsions of his coming startled her out of her own body; tenderly, wonderingly, her white hands flitted on his arched black back, seeking to heal the great rending he had enjoyed in her gummy depths, in the web of her silken limbs. His panting ebbed; his voice became reasonable, considerate: "Did it hurt?"

"Yes. Oh God yes. Just like the nuns said it would, for the sin of Eve." Yet her legs, her arms, tightened their embrace of him, as his chivalrous impulse to re-lieve her body of his weight communicated itself.

"Dear Isabel," he sighed, embarrassed for better words, and still feeling shy with her name. One task heroically performed did not entitle him to equality with this patrician beauty. When he at last was permitted to remove his penis, it was coated with her blood, and she seemed to blame him for staining the scum-green satin quilt.

"Maria will see and tell my uncle!" she exclaimed.

"She is his spy?"

"They are—friends."

She had leaped up and brought from the bathroom a wet washcloth, with which she dabbed and scrubbed at the stain. It was an irregular stain, shaped, by his offer to stop, like a chalice, with a bowl, a base, and a thin red stem between.

"You should have spread a towel," he said, vexed at her appearing to blame him for her own blood, and to be rushing from their exalted moment together into details of mere housekeeping.

She heard his offended note, and sought to mend his pride, turning from the bed and docilely pawing with the reddened washrag at what was now returning to its cashew shape. As it retracted, her virginal blood sank brownish into the wrinkled, eggplant-colored skin. Feeling the pain between her legs increase as the high drama of herself supine in defloration wore off, she impatiently pushed the wet wad into his hand.

"Here, Tristão; it's your mess too."

Though imbued with the fastidious pride of even the poorest of Brazilian men, Tristão accepted the washcloth and comprehended her mood; she was giddy with the daring of what had been done, what could never be undone. Their uncontrollable moods are the price men pay for women's unearthly beauty and their habitual pain.

When Tristão returned from the bathroom, wearing his damp bathing trunks, Isabel was still naked, but for the DAR ring and on her blond head a straw hat, like the black straw hat she had worn to the beach, but dyed strawberry red. The rainbow shelves along two of the four walls of her little room held a number of playful hats, along with the wealth of toys provided by an uncle who wanted to keep her forever a little girl.

She cocked her head and posed like a *boîte* dancer, white buttocks outthrust and one knee bent above an arched foot up on its toes; her toes were whitened by the pressure of the pose and a drying streak of blood showed on the inside of that leg's thigh. It was wonderful, she was thinking, to have a man see you naked, to need to have no shame in front of him. "You still like me?" she asked, with a mournful seriousness, her upcast eyes just showing beneath the impudent hat's rim.

"I have no choice," he told her. "You are mine now."

iii. *Uncle Donaciano*

"**N**o, I don't think so, my dear," said her uncle Donaciano, his supple portliness sheathed in a gray suit that at certain angles of light flashed like aluminum, "I don't think this is within the bounds, within the bounds at all, even of our permissive age, in this all-too-progressive society."

A month had passed. Maria had told her employer of the boy's visit that day, and of Isabel's constant absences at the beach—absences so long that since she returned without sunburn she and the boy must be going to the cinema together, or resorting to a by-the-hour hotel. Certainly she was not going off to be with Eudóxia; Eudóxia's parents had taken the girl, with her three brothers, from Rio to the mountains, to escape the summer heat—to Petrópolis, where the court of Dom Pedro II had erected a palace, now the Museu Imperial, and horses and carriages were still used, along the canals and curving hillside streets of mansions, and then for some weeks to Nova Friburgo, where a colony of immigrant Swiss had once built homesick chalets. Rock climbing, tennis, boating, horse-riding, flowers in perpetual bloom: Isabel when younger had often experienced these pleasures with her uncle and his wife, elegantly slender Aunt Luna, before their unfortunate separation—their *desquite*, since divorce was illegal. Aunt Luna came from the thin upper crust of Salvador and now lived in Paris, from which she sent Isabel a Hermès scarf or Chanel belt each Christmas. She was the closest approximation to a mother the girl had ever known. In Petrópolis, on rare occasions, Isabel's father would steal a weekend from his official duties and fly from Brasília. How exciting that had been, to sit beside him in the grand hotel restaurant, dressed like a real woman, preening and prim, the starched ruffle of her décolletage gently scratching her bare skin while a thin waterfall glittered between the distant green cones of two mountains in the view through the big window that gave on the blue lake where waterskiers left swerving trails of paler blue! But those pleasures had belonged to childhood, as small as the smiles in a snapshot.

"What bounds are there, in Brazil?" she asked her uncle. "I thought this was a country where each man made himself, regardless of color."

"I do not speak of color. I am color-blind, like our constitution, in tune with the national temperament we inherited from the grand-spirited sugar planters. This is not South Africa, thank God, or the United States. But a man cannot make himself out of thin air, he must have materials."

"Which are in the hands of very few, where they

have always been," said Isabel, drawing with impatient vigor on one of her uncle's tinted English cigarettes.

Uncle Donaciano rooted his ebony-and-ivory cigarette holder—empty, since he was trying to stop smoking, and used the holder to pacify his habit—deeper in the side of his mouth, giving his lips a sage and sinister twist. His lips were thin but ruddy, as if freshly scrubbed. "The hands of the many would tear everything up," he explained. "Even so, the Rio of my youth has been turned into one big slum. So beautiful it was, so amusing—the tram along the Botanical Garden, the cable car to Santa Teresa, the Casino where Bing Crosby would come and sing. So quaint and charming, like an exotic piece of Venetian glass, unique. Now, in the shell of its beauty, it has gone rotten. There is no air, there is no silence. All the time, traffic noise and music, the music of the brainless samba; everywhere, the stink of human secretions. Everywhere, *bodum*."

"We do not stink, you and I? We secrete nothing?" Puffs of smoke kept coming from Isabel's mouth with the syllables, like puffs of anger.

Donaciano appraised her, trying to muster uncle-love back into his sneering features. He removed the empty cigarette holder from his lips. His long smooth brow—tanned a constant butternut-brown under a carefully controlled regimen of sunbathing—furrowed as if mechanically crimped as he leaned, with new urgency and frankness, toward her. "You have used the boy. I would not have advised it, but yes, you are right, some of one's life cannot be lived by the advice of elders. Some steps must be taken defiantly, against the grain. There is no growth without a bursting, without pain; primitive peoples in their wisdom place pain at the center of initiation. All right, my dear, you have been initiated. You went to the beach and picked up a tool with which to mutilate yourself. You have become, with this living tool you used, a woman. You have done it out of my sight, and this was considerate, and proper. But a lasting attachment will take place *in* my sight, in the sight of society, in the sight of your distinguished father. Even, if you believe anything of what the nuns have told you, in the sight of your dear mother, our lovely lost Cordélia, gazing with tears down from Heaven."

Isabel shifted on the sumptuous crimson sofa—its ribbed velvet whispering against the underside of her thighs—and stubbed out her cigarette; she did not want her mother spying on her. She did not want another woman inside her life. Her mother had died attempting to give birth to a brother: Isabel had never forgiven her for this double betrayal, though she often compared photographs of her mother—misted and dulled, all of them, by the fact of her death—with her own face in the mirror. Her mother had been darker than she, more typically Brazilian in her beauty. Isabel's blondness had come from her father's side, the Lemes.

"So," Uncle Donaciano was concluding. "You will no longer see this *moleque*. After Carnaval, you will begin your studies at the university, our illustrious Pontifícia Universidade Católica do Rio de Janeiro. While in attendance there, I expect, you will entertain fashionably leftist fantasies and engage in anti-government protests, demanding land reform and the cessation of atrocities against the Amazonian Indians; while engaging in such quixotic agitation, you may fall in love with a fellow protestor who will become, upon graduation, despite his youthful scruples, a member of the professional class and perhaps even a member of the government, which by then, perhaps, the military will have freed to resume its civilian guise. Or—don't interrupt yet, dearest; I know how distrustfully your generation views suitable marriages, though, believe me, suitability remains when attraction fades—you may choose to become yourself a lawyer, a doctor, a Petrobras executive. Such opportunities now exist, for women, in Brazil, though very grudgingly. Women must still do battle against our worthy forefathers' conception of women as ornaments and breeders. Nevertheless, if you are willing to forgo motherhood and the traditional amenities of homemaking, you may enter upon the power game. Ah, believe me, my darling niece, it is a boring game, once the rules are learned, and the first few tricks are played."

He sighed; as was the way with Uncle Donaciano, boredom was draining the energy from his words; after fifteen minutes, everything bored him. That is how we shall brush him aside, Isabel said to herself. The young are not so easily bored.

But he had become animated again, by a new thought. "Or—here is an idea that makes me envious, frankly—why not go abroad? Why, after all, on this dwindling globe, must we confine ourselves to Brazil, with its atrocious history, its sordid stupid masses, its eternal underdevelopment, its samba on the edge of chaos? We are not Brazilians only—we are citizens of the planet! Go to Paris, and live under your Aunt Luna's wing! Or, if that savors too much of clinging to the nest, take a year in London, or Rome, or even dowdy old Lisbon, where they speak Portuguese so rapidly you cannot comprehend what they say! In San Francisco, I read in the newspapers, something called flower power has come to bloom, and Los Angeles is the capital of something called the Pacific Basin!" He leaned closer toward her, cocking his long thin eyebrow, blonder than his butternut brow, in a fashion that had signalled dozens of women before her that a fascinating proposition was being eased forward. "Isabel, let me speak naughtily, in my own avuncular voice, knowing my staid brother would not approve, would certainly *dis*approve: if you are determined to be unconventional, become an adventuress—an actress, a singer, a phantom within that electronic world which more and more supplants the dull world of heavy elements and three dimensions! Leave us behind! Travel to the stars! A dizzying wealth of possibility remains, if you give up this, this—"

"Tristão," Isabel interrupted, rather than hear his epithet. "My *man*. I would rather give up my life."

Uncle Donaciano made a curious red mouth, quick and small, and noticed that his tall glass, which had been full of a drink as silvery as his suit, was empty.

"This is gutter talk, my dear. Vulgar romanticism of the sleaziest kind, which is all that the poor have to make life tolerable. But *you*, and *we*, are privileged to be rational beings. On our ability to reason, after these dismal centuries of Iberian fantasy and mongrel greed, rests the hope of Brazil."

Gaily Isabel laughed, knowing the pattern of her uncle's days—the post-dawn promenade along Ipanema and Leblon beaches; the mid-morning call to his broker, a clever *mulatto claro* who had gone to the London School of Economics and who did all the necessary financial thinking; the mid-day lunch and siesta with one of his mistresses at one of their embowered suburban homes; and then the late afternoons on the terrace at the Jockey Club, filling himself up with gin as the sky beyond Corcovado filled up with sunset pink. Gaily she kissed his butternut-brown forehead and sauntered from the living room and up the spiral stair, believing (falsely) that her uncle had simply been going through the obligatory but empty verbal motions, to placate the family ghosts.

Since beginning to sleep with one of the poor, she felt more at ease with Maria—less afraid of her bitter Indian blood and taciturnity. "My uncle," she sneered in the kitchen. "He forgets I am no longer a child in the care of the nuns."

"He loves you very much and wishes only what is best for you."

"Why do you tell him everything? I can no longer bring Tristão to my room, you are such a traitor to us."

"I will not deceive your uncle. He is very good to me."

"Ha!" Isabel mocked, while helping herself to a plate of *caruru* with which Maria had intended to feed herself. "He pays you a dog's wage, and fucks you and beats you. I know he beats you, because I hear the noises from your room, though you never cry out."

The other woman, her broad cheekbones tidily nicked by two pairs of small diagonal scars, gave Isabel a conspiratorial glance. Her eyes were glittering slits deep-set in her puffy, reddish-brown flesh. "Your uncle is a kind man," she said. "If he ever strikes me, it is because he is angry with himself. It is because he is furious with the stresses of being a rich man in a poor country. He is frustrated, because this country does not offer enough scope for a refined man like himself. It is being taken over by roughnecks from the *sertão*. I understand that it is not me he is striking. His blows are soft, like that of a kitten batting a paper ball."

"And his fucking? Is that soft too?"

Maria made no answer; in Indian silence she reached down another plain plate from the cupboard, and divided the *caruru*, hot with grated *malagueta* peppers mixed with okra paste and *dendê* oil, topped by fried pieces of *garoupa*, into two portions, as if to say that they were equals, now that Isabel wanted to talk about fucking.

"Your uncle is a kind man," she repeated. "But you

must not push him too hard. You must go to university, and go with nice boys. Tristão is not for you. He is the sort of boy I could have had, when I was younger. A handsome street boy. He is pretty, like a bird from the jungle, but he will not make a meal. He is all beak and claws and showy feathers."

Isabel flicked back her hair so it did not trail into the forkful of okra paste she was bringing to her mouth and then, when she had swallowed, held her face with her chin thrust out in a brave, experimental way. She knew that defiance became her, accenting the pert thrust of her face. "We sought each other out," she said, "on the beach, among multitudes. We will never let each other go. What can my uncle do about it? Nothing. I am eighteen. These are not the old days when young virgins could be penned up in the big house in their *alcovas*, smothered in lace and black taffeta, peering fearfully out through lattice windows, waiting to be bred like pigeons."

Maria said, "He can have you taken to Brasília, to live with your father. No one escapes from Brasília; it is surrounded by wilderness, I have heard, and has a giant moat."

Isabel hopped from the kitchen stool as if the seat were hot; she moved rapidly about the kitchen as if every surface were hot, to be touched only for an instant. "Did he say that? Is that what he told you, Maria? To Brasília to live with my father? *Tell* me!" Any threat of going to Brasília terrified a true Carioca.

Within Maria's silence a stubborn battle of loyalties

31

was being waged: to her employer and lover on the one hand, and on the other to this young sister in suffering, captive to the power of love, the slavery that sex brings to women, though Isabel innocently proclaimed herself free. "I know nothing for certain, little mistress," Maria said at last. "But he and his brother converse on the telephone. I think, if you do not give up this boy, do not expect to spend Carnaval this year in Rio."

iv. *The Shanty*

THE INTERIOR of the shanty Tristão's mother occupied was here and there pierced by bright shards
of light leaked between sheets of zinc overhead and the
pieces of painted wood and printed cardboard that composed the walls. The blue brightness thus admitted in
these sharp splinters penetrated but a little way into the
dense atmosphere, an air thick not only with the smoke
of tobacco and cooking fires but with the dust of the
earth floor and of the friable materials, constantly renewed by layers of theft and appropriation, that held off
the weather—the baking sun, the pounding rain, the
ocean wind on moonless nights. The shack was bathed
in nature, for it perched on one of the highest and steep-
est slopes of the Morro do Babilônia, and when its inhabitants groped out past the curtain of rotting rags that
hung in the place of a door, a cruelly splendiferous view
of the sun-hammered sea, with its sailboats and islands,
opened before their wincing eyes.

Isabel, who had arrived in darkness and not yet dared
thrust her head into the sunlight, was struck by the flu-

idity of this hazy space, in which she still did not know how many people, besides herself and Tristão and Tristão's mother, were present. The rooms were somehow several, at different levels; she had already visited one that served as bathroom, its floor a yielding piece of plywood above a dazzling slide of naked orange earth where excrement and urine flowed down out of sight, into another squatter's terrain. Tristão's mother's voice, slurred and heavy, emanated from no distinct spot, but from a corner, the darkest and most weathertight, where the floor became uneven, showing pale profiles of swells and depressions such as dawn light etches on a far mountain range.

His mother's name, Isabel had learned, was Ursula. Ursula Raposo. The woman had been awakened, last night, by their breathless entry. It had been a long scramble up the slope of the Morro do Babilônia. After the moon-blanched zigzags of the mountain streets, the inside of the shack was as dark as a bottle of ink. A match had flared, come close enough to Isabel's face to singe her long eyelashes, and been blown out, in a gust of breath sweetly rank with the fumes of sugar-cane liquor.

"This white girl somebody's," the voice attached to the match and the foul breath had said. "How come you steal her?"

"Not steal, Mother. Rescue. Her uncle was about to send her to her father. She doesn't want to go. She wants to be with me. We love each other. Her name is

Isabel." All this Tristão whispered, urgently, inches from Isabel's ear.

The darkness grunted, and then suddenly rustled, making a breeze of motion. From a flat soggy sound close by her head Isabel gathered that Tristão had been struck by a fist. "You bring me money?"

"A little, Mother. Enough for a week's *cachaça*."

There was a smaller, papery rustling, and the sour-sweet cloud of alcohol, with the body-warmth attached to it, moved away, and Isabel felt her lover's strong hand pull her lightly in a direction where she scarcely dared step, for the floor beneath her feet was uneven and littered, and the darkness still absolute. Things—scorpions, or the antennae of giant centipedes—brushed against her ankles, and once she rammed her elbow against a shaggy wood support that Tristão had slithered around, still keeping his grip on her hand. She felt in him the tension of embarrassment, having her present in his home.

"Here, Isabel," he said; his tense grip tugged her down, into a narrow space where the bare clay was overlaid with scratchy lumps, rough bags stuffed, from their faint fragrance, with what might have been dried flowers, or the skeletons of very small and delicate dead creatures. Stretching out her own delicate bones, thinking herself as safe from pursuit now as a body in its tomb, she whimpered in an approach to pleasure.

"Quiet," Ursula's voice instantly snarled, right against, it seemed, Isabel's ear, though they had groped a good distance away, through this breathing blackness burdened with other shapes and presences. Close by, soft snoring arose, or an overlay of several sets of rhythmic lungs, and Tristão's mother began to sing, incoherently, softly, incessantly, the song going up and down but refusing to come to an end. The sound was not disagreeable, and merged with the murmur beyond the shack's unseen walls, of conversations and foot traffic lower down in the *favela*, and the nocturnal rush of Rio automobiles still further down, and a tingle and throb of samba first from one direction in the city below and then from another, higher still on the mountain, as if even the angels were anticipating Carnaval.

Perilous and strange though her situation was, Isabel felt luxuriously sleepy, after the hectic escape from Ipanema and the run along Copacabana Beach and the long climb up the *morro*, where the *favela* hung like a frozen avalanche in moonlight. Tristão's body was hard and vigilant beside hers, and he had given her, to pillow her face in, a wadded rag musky with a smell of another's sweat; an intestinal space curved close about her, murmuring with this omnipresent drunken mother's blood and breath.

Her lover was tense and restless, and had placed between them, with several anxious adjustments, what they had lugged up the hill, the two duffel bags containing her clothes and the expensive treasures they had stolen from Uncle Donaciano's apartment—the silver cigarette box, the crystal candlesticks, a begemmed gold cross once stolen from an eighteenth-century church in Minas Gerais and sold to her uncle by an antique dealer, and a cube-shaped wad, secured with many rubber bands, of ten-thousand-cruzeiro notes which they had found tucked among his perfumed pastel underwear—underwear fit for a woman, Tristão had observed in astonishment. As he anxiously pressed the bags tighter between them, the sharp edges of their booty dug into Isabel's flesh; the jabs seemed to tell her that she had left coddled girlhood behind, she had embarked upon the path of woman, which is a path of pain. Tristão's mother's rambling drunken low-sung song told her the same thing. Nevertheless nothing kept her from sleeping, amid these warm entrails of squalor, while her husband (so he now seemed) turned tensely beside her, plotting their future in the inky blackness.

When she awoke, day declared itself in the blue knives of light suspended about her, each with its halo of smoke. Someone was cooking—a girl, twelve or thirteen, squatting to a fire over which was propped a round oil-drum lid, for a stovetop, near the ragged doorway for ventilation. Isabel recognized the smells as coffee and *angu*, corn cakes made mostly with water and salt. Other bodies were stirring; she recognized, from that day at the beach, the squat form of Euclides as it moved in the gray dawn light. He looked in her direction but did not seem to see her. Tristão showed her the room from which excrement slid down the hill. After his troubled night he seemed thinner, and older, like a piece of smoked meat, and the black of his skin duller. It saddened her to see that his acquisition of her had so soon proved a withering burden.

She now thought, in her innocence, that if she could form an alliance with his mother it would lessen his burden. Ursula was still in her bed; a little man lay beside her, on the wide and dirty, sweetly stinking straw-stuffed pallet, still unconscious, with his face pressed against her side like a dark leech. His matted hair had gray in it; his face was eclipsed by the great brown breast which sagged sideways in Ursula's torn cotton dress. Her skin was a sludgy bistre quite without Tristão's shimmer of African blue; the blue must come from his unknown father. The whites of Ursula's eyes had been yellowed and curdled by drink, and some of her teeth were missing. "White girl, what you want here?" she asked, seeing Isabel standing at her feet.

"Tristão brought me. My family wants to part us."

"Smart folks. You two pure crazy," Ursula said, yet not taking her curdled eyes from the face of the fair intruder, trying to fathom what advantage to herself might come of this visitation.

"We love one another," Isabel announced. "We want to live together forever."

Tristão's mother did not smile; her sullen features in fact sank a little deeper into anger. "Lucky if love lasts as long as a fuck," she said. "Trash of mine got no right to go loving any fucking body."

"He is beautiful," Isabel told the woman, of her own son. "I feel incomplete when I am not with him. I cannot eat, I cannot sleep. Last night, I slept like a baby." More than a baby, she thought to herself: like a fetus. "I love you, Ursula," she dared confide, "for bringing a boy—a man—so beautiful into this world." She was determined to lift that sludgy brown face up from hostile stupidity and to win its acknowledgment of the wonder of her and Tristão's love.

"Porra!" the woman obscenely exclaimed, yet grinning. As if to quench the grin, with its pathetic toothless gaps, her lips tugged at the unlabelled bottle lying in the confusion next to her pallet. When Ursula's eyelids closed, beauty swept back across her face, the beauty Tristão had, of an eclipsed sun. Though her body had become obese, a mere absorbent mass, her head was oval and petite, under a nest of unravelling corn rows. On her face an erratic pattern of scars—not symmetrical and meaningful, like Maria's—testified to old beatings and injuries.

Tristão, who had been hiding from this confrontation between Ursula and Isabel, in the section of the shanty beyond the rough wood pillar that held up the roof of overlapped zinc sheets and divided the space into a suggestion of rooms, now came forward. "We will not stay here, Mother. It is too disgusting."

Disturbed perhaps by the reverberating male voice, the sleeping small man rolled onto his back, displaying a saliva-webbed open mouth; Ursula with her free arm twisted his head back to her breast, where with a slurping noise he became still again. "Trash with high ideas the ones that disgust me. How much you think her rich folks pay to have her back?"

"Plenty, I am sure," said Euclides, who had been speaking with the girl tending the cooking fire. Of Isabel he asked, "Where is your friend Eudóxia? She and I had a good long talk walking the beach all the way to the Leme end and back, on Catholic communalism versus Marxism. Both, we concluded, were quixotic."

"Her family have taken her to the mountains," Isabel told him. "She is a typical bourgeois girl, full of bold chatter but with no courage for life."

Euclides squinted and said, "Too much courage becomes the love of death."

"We love one another," Tristão continued to his mother. "My plan is to take the train to São Paulo and find work in the auto plant, with the help of my brother Chiquinho there. Mother, I need to know his whereabouts."

This was the first that Isabel had heard of a third brother. The mother of them all looked blank, but then slit her eyes as if to declare cunning. "Another trash," she said. "Never sends a penny home, and a rich man by now, making those *fuscas* everybody drives. If the medicine man give me a decent potion, none of you trash be burdening Mother Earth."

The girl by the tin-can cookstove asked now, "Do we feed *her*? The batter only made eight cakes."

"Give her mine," Tristão said.

"No, you need your strength," Isabel said, though in fact she was faint with hunger. This lightness in the head, this incessant salivating—did the poor live with these sensations all the time? She counted the people in the shack, and there were six, including the man still asleep.

Tristão saw the darting of her eyes and read her thoughts. He explained, "There is also Granny."

Out of the tangle of mats and bags and shadows in the far section of the shack a sweetly smiling assemblage of dark rags and bones had lifted up; an elderly emaciated woman wearing a turquoise bandana wrapped as a turban shuffled forward, touching the patchwork walls for guidance. Her eyes had no irises; she was blind. Her skin was cracked like black earth after a long drought.

"Is this your mother?" Isabel asked Ursula. Though the other woman gave her no encouragement, Isabel felt impelled to draw close to her, as a potential instructress in this new art of womanhood.

"My mother, I had no fucking mother," came the answer in a mumbled monotone. "Old Granny say she the mother of my mother, back in Bahia, but who can prove? She stays here, she has nowhere else to go, everybody comes here, crowding in to be supported by my cunt. My poor cunt worn out by penniless trash like this." She angrily snapped her side, so the man clinging there was jarred loose, onto his back again. His eyes slightly opened, like the eyes of a lizard when it flicks its tongue. "Nothing in his pockets but his balls," Ursula told Isabel, and, as if sensing her need for instruction: "Always make 'em pay before you do a fucking thing, and up the ass is extra, because it hurts."

Granny made seven. There would still be one spare *angu* cake, Isabel was calculating. She and Tristão could split it. Her hunger was like a solid object viewed

41

through the transparent veil of the life around her. The very walls of the shack, with their fuzzy blue shards of daylight, felt transparent, as the sounds of the stirring *favela*, and the roar of Rio traffic far below, and the vertical pressure of the morning sun, intensified. In the corner out of which Granny in her *torço* had emerged, two other bodies, those of a stocky man and woman past first youth but not yet old, rose up and groped through the smoky doorway to the out-of-doors, each deftly lifting a cake from the stove as they went.

Isabel marvelled at how many people she had slept so soundly among. These poor, like animals, had developed a tactful politics of space. The whole shack, now that she could gauge its dimensions, was no bigger than her uncle's master bathroom, without its massive sunken tub, the lavender toilet with its padded seat, the matching bidet, the two basins side by side before a single huge mirror, the two cabinets (one for medicine and one for Aunt Luna's deserted cosmetics), the clothes hamper, the towel racks, the heated towel rack rounded at the top like a church window, the separate shower stall with frosted glass and a tiled floor you stepped down onto, the closet where Maria kept stacks of folded towels of all sizes—like fuzzy stairs, it had seemed to her as a little girl. When she grew up, she would climb those stairs and become a housewife like Aunt Luna, only with even more towels, and nappier ones, and a husband even handsomer than Uncle Donaciano.

v. *The Candlestick*

A FIGHT was brewing; Euclides, who had seemed such an amiable broad-faced pup on the beach, was insisting to his brother that their possession, in a sense, of this pale rich girl must somehow turn them a profit. Tristão had taken up the two duffel bags, both under one arm to leave his right hand free. His hand rested on the belt of his shorts, near where Isabel knew his razor blade lived. "She is mine," Tristão was saying. "I have promised her no harm would come to her. You heard me promise."

"I heard you, but I myself promised nothing. I merely watched you strut into folly. Luckily for us, she proved as great a fool as you. A note to her father will produce millions. Tens of millions."

"When I meet her father, it will be as two gentlemen, not as a thief and his victim, not as a beggar and a prince."

"Tristão, you always dreamed too much. You always believed in spirits, in fairy tales. You believe your life is a story, to be told in another world. You think there are recording angels up above dipping their pens in liquid gold. There is nothing, in truth, but dirt, and hunger, and finally death. At least share the contents of these bags with your family."

"They hold only my woman's clothes. Isabel is my family now. Our mother calls us trash and would have killed us in her womb had she had the science. You, I called you my brother, we were partners in crime, but now that I have a treasure, you wish to rob me."

"I wish you merely to share, you fatuous scrotum. Make your mother rich, so she can close up her cunt."

"Riches do not produce that result, you insignificant rat-turd. You squinting little slimy frog-pecker. Our mother is a whore. Whoring is all she knows, whoring is her happiness." Sensing that Euclides was enough enraged to attack, Tristão dared look toward his mother with only a split second's sideways glance, to see if he had insulted her.

"Kill him," she advised the air, in her floating, *pinga*-betranced, omnipresent voice. "Kill each other and erase a poor nigger woman's natural mistakes."

"Who are we?" the man attached to her side asked, awaking and staring at the ceiling through a thunderous headache. Perhaps he had meant to ask another question.

"I smell a stranger in this house," Granny announced, in an old-fashioned Portuguese redolent of colonial Bahia, with its courtesies and barbarities.

"Seven persons, six cakes left," the girl by the stove announced.

"Take mine," Ursula told Isabel. "My teeth are fit only to drink with."

"Oh!" Isabel exclaimed in surprise. Politeness urged that she refuse, but larger imperatives overruled. "How kind of you! I will not refuse. Thank you, Ursula, with all my heart." It took her a moment to eat the *angu* cake, hot from the old oil-drum lid. When had food ever tasted so good to her, so instant in its union with her essence, the burning within her nerves and veins? Gliding a few steps forward, she unzipped the lumpier duffel bag under Tristão's arm. "In exchange, and in acknowledgment of your hospitality, I have something to give you." She had quickly decided what she would give Ursula: one of the crystal candlesticks. This would leave the other in her possession, as a bond, a pledge. When she held out the intricately faceted object, a beam of sunshine from a gap in the wall set off a froth of rainbows, skimming about the room like iridescent dragonflies obedient to the twist of her wrist and the tremor of her fingers. "It came, I believe, from Sweden, a land of snow and ice. Please accept it, Mother, and allow me to give you that name, since though you were not mine you are mother to the person dearest on earth to me, and whose life has merged with my own."

The woman drunkenly sunk on her bed hesitated, her curdled eyes bothered by the precious object's brilliance. "Trash," she at last pronounced. "We sell it, the fuzz trace it, hoosegow for everybody. This girl try to kill her boy friend's mama."

"Take it to the store of Apollonio de Todi, in Ipanema," Isabel said. "He will give fair value, and hold it for redemption. Mention the name Leme."

"Granny, do you smell a trap?" Euclides asked the old blind seer. To the others he said, "In my opinion, my brother's pride and conceit are bringing complications upon those of us who wish only to live humbly, beneath the notice of the powerful, stealing and whoring no more than we must to stay alive."

Tristão produced, with a silent flicker, the razor blade and held it against his brother's broad and sallow cheek. "You deserve another face," he said, "for spitting on this lavish offering from my wife."

In Brazil, one says "wife" and "husband" not after some stilted legal ceremony but when one's heart feels married. That ceremonious feeling had come to Tristão and Isabel after one night spent together in the utter darkness of Ursula's shanty.

Euclides said carefully, holding his face motionless, "We are unaccustomed to such gifts. Beasts such as we are generally safe from the operations of bourgeois guilt. Marx says that sickly philanthropy is worse than blunt, healthy oppression, which at least alerts the working class to the war that exists. Forgive us, Isabel, if we are rude."

"Pretend that you have stolen the candlestick," Isabel told him lightly, "if that will ease your sense of honor." She realized that rivalry existed between the half-brothers, and jealousy in her behalf, in part because Eudóxia had eluded this nearsighted, philosophical child of poverty, and fraternal reciprocity had been broken. "Euclides, forgive me for taking Tristão from you."

On the beach, we seem each free, naked and idle and absolute, but in fact no one is free of the costume of circumstance; we are all twigs of one bush or another, and to gain a wife means to lose a brother. "Embrace," she told the brothers, and told her lover, "We must go." To Ursula she added, "Keep my gift, if you prefer, and light a candle against our return some dark night."

"Too damn much pussy in Brazil," Ursula mumbled, as if to explain their poverty, and their shameful willingness to accept this payment for hospitality.

No one obstructed the couple's leaving of the shack, though Granny, annoyed with being ignored, set up a small commotion of prophecy. "Bad luck, bad luck," Granny was shrieking. "I smell bad luck coming. It smells like flowers, it smells like the forest. The old forest, it is coming back, it will eat all the poor! Oxalá, have mercy!"

Outside, on a rough bench set up on the packed dirt, between milky trickles of sewage, the stocky couple was sunning. Tristão introduced them as his cousins, who in the glory days of Kubitschek had performed an onstage sex act in one of the *boîtes* of the Lapa district, close to the old aqueduct. Twice a night, and thrice on weekend nights, they achieved orgasm on a hotly lit stage, before a jeering, distracting audience. Suddenly, it seemed, they had become too old for this feat to be interesting to others, and now they waited here for their fortunes to turn. They had kindly, wrinkled, non-involved faces, like those of vegetable sellers in the market, expectant and amiable but not pressingly so. Isabel wondered, with an inner shudder, if she and Tristão might end like them, all that sexual bliss vanished like rainbows in the sea-spray. As, hand in hand, they descended the steep hillside, the sea was enormous before them—a breastplate of shining metal—and they could hear all around them, operating on stolen electricity, the sequestered seductive chatter of television sets.

vi. *São Paulo*

THEY TOOK THE TRAIN to São Paulo. It wound south-west along the Atlantic coast. The faded plush seats could be seen to be emitting dust when the tracks curved so that shafts of sunlight slanted in through the dirty windows. Isabel was wearing her little straw hat, the black one, and the DAR ring Tristão had given her. On the left of the train streamed red-tile-roofed small fishing villages, conical old sugar mills, nodding palm trees, sickle-shaped white beaches shining in the sun as they were whetted by the rhythmic abrasion of the glittering blue sea. On the right loomed green-crowned domes of rock, upright loaves of granite. Most of Brazil is a vast, gently mountainous tableland; the coastal mountains are the legs of the table. As the train, laboring to climb the Serra do Mar and patiently stopping at stations where no one got on or got off, carried Tristão and Isabel into their future, the lovers napped, their heads resting heavily as sacks of sugar on one another's shoulders and their hands numbly intertwined in each other's laps. Awake, they talked of themselves. There was still so much to learn, to know.

"I loved your mother," Isabel said, "though she did little to encourage me." Tristão admired the way, when Isabel delivered herself of a remark meant to prompt a response, her whole face showed tension, a kind of bright brimming, as of a plump dewdrop about to break and run. Her mouth in such moments slightly pursed, so a row of tiny wrinkles broke out along her upper lip, beneath the almost invisible fuzz.

"That was beautiful of you, but she deserves no respect from either of us. She is viler than an animal, for at least an animal has motherly instincts. Birds hatch and feed their young, but my mother has no more feeling for me than for a piece of her own shit."

"Didn't you think she liked me? Did you see her fight back tears when I gave her the candlestick?"

"I did not see that, but the light in the shack is poor."

"Who was the girl at the stove?"

"My sister, I think."

"You do not know?"

"She appeared, one day."

"Have you slept with her, ever?"

"I forget. Until I saw you on the beach, I felt nothing profound for any female."

"You lie, Tristão. I think you have slept with her. That is why she did not want me to have any food. When was your first girl?"

"She was a woman, a woman who seemed old to me, an associate of my mother's. She made me enter her, front and back. I was eleven. It was disgusting, horrifying. My mother watched."

"And then? Then there were others, less disgusting?"

He resisted more talk on this topic, but finally admitted, "The girls of the *favela* are easy to seduce. They know their lives will be short and so they are generous and reckless."

"Were there ever . . . any you especially loved?"

He thought of Esmeralda, her bushy hair, her thin dusky limbs, her streak of madness like that of a pet too stupid to be trained, and wished to hide her in the whorls of his memory, and felt guilty on this account. Isabel sensed this withholding, and was wounded by it, and as if in revenge confided to Tristão the daydreamings of her eighteen tender years about boys, sons of the friends of Uncle Donaciano and Aunt Luna, boys glimpsed across the dining room or swimming pool in the heat of January vacations in Petrópolis. He fell asleep when she was talking, his long-fingered brownbacked hands cupped in his lap, the palms the color of silver polish, with creases like engraved lines. Outside the windows, rolling miles were blanketed in the excessively bright green leaves of coffee trees.

As they arrived at the Estação da Luz in São Paulo, a heavy thunderstorm broke, sending sheets of water running down the streets and hiding the tops of the tallest buildings in cloud. People raced from doorway to doorway with wind-tossed newspapers over their heads, and huddled in the terminal archways, emitting a damp herd smell. The terminal was all of iron, sporting lacy balconies and many Victorian girders. Already, they sensed that São Paulo had no limits; it was not pinched between the sea and the mountains like Rio, it was part of the vast *planalto*, a port on its edge. Cattle and coffee from the hinterland had funnelled through this place and made it rich, heartless, and enormous.

When the rain cleared, and a weak yellow sunshine gilded the puddles and the still-running gutters, and the green telephone booths and the newspaper stands where *O Globo* and *Folha de S. Paulo* were clothespinned to lines like drying wash, they found a taxi and told the driver to take them to the only hotel of which Isabel knew, the Othon Palace, where ten years ago she had stayed for a weekend with her father. Her mother was already dead, and there had been a tall woman who had been too warm to Isabel. She had bought her candy and trinkets and given her hugs like an actress trying out for the rôle of a mother, but too glamorous and young for the part. Now, at the same hotel, Isabel proved too young for the part she wished to play, that of wife; the hotel clerk, a slender young man with big red ears and centrally parted hair slicked very close to his skull, glanced at her and then at Tristão, his thin blue cotton shirt—his best—and sun-faded shorts exposing his long black limbs, and told her they had no rooms. Isabel fought back the tears percolating in her eyes and asked where, then, could they go? The clerk seemed nice to her, though he was trying to master professional hauteur; he reminded her of some of her cousins. Sliding his milky blue eyes—with lashes almost white, like

52

those of a pig—this way and that to make certain he was unobserved, he wrote, on a piece of Othon Palace notepaper, *Hotel Amour*, followed by an address he softly explained how to reach: across the Viaduto do Chá to the Avenida Ipiranga, and bear right, and then take many intricate turns. Walk rapidly, he advised, and do not talk to strangers.

The hotel's name was written on the dusk in flickering neon, in a careful lean script such as the nuns had tried to teach Isabel. Instead, her handwriting was upright and rounded. The hotel had been a coffee planter's mansion, with airy vaulted chambers, now subdivided and furnished in synthetic substances from the 1950s. The bed was a blunt platform and the pictures on the wall were staring urchins with enlarged eyes, but a fan hung on a rod from the ceiling's center turned its four lazy paddles at the flip of a switch, and there were several gilt-framed mirrors and a chest and armoires of a sweet-smelling dark wood. Isabel felt like a woman of the world, unpacking her clothes into drawers and arranging herself on the sofa and dialling room service, commanding in level tones that food and drink appear. The clerk downstairs was a fat Italo-Brazilian in a collarless shirt and had not hesitated to rent them a room, though the mulatto bellhop who had carried their duffel bag and knapsack waggled his hand until they had enlarged the tip, and audibly spat on the hall floor when he had closed the door. But the staff came to like them, as the days wore on; few guests stayed more than an hour or two. There was a small courtyard where a neglected bougainvillaea vine had grown to enormous size, and there in its shade, on a worn wooden bench where the old planter and his wife must have often rested, they took coffee, when returning at noon from shopping.

Their packet of cruzeiros was diminishing in value, and it seemed thriftiest to spend it rapidly. They went out onto the Avenida Paulista and the Rua Augusta and bought themselves clothes suitable to city life. They ate in restaurants where elegant women sat at small tables in pairs, drinking cocktails from slender glasses and managing not to get their noses involved with the fruit slices clinging to the rim. Under the round white tables their long legs whispered in silken pantyhose, exposed up to their hips by newly fashionable miniskirts. Around them, in tall buildings of cement and glass, São Paulo was rising, manifesting the economic miracle of the generals. Emerging after eating breakfast and making love and taking a shower together which often ended in making more love, Isabel and Tristão would step onto their little balcony and be dizzyingly greeted by the chasm below, by the glittering mosaic of street noises and the wilderness of poured-concrete buildings still mottled by the previous night's rain. The anonymous vastness of São Paulo then seemed an expectancy, a vast rapt audience cumbersomely applauding. Isabel felt within a new, operatic self, vauntingly female.

Serving Tristão financially with money stolen from her uncle, she became obsessed with serving him physically. His penis, so little when limp, a baby in its bonnet of foreskin, frightened her when it became a yam, stiff and thick with a lavender knob and purple-black ripples of gristle and veins. She would master this monster with her fragile white body. The extremity of pleasure she would give him would measure the limits of her womanhood. They watched pornographic films on the hotel's pay channel and she studiously imitated what the women did there. Mouths she had known about but she could not at first believe that women's bottoms could be used the way they were in these movies. Up the ass is extra, Ursula had said. Tristão found the practice disgusting but she insisted. After a while, yes, she felt something beyond the pain, an illumination of her depths. This, too, was part of her being, a boundary probed. Submission was a darkness from which she re-emerged purified.

"I am your slave," she told her lover. "Use me. Whip me if it pleases you. Beat me, even. Only, do not break my teeth."

"Dearest, please." Tristão almost simpered. He was becoming a little plump, and effeminate in his gestures. He wore pajamas of figured silk from a store in Consolação called Krishna. "I have no desire to hurt you. The men who hurt women are those too cowardly to do battle with other men."

"Tie me up. Blindfold me. Then touch me lightly, lightly, and then be rough. I crave a world in which only you exist, all around me, like the air I am constantly eating."

"Darling, really," her knight tut-tutted, reluctantly accepting all the sexual favors she thought up for him. She rode his yam backwards, tongued his anus, swallowed his sperm. After seeing several such scenes on the blue pay channel, she decided it would fulfill Tristão to have her in conjunction with another man, for two men to communicate with each other through her body. She chose the bellhop who had spat in the hall, a brown broad-faced boy who reminded her of Euclides. His almond-shaped eyes made shy contact with hers, for a questioning half-second, whenever she passed through the lobby. Blushing as she described what she wanted, she bribed him from the diminishing little packet of cruzeiros. Tristão was appalled when she described her plan five minutes before the embarrassed boy, out of his uniform and in a touchingly clean shirt and pair of polyester slacks, appeared at their door.

She feared Tristão would toss the boy out but, gallantly obedient to her in all things, he allowed the tableau to take place, and played his rôle in it. In mirrors arranged along the floor, Isabel saw her whiteness wedged between brown and black, a human bridge receiving traffic in two directions. But even at the technically triumphant moment of double climax, the stranger's throbs muffled in her vagina and Tristão sourly exploding in her face, she felt the experiment to be a mistake. Some boundaries were not purely her own. The boy, both shamefaced and faintly swaggering, waited an awkward moment as if for his tip, or an invitation to return, and then left, feeling the danger in Tristão's glance. He had been her first other man.

Tristão was magnificently haughty in the wake of this tableau she had staged, and not all of her tears and frantic excuses could bring down the tower he had become. Outside their windows, night enveloped São Paulo's infinite buildings, and only a few wan lights came on in the windows, as if every room held a quarrelling, sorrowing couple like themselves.

"You dirtied me," he said. "You would never have played the whore like that with a husband from your own set. You think because I am black and come from the *favela* I have no shame, no civilization."

"I was trying to *please* you," Isabel sobbed. "I can see on television what men like. I was trying to enrich our love, with the presence of a witness. Do you not think I felt degraded? I hated feeling him in me. But your pleasure is my pleasure, Tristão."

"That gave me little pleasure," he said stonily, having propped himself up in their bed on all the pillows, his and hers. He wore only the bottoms of his silk pajamas, like a woman in harem pants. "It was you who had the pleasure of being a slut. You let yourself sink into the warm shit, *porra* at both ends."

"Sim! Sim!" she cried, letting herself be knocked flat as if by a revelation onto the bed beside him. She showed the extreme of her self-abnegation by not asking for her head even a corner of one of his many pillows, instead lying level like a corpse on the mortuary slab. "I am a slut, worse than your mother, who has the excuse of poverty."

"You think *I* am shit, because of my color. Like the

mincing clerk at the Othon Palace. You think I come from depths where order and honor never penetrate. But hopes of order and honor are everywhere—the spirits bring them. We all know what order and decency and honor are, though we never see them."

"Let me lick you everywhere on your angelic body, Tristão. Tell me what to do to win back, I dare not say your love, but permission to continue as your slave." She lifted herself up from the bed enough to flutter her tongue on one of his nipples. The dear little useless nub stiffened, despite his lordly fury.

"Our lot is cast together," he said, as if pronouncing his own death sentence, and hit her, with a flat hand knocking her face away from his chest. "You gave that clod your cunt; suppose you become pregnant by him?"

"I didn't think. I wanted him where I could not see him, and you where I could see and taste everything."

"Then taste this," he said, and hit her again, but with an open hand, to leave no mark, unlike those women against whose cheeks he leaned his razor blade. As he had promised, he would do her no harm. That night he did beat her, but judiciously, on the upper arms and buttocks, and fucked her, alternatingly, as she clung to his hardness in its renewed convulsions of masculine vitality.

"If I made a mistake," she at last dared plead, during this long night of their mutual deepening, one into the other, "it was out of love for you, Tristão. I do not know any more how to be selfish."

He snorted in the dark, jolting her head where it lay

on his breast. "For a man to love, to surrender his defenses in the war of all against all, that is unselfish," he told her. "For a woman to love is selfish; it is her nature to love, giving and receiving is all one to her, as the in and out of screwing is all one to a man. Loving is necessary to her, as hating is necessary to a man."

Humble and clinging in the dark (which yet in the high-ceilinged hotel room was not absolute, light leaking into it from circumambient São Paulo, as a television screen continues to glow when switched off), her bruises smarting on her body like a hot-lipped beast's kisses, she thought, God, can it be true, this flowing outward of love like milk through each pore is what we have instead of a man's passing bliss of ejaculation, his brief and viscid coming that makes him whimper as if wounded? It was brief and pointed compared with a woman's unstoppable outflow. This giving, this shedding, this vapor of love arising from the lake of herself was as well a voluptuous feeding, for love takes all the beloved's details into itself, as the fabled cannibals of the Amazon eat one another's brains. Just saying his name, sinking her voice into the nasal sound at the end, gave Isabel voluptuous pleasure. During this long night in which she scarcely slept, awakened more than once by Tristão's renewed vigor of outrage, which pumped his sperm into her to pursue and kill that of the other man, she learned, with the gloating greed with which young lovers accumulate their lessons, this: the soft low flame she had lit within him, which illumined her face and name even in his sleep, could not be blown out, merely made to shudder, like a votive candle when a church door is opened at the far end of the nave, by whatever events overtook her resilient, flexible body. Someday soon he himself, she silently predicted, would suggest having the bellhop in their room with them again.

vii. *Chiquinho*

TRISTÃO began to feel queasy, as if he was living on a diet of sweets. He would be glad when the packet of cruzeiros was used up and he and Isabel would be cast upon the world, with him as defender. In preparation for that day, he intensified his search for his brother Chiquinho. He had been given no address, and the city was a great maze, without an ocean or mountains to orient oneself by. Vast neighborhoods held only Japanese, and others Italians; there were even neighborhoods for Jews and Arabs, with signs in unreadable alphabets. There were fewer black people than in Rio, and the climate was harsher, unsoftened by the sea; violent thunderstorms and spasms of wind swept in from the ocean of land to the west. Tristão no longer felt like a roving predator on his own territory, though he robbed a few conspicuously ripe white people with his razor blade, to keep in practice. He felt shy, clumsy, potentially a prey of the immense forces gathered here.

The people here did not spend all morning at the beach as in Rio but instead bustled efficiently about like

Europeans, selling each other things, hatching deals with the excitement of Cariocas generating a romance—men in dark suits marching three and four abreast along the sidewalks gesticulating and shrieking with the excited love they felt for one another and for the business of money. Only here and there, in the blank-faced prostitutes stalking the Rua dos Andradas on their long legs or in the candles dribbling wax at the foot of the large crude statue called African Mother near the Viaduto do Chá, did the city betray that true life, the life of ecstasy and the spirits, persisted beneath the hurry of business. Tristão bought maps of São Paulo but no two agreed; the bus routes wound about like tortured snakes, and when he emerged, sick from the twisting and swaying, he walked south when he meant to walk north. Nevertheless, leaving Isabel sleeping off the night's love or immersed in a romantic novel, he found industrial districts—endless crowded houses little bigger than Rio's shanties, but built of more solid materials, on rectangular lots, and drab factory buildings, buildings expressive of work yet often appearing empty and idle, as if work came in large rhythms like the weather, drought more common than flood. From behind their sealed walls he heard the sounds of machines rapidly knitting, pounding, mixing, compressing, capping. Between these buildings—irregularly placed, with some windows blackened like absent teeth—were rusting rails, of track where no trains ran, and fenced-in spaces where enigmatic stacks of concrete blocks and wooden crates were slowly weathering back into nature. At odd corners little downtowns, made of *mercearias* and bars, barber shops and oculists, fortune-tellers and establishments for shoe repair, clung to life, fed by a trickle of customers who, compared to the poor of Rio, seemed to Tristão disconsolate and dirty, dully dressed and grim— a proletariat. He stopped some of these people and asked if they knew a man called Chiquinho; none of them had, and laughed at Tristão for thinking that a single name could pluck a man up from the vastness of São Paulo, the greatest city in South America. Chiquinho Raposo, he said, and still they laughed. There were hundreds of Raposos, they said. They distrusted him, a Negro in fine clothes, with the Carioca accent, that turned the *s* sound into a soft spray, *sh*.

His older brother had left the *favela* when he was eleven or twelve and Tristão not yet six. Tristão remembered only sadly pale eyes and a painfully thin neck. Chiquinho had moved through the shadows and stark sunlight of their existence with an air of brittle abstraction; he moved without elasticity and his hands flapped awkwardly at the end of his bony arms. No doubt he would have changed beyond recognition in thirteen years.

But in truth he had not: Tristão recognized him without any difficulty, on the broad sidewalk outside the hotel one day. "Brother," the tall thin man said, unsmiling. He appeared to have been waiting.

Chiquinho, the chalky brown color of cheap patio tile, was decidedly paler than his brother; his father must have been a white man, or more likely a gray man, whose cold aluminum eyes gazed out through crinkled lids. Since Tristão had seen him he had gone from boyhood to manhood; there were small dry wrinkles where squinting and grimacing had stressed his skin. Even Chiquinho's thin neck had wrinkles, like a cloth wrung dry. "Oh, how I have been looking for you!" Tristão told him, after their *abraço*.

"Yes, I have been told of your inquiries," Chiquinho said. "But I was never in the exact place where you asked. It is a miracle that we meet in such a metropolis, where hundreds arrive every day." He spoke in a thoughtful manner that was not pleasant, his mouth moving while his gray gaze did not change.

"Chiquinho, I am not alone. I have a wife now, a *companheira*, and I must have a job in the automobile factory."

"I am no longer making *fuscas*. I am into a new thing, electronics. But my education is too poor for the work, so I am stuck at the lowliest level, cleaning the factory so there is not a fleck of dirt. In the intricate thing we make, which solves all mathematical problems in a little stroke of directed lightning, a fleck of dust is like a rock in the engine of a car. Under the enlightened capitalist policies which have supplanted the dangerous socialist experiments of Quadros and Goulart, I have been privileged to head the team of cleaners, while taking night courses that educate me in the mysteries of the new technology. But why would you speak of work? You are dressed like a rich man. You reside at this hotel of hourly rates, day after day."

64

"My wife and I stole some money, but now it is all but used up. Inflation has stolen it back; that, and our self-indulgent life-style. Come, you must meet her; she is beautiful, and a saint in her devotion to me. Her name is Isabel Leme."

Chiquinho made some ungainly hand-flapping gestures across his chest, indicating his tattered shirt. It was a white shirt, short-sleeved, of the type that engineers wear, even to the plastic protector in the pocket, but the pocket had no pens in it, and the pointed collar was frayed. "I would be ashamed to meet her, dressed as I am. You must come to see us. I, too, have a wife. Her name is Polidora. Here is my address, dear Tristão. Our street now has electricity, and the city promises sewers. Take the bus to Belém, and walk south into Moóca, as I will indicate." He swiftly drew a map, and named the next night, adding, "There is work in São Paulo, but also there are many from the *nordeste*, who drive the wages down, and think nothing of cutting the throats of those who threaten them. But I will make inquiries, for our family's sake. How does our blessed mother fare?"

"She lives, much as ever, cursing everything."

Chiquinho permitted himself a smile, and a bleak nod. From the aluminum calm of his eyes Tristão gathered that the information had not been news, and his asking had been a mere formality. As they parted, Chiquinho emphasized, "Polidora and I will expect the two of you. Do not leave your wife behind."

It had been uncanny, their meeting so opportunely, in a section, Campos Elíseos, where Chiquinho must have rare occasion to walk. Still, Tristão accepted gratefully, and turned back into the hotel to tell Isabel that their true life together—their life in the real world, and not this rented chamber—was beginning. In their idleness she had become addicted to the afternoon soap operas on the radio, and to the dubbed broadcasts of such imported television shows as "I Love Lucy." Like Tristão, she was putting on weight.

viii. *The Ranch House*

WITH THE LAST OF THEIR MONEY they took a taxi, following Chiquinho's directions, through a flat neighborhood that had recently been a coffee plantation but that now boasted electric wires and street signs. Though the ground underfoot was unpaved and littered with industry's glinting detritus, and the sky overhead was smudged by smoke, the houses had yards and verandas and several rooms, spreading sideways beneath roofs of red tile. Chiquinho at the door seemed more brittle than ever, his smile of greeting a tight gash in his face, and his head precarious on his thin neck. His wife, Polidora, like a ball of freshly baked bread, was round and spongy and a toasty golden brown; her hair was rinsed with henna and had been teased and baked into a stiff beehive. She had round eager eyes but as if to match Chiquinho's cautious squint kept her lids half lowered. Her doughy features gleamed with a sweat that Tristão blamed upon the beauty and prestige of her female guest; she greeted Isabel with an excessively familiar embrace and then pulled her, not relinquishing her adhesive grip on the girl's slim white hand, into a larger room beyond the tiled entrance hall, Tristão following as Chiquinho's bony arm interlocked purposefully with his. In this second room two men in silvery-gray suits rose and showed the guests their guns.

Tristão thought of the razor blade but realized he had not even that. He kept it generally in the little change pocket of the bell-bottomed denims he and Isabel had bought for him at a store called Polychrome, but this evening, dressing in the hotel, they had decided such informal trousers might seem disrespectful to such a petit bourgeois as his brother had apparently become, and he had opted instead for a flowing silk shirt, with white French cuffs on mauve sleeves, and cream-colored linen slacks, with tasselled loafers. So he had no razor blade. But what could a razor blade do against two guns?

The older of the two men, a heavy handsome man who had grown gray and melancholy in the service of the rich, gestured with his gray barrel for them to sit on the sofa, a plaid Hide-a-Bed set against a yellow wall decorated with two plaster parrots, gaudily enamelled bas-reliefs of a piece with the rounded plaster frames. The parrots' tails and beaks overlapped the frames—a caprice of the artist's, asking you to consider, What is reality and what is artifice?

On the sofa Tristão felt Isabel's body trembling beside his like that of a woman in heat, who is gambling her life in a moment of sexual abandon. He dismissed any thought of how her body from the start had led him into embarrassment and danger, and put his arm about her, to shield her with his own body if need be. Though he, too, was trembling, his mind was immensely clear and quick, the electricity evoked by this emergency running along the forked paths of possibility. All that was now said he had understood in a flash.

"Do not be alarmed, my friends," said the man with the handsomely grayed temples, and a measured gray mustache. "We are here only to escort the young lady to her father in Brasília. There is a plane from Congonhas at a little after ten; there is plenty of time. We thought you might be fashionably late. Let's all have a drink."

"I would spit in the glass offered me by my Judas of a brother," Tristão said. Directly of Chiquinho he demanded, "How can you justify to yourself this betrayal?"

Chiquinho worked his arms about on his chest as if brushing away flies without using his hands. "This relationship is degrading to you, brother. You have lost your edge; you look soft and sleek, like a kept man. Better I betray you than this platinum girl. The rich always retreat back into their own. The little money her people have spared me for my collaboration will finance my education; I will become a certified electrical engineer!"

Isabel's dear monkey face was twisted by the torque between indignation and tears; yet her body beside Tristão's on the plaid sofa was, under his arm, oddly limp. Something in her had relaxed. Our deep selves welcome our catastrophes. Her own education was moving beyond sexual stunts and daytime soap operas.

"How did you know about us?" she softly asked Chiquinho. "Was it Ursula?"

Tristão grieved for her, for he knew that in deciding to love his unlovable mother Isabel had set herself a task precious in its perversity. Loving his mother was her invention, the first vulnerable offspring of their marriage.

"Ah, no, miss," Chiquinho responded, as if mercifully. "Our blessed mother lives beneath the level of electronics, of communication with the unseen. Since at the age of fourteen the idea of selling her own body was thrust upon her, she has had no further profitable ideas. It was Euclides who warned me, via our not always undependable post, that Tristão would be coming to São Paulo with a treasure. At first I waited for him to find me, but the city's vastness defeated him. So I found him. The Othon Palace was suggested as a possibility, and the clerk there was helpful. He remembered the two of you. He asked me to assure you that the reason you were turned away was not racial prejudice on his part, but respect for the feelings of the other guests, many of whom come from abroad, from less tolerant societies."

"What will happen to Tristão?" Isabel asked, with a gasp of panic that left her mouth open, displaying her pearly teeth, her velvet tongue. Her mind, accustomed to the logic of wealth and power, had grasped more quickly than Tristão the crux his own person posed: Left free, he would make trouble. He might seek out his wife in Brasília, he might try to abduct her back, he might even—grotesque thought!—go to the police.

Sensing her panic, Tristão now saw that the surest way to end Isabel's attachment was to kill him. As if an electric current had been switched on, or one of those sudden and terrific thunderstorms of São Paulo had darkened the air so that everything appeared in negative, with shadows white and plaster walls black, he saw how completely the quiet presence of the two guns had altered the room. Death, that unthinkable remoteness, had been brought abruptly near, a pace or two away, giving everything a papery, permeable texture. All the lines in the room, from the shadowy corners to the seams of the plaid sofa and the hexagonal floor tiles the color of Chiquinho's skin, were aligned on a new perspective; a solemnity had been introduced in which everyone spoke softly, and everyday gestures were performed with a sleepwalking stateliness. Polidora brought in a tray of drinks—tall pastel *sucos* for those who wished no alcohol, and for the others *caipirinhas* blended of *cachaça*, lime, sugar, and crushed ice. Isabel took a *caipirinha*, to quell her emotions; Tristão, a *suco*, in case an opportunity arose for clear wits. A warm smell of stewing beef swam out from the kitchen.

The younger gunman, who lacked a mustache and silvery temples, answered Isabel comfortingly, "He will become my friend. César will accompany the young lady to Brasília, and I will stay here with the young man, whose mind at first will naturally be bewitched by thoughts of rescue and vengeance. This is an ample house; we can all be happy here, for a week or two, until the young lady is safely restored to her father's influence. My name is Virgílio," he added, to the couple on the sofa, with a small bow that did not lower the level angle of his gun barrel.

Polidora protested, "Sir, we have two children sleeping here."

"Madame, you will be paid."

Isabel burst out, "I will *never* be restored to my father's influence! I am a woman now, with my own rôle in the world. My entire life, since my mother died when I was four, has been spent without a father—he left me in the care of his foppish brother!"

César, scandalized, was moved to defend his employer, and perhaps all those men, of whom he was one, of graying middle years, who understandably could not meet all the demands converging upon them. "Miss Isabel, your father is an important man, who has given his life to the government of the country."

"Then why does nothing seem governed? The poor remain poor, and the rich rule with guns." As if fulfilling her uncle's prophecy of her radicalism, she rebelliously stood and taunted the gunmen: "Why should I do what you say? You would never harm me—my father would have your hides."

Courteously César agreed. "That is true. But the same does not apply to your black friend—your husband, if you will. The world would not miss him. Only you would miss him. His death would not leave even the smallest gap in the records, since he has no doubt evaded registering for the draft. And if he is not hostage enough to win your coöperation, think of our hosts"—

the gun barrel twitched toward Chiquinho and Polidora, standing waiting to serve them all dinner—"and their two children. These children could return from the streets to find their parents dead, and though these deaths would be noticed, our police are overworked, and would not find the killers. Do not think these threats are bravado. Reality is, more and more, statistics, and in a country as big as Brazil we are very small statistics."

Now it was Chiquinho who protested: "It was my voluntary information that brought you here, and now you threaten my life!"

Virgílio told him, "The man who betrays his own brother deserves to die." To Tristão he added, with a smile that revealed winningly irregular teeth, overlapped like feet doing a dance step, "You see what a good and loyal friend I am already? Better sometimes a spiritual brother than a blood brother."

Isabel, on her feet, seemed stretched and twisted as if pulled by invisible threads; it was strange, Tristão reflected, how the two gray guns had, like pencils, redrawn the space of the room, reducing the infinitude of possibilities to a few shallow tunnels of warped choice. Their spirits had all become very thin, walking the taut wires of the situation. Isabel now said calmly, "If I am to be taken to my father, then, I must have my clothes. They are back in the hotel. There is no time to eat, if we must be at Congonhas by ten. We must go now," she said to her new escort, the paternal, gray-suited delegate of the power that had formed her.

"It is so," César said, pleased. To Polidora: "Our regrets. The *feijoada* smells excellent; my healthy young associate will eat my share." To Chiquinho: "You have half your reward in your pocket. The other half depends upon your continuing coöperation and hospitality." To Tristão: "Farewell, my friend. It will be unfortunate for one of us if we ever meet again." To Isabel: "Come, miss. As you say, the plane will not wait."

Isabel bent down and bestowed upon Tristão a languid kiss, soft as a cloud and warm as the kiss of the sun, that said, *Keep faith.*

But could he trust her? His wife, from the back, looked uncannily at ease on the arm of her distinguished-appearing abductor. Back in the hotel, she had put on a pert, neither formal nor informal dress of small red flowers on a navy-blue ground, changing costume two or three times to find the perfect match for his slacks and casual yet French-cuffed shirt—respectfully elegant, but not overbearingly so. This was to have been their first night out together, as an established couple, visiting one of her in-laws. Perhaps they had reached too far, too fast.

With Isabel gone, Tristão felt more his old self, and, as Polidora brought her pot of peppery *feijoada* to the table, all of them relaxed. Virgílio removed his gray coat and tucked his gun into his armpit holster, and Chiquinho replaced their tall glasses with bottles of Antártica beer. Tristão's little niece and nephew, Esperança and Pacheco, came in from the dark streets—toasty-skinned, gray-eyed tots of three and five—and the importunate innocence of children infected the table with merriment. Their stares fixed upon Virgílio's gun; its handle jutted from the holster like the rear end of an animal diving into its burrow, and, sensing their fantasy, the gunman enacted it, moving the gun in and out like a scurrying animal, miming its fright on his face, his crooked teeth chattering. *"Fora! Opa! Dentro! Bom."*

When the beer was depleted, transparent *cachaça* appeared, and the table of four adults overflowed with jokes against the world outside the thin walls, above the fragile roof—the others, the rich, the *poderosos*, the gringos, the Argentinians, the Paraguayans, the German and Japanese farmers in the Região Sul, with their ridiculous accents and insular, puritanical, work-obsessed habits. The true Brazilian, they jubilantly agreed among themselves, is an incorrigible romantic—impetuous, impractical, pleasure-loving, and yet idealistic, gallant, and vital.

Tristão was dizzy as he went to bed. The room's angles surged and tipped much as they had under the magnetic pressure of the guns. He was assigned the children's room; the children were shifted to their parents' bed. Tristão had one cot and Virgílio slept in the other, placed across the door to bar escape. The room's only window was secured with fixed outside bars against thieves, who flocked to this neighborhood of slowly rising working-class prosperity.

It had been many weeks since Tristão had lain down without Isabel beside him. Her being had become hard to distinguish from his own. She burned inside him like a peppery lining to his stomach, a luminous longing eating him alive. Being alive, he perceived, is a relative condition, not worth everything. It was not worth Isabel's absence—her cunt moistly enwrapping his stiff yam, her voice pattering into his half-attentive ear, the warm cloud of her lips descending upon his, saying *Keep faith.* She was not death but her whiteness had death's purity. He stifled his tears, lest he wake his new roommate. He schemed, and then he dreamed.

ix. *Brasília*

S EEN AT MIDNIGHT from an airplane, Brasília's lights
trace the shape of an airplane, with long curved
wings, on the vast black slate of Brazil's interior. The
city seems to float on emptiness like a constellation,
and then to tilt, as if wheeling toward takeoff past your
own stationary position in space. You land with a whisper, as if not on solid earth. The air in the airport is
cool, and surprisingly crowded with comings and go-
ings, late as the hour is, for this is a place where few
want to be, yet where many must come.

César directed the taxi to Isabel's father's apartment,
on the Eixo Rodoviário Norte, in one of the great vertical slabs where government higher-ups maintained ad-
dresses. Her memories of Brasília went back to her
girlhood, to overhearing Uncle Donaciano and her father quarrelling over President Kubitschek's determination to make good on his campaign vow to build an
inland capital. It is an ancient Brazilian dream, her father said—as old as the dream of independence, going
back to the Inconfidência Mineira. Then keep it as a

dream, her uncle had responded—if we make all our dreams come true, the world will become a nightmare. The rumored event had made childish Isabel feel strange, as if her heart were being tugged off-center, or as if an earthquake had moved her beautiful Rio out to sea. Then, a year or so later, a skidding, bobbing flight in a Piper Cub landed her, with her father, amid mountains of fresh red dirt and thousands of poor peasants from the *sertão* slaving like ants to effect an inscrutable plan. When she and her father returned again, skeletal buildings were up, giant yellow trucks roared back and forth importantly on unpaved roadways, and the sunken round shape of the cathedral had sprouted its crown of concrete thorns. Now the plan was realized, the stony capital was built, like a beautiful statue still waiting for life to be breathed into it. The black space of the *sertão*, the blank calm of the inhuman night still presided beneath and above the schematic lights, the dazzling blackboard diagram.

The security guards at the apartment building had been forewarned of Isabel's coming, for both of them—small, high-cheeked men, with a *caboclo* wiriness—were awake and wearing neat olive uniforms. Nevertheless, César insisted on accompanying Isabel into the elevator and up to the floor where her father's vast apartment spread its wings like a miniature of the city itself. As César surrendered her and her luggage to the tall stooped servant who met them at the door, he lifted her white hand to his lips and kissed the backs of her fingers, which were curled and cold in her resentment.

"Now, do as your papa says," he affectionately advised her. "Brazil has few leaders; the Portuguese did not bring to the New World the discipline and austerity that the Spanish did. If we were not as cruel as they were, merely brutal, it was because we were too lazy to have an ideology. The Church was too lenient; even the convents were brothels." This was the summary, as if from a professor whose time had run out, of the lecture he had been giving her in the airplane. César was a considerable self-improver: he made a point of reading at least one book per week and had taught himself a reading knowledge of Spanish, French, and English. German he had found a bit thick, as yet. He hoped, when his days as an enforcer and assassin were over—"It's a young man's game, miss; when you get old, you become too soft-hearted"—to buy his own limousine and become a tour guide. Not just in the cities, mind, where all the visiting businessmen care about is finding a sexy mulatta, but into the countryside, where the rich widows and Canadian schoolteachers will want to visit the picture-book towns like Ouro Prêto and Olinda, redolent of our colonial history, and the eighteenth-century churches with their soapstone carvings by Aleijadinho—"A dwarf and a cripple, miss, and his mother a black slave; who says a good man can't get ahead in Brazil?"—and of course the fabled Amazon, the world-famous opera house in Manaus, and the vastness itself, which will become a tourist attraction in its own right, as the world runs out of space. Only Siberia and the Sahara can rival Brazilian vastness, and they have deplorable climates. That is why the government in its wisdom has settled Brasília and is pushing roads through all the virgin forest—"Roads are progress, miss, and the man who can drive them is a man of the future."

With all this false paternity ringing in her ears, which were still unpopped from the airplane flight, Isabel went to bed in the chamber at the end of a long, gently curved hall. The room, furnished with a narrow bed and a bare desk, was "hers," though she had spent in her eighteen years not a hundred nights in it. Her father, who had just that day flown in from Dublin, was of course asleep. She could picture him, motionless as a doll in his black eye-mask. Years of jet travel had taught him how to sleep at will. He looked forward to conferring with his daughter in the morning, at breakfast at nine-thirty, the tall servant, a *pardo* whose complexion bore a lugubrious touch of green, explained. A chubby short woman, perhaps the servant's wife, in a maid's uniform of starched blue, asked her if *senhora* required anything—a *vitamina*, a sleeping pill, another blanket. The couple—one lean, one fat, and both of them obsequious yet watchful—reminded Isabel of treacherous Chiquinho and Polidora and she wearily brushed them aside, wishing to be alone with her sorrow, to taste its bitterness and assess its limits.

She perceived that her rebellion had won her new respect and consideration from those who held power over her life. Thus the world's authorities betray their basic fragility and cowardice, she reflected, slipping herself naked into the prim, virginal bed. She was too weary to search out a nightie in her baggage. Her nakedness felt like a defiance of the rectilinear city about her, Brazil's heart's prison, and a rejoining of her body to Tristão's blackness. She wished to pray for his safety, but in thinking of God she could only think of him, the black gaze of longing and potential command Tristão had first fastened upon her, on the radiant beach.

Her father, whose given name was Salomão, was older than Uncle Donaciano, and more powerful, yet smaller, with a bulging forehead that leaned forward anxiously from his balding head, as though he were melting. At breakfast he wore a maroon silk bathrobe over his gray-striped trousers, and slippers over black ribbed socks that would soon be enclosed in the narrow polished shoes of a diplomat and politician. Isabel perceived that she was just an appointment within his day, to be followed by others. Already he was engrossed in the stack of newspapers by his plate, in a number of languages; he stood to greet her with an air of having been interrupted.

"My beautiful errant child," he said, as if stating the meeting's topic. He bestowed upon each of her cheeks and then her lips a kiss whose coolness had since childhood seemed to her tinged, like luggage stored in the unheated hold of an airplane, with the extra-terrestrial cold of the stratosphere. Always in her memories he had been coming to her from a great global distance; the apartment, though so laterally vast as to never (unlike Uncle Donaciano's) feel crowded with acquisitions, abounded with souvenirs of his travels and posts: a seven-foot-square Tibetan *thang-ka*, its cosmic tree glinting with spidery lines of gold paint on a ground of pre-Creational purple and green, hung behind a Louis XV marquetry *coiffeuse* supporting a Ch'ing *famille-noire* vase and a Dogon wooden ancestor figure from Mali. Uncle Donaciano's high-ceilinged Rio apartment held big slashing abstract canvases in the current mode; her father favored small engraved prints of historic scenes and edifices, or duo-chrome Japanese prints whose formality of composition denied the violence of their subject matter.

He sat down opposite her at the low breakfast table, whose inlay contained an oversized chessboard. He opened the meeting: "I hope you slept well."

She could see he was determined to give her all the respect and intensity of attention that a fellow diplomat would have received. Nevertheless, his eyes did keep nervously flicking to the top newspaper on his pile, whose headlines told of riot, tactical war, and impending revolution throughout the globe. "I fell asleep promptly, Father, since I was exhausted from the journey your henchman forced upon me. But I awoke at four in the morning, not knowing where I was and then terrified at the realization that I could not get out—that I was being held captive. I nearly screamed with panic. I thought of jumping to my death, but of course the modernistic windows do not open." She dug into her new-moon-shaped slice of honeydew melon, having already consumed a buttered roll and three crackling pieces of bacon. She no longer had a virgin's picky appetite.

"And then," her father asked, "did you stay awake?"

"No," she sullenly confessed. "I fell back asleep for an hour or two."

"Well, then," he said, somewhat triumphantly, and eyed the top newspaper again. "We adjust to circumstances quickly, so quickly the spirit thinks the body is a traitor."

"I fell asleep," she said, "by imagining that I was back in the arms of my husband, where I belong."

"Just as you belong in the Hotel Amour, running up extravagant bills and corrupting the bellhop. You have had a little holiday, my Isabel, and I have been constrained to bring you back to real life." Yet he spoke, she was almost sorry to observe, with a certain tentative delicacy, his eyes darting down to seize the morsel of another headline, his lips wincing back at the end of a sentence, exposing a child's small round teeth, yellow with age. Her father, she dared see for the first time in her life, had been a small and delicate boy, easy to bully, pedantic in his plans for revenge. Earthly power was his revenge, and it was proving hollow.

"Brasília is scarcely real life," she told him, "nor have you been a very real father to me. You have been to me a hazy, unapproachable star, which is perhaps what a father should be, but now I must be allowed to transfer my affections to a man who has burst upon me like the sun."

Her father's thin eyelids fluttered in a pained manner. He had developed a tic in the translucent bluish skin beneath one eye, and a pulse in the hollow of his temple. His gaze, when he could lift it from the newspaper to her face, had something of the slumping heaviness of his pallid brow. Compared with Tristão, her father seemed unformed—the skin thin and colorless as if interrupted in its development, the eyes a weak watery gray-blue, the skull clothed not in an impervious cap of tight oily circlets but in lank parallel strands that let the infantile scalp show through, the neckless square body shaped for nothing but sitting in a chair. Yet he spoke with an unabashed precision and authority, as if all his manliness had gone into his voice. "Do you remember," he asked her, "your visit to the Othon Palace, the lady who accompanied us?"

"She tried to be a mother to me," Isabel recalled, "and I resented it. It was a false attempt."

"I, too, felt the falsity of her attempt to endear herself to my daughter, and it helped end our romance. Everything can be forgiven of a woman but awkwardness; that clings to the mind."

His Portuguese, compared with that of Tristão or Uncle Donaciano, had a flavorless neutrality, it seemed to Isabel. He knew so many other languages that his mind was always translating; his tongue had no home.

"She to me," he continued, "had been a revelation. Four years had passed since your dear mother's death; except for periodic visits to *raparigas*—a matter solely of physical hygiene—I had lived chaste, first out of decent observance of mourning, then out of habit. Eulália—that was her name, in case you have forgotten—Eulália transformed me into what I had never been with your mother, for all her virtues: a sensual man. For the first time, I saw that the old Church was right and the Protestants and Platonists were wrong—we *are* our bodies, and resurrection is the only answer. Eulália resurrected me. She *created* me, in the way that you feel this boy has created you. In sad truth, he has exploited you—your sexual innocence, your bourgeois boredom, your youthful idealism, your Brazilian romanticism. Just so, Eulália exploited me—my easily flattered virility, my accustomed habits of cohabitation, the dependence on women that a mother's weakling child develops. Only when I saw her seek to seduce my eight-year-old daughter, and clumsily fail through overacting, did I begin to awaken—for love is a dream, Isabel, as all but the dreamers can see. It is the anesthetic Nature employs to extract babies from us. And when, as in your ineffable mother's case, the operation proves fatal, what does Nature do? She shrugs and walks away. Nature doesn't care, my darling, about us; therefore we must care about ourselves. You will not throw away your life on a black slum boy. You will not see Tristão again. You will stay here in Brasília and live with me; you will be in every night by midnight. You will attend the university a few blocks from where we sit now. Since our new government in 1965 was constrained to close it and cleanse both faculty and student body of radical undesirables, the university curriculum may be mediocre in its specifics but is sound in its overall values. Protests and nihilism are kept to a minimum—a far cry from the hotbeds of anarchy and sedition in the coastal cities. Perhaps you will meet in one of your classes a charming general's son."

"And what if I refuse to go? What if I run away?"

Her father's pendulous watery gaze lifted smilingly, as if the array of breakfast glasses and dishes between them were chess pieces, and she was mated. "Then this Tristão, whom we can now identify and trace, may painlessly disappear. Not even his mother, I understand, will trouble the authorities. She is an unnatural mother, or perhaps we should say all too natural. It would be, my angel, as if you, and you alone, had dreamed of his existence." His smiling lips were not ruddy, like Uncle Donaciano's, but pale, like the skin that peeped through his thinning hair, and were made whiter still by the powdered sugar topping the fried bun of which he had taken a surprisingly greedy bite, rolling his eyes downward toward the newspapers as he did so.

x. *The Two Brothers*

FOR TWO YEARS Isabel attended the Universidade de Brasília, studying art history. Slides of cave drawings and cathedrals, historical tableaux and Impressionist landscapes appeared in the darkness of the lecture hall and disappeared. All were French. Art was French, and the lecturers twanged out the French nasals and the rasped *r* as if returning home. Oh, there were some Cambodian temples, and German woodcuts, and after 1945 one had to take some note of the New York School, but in the end it was all dim spinoff or especially ingenious savagery, compared to Chartres and Cézanne. True culture, Isabel learned, was a surprisingly local, a purely European, and mostly a French, affair. Only biology was global—billions of copulations, adding up.

If she did "date" some of her fellow students, conservative and pusillanimous but handsome and admiring sons of the oligarchy and its servants, what of it? She was young, full of nervous energy, and on the Pill. One can be faithful in spirit, especially if at the moment of orgasm one closes one's eyes and thinks, *Tristão*. Removed from her life, changeless in his absence, he had become inviolate, an untouchable piece of herself, as secret as a child's first sexual inklings.

Her father, observing what seemed to be her acceptance of her situation, congratulated himself on the success of his strategy. He came and went in the vast apartment like a strange slug, with his thin bluish skin, his pale-lipped smile, his balding brow toppling above the oppressive vague benevolence of his gaze, like that of the nuns who had taught her and Eudóxia at school. He had asked a year and a half's home leave, before embarking on his new ambassadorship, to Afghanistan. At night she could hear him in his bedroom practicing Persian and Pashto—the deep, swaying, sometimes guttural voice so Islamic in its passions that she imagined him in a loose turban and flowing robe, haggling for carpets or decreeing death to blasphemers. He modestly explained that neither language was too difficult, both being branches of Indo-European. Once in a while he took her to a concert or play, in the capital's scanty round of cultural events. But for days at a time they scarcely spoke, each preoccupied with different duties and circuits. Isabel held to her collegiate path in a kind of trance, under the spell of a vow for whose inner emblem two gray gun barrels served instead of a cross. She would not cause Tristão's death, and held him in her heart like a prisoner safe in a locked cell.

Only when Uncle Donaciano visited did Tristão in a

sense escape, for her uncle brought with him into stark Brasília—its vacuous grid, its fake lake, its red dust devils swirling where the grass of the enormous median strips had been allowed to die—the debonair sea breath of Rio. In his ice-cream suit and two-toned wing-tip shoes and red-ribboned Panama hat, he brought her presents too young for her age—a bouquet of cunningly made cloth flowers, a pottery tricycle with lumpy wheels that actually turned, a little circus of performers made of gold wire wrapped about semi-precious gems from Minas Gerais. He wanted to keep the girl in her alive, and he embodied Rio's childish, playful atmosphere, in which adults walk the streets in bathing suits and all year is spent constructing the quickly shattered toy of Carnaval. His soft-voiced bantering and the smell of his English Oval cigarettes in his ebony-and-ivory holder reminded her of the apartment with the snaky-armed brass chandelier and white rose of a skylight where she had first given herself to Tristão and her virgin blood had left a chalice-shaped stain on the quilted satin bedcover. Uncle Donaciano embodied love, of sorts; she twisted the DAR ring on her middle finger and asked him about Maria.

"Ah, Maria," he said, his eyes undercut by mauve shadows and a few strands of his graying honey-blond hair disarrayed by his aura of *distingué* melancholy. "Maria grows older."

"And less desirable?" Isabel teased him, blowing smoke upward toward her father's low ceiling. Salomão had sensitive lungs and Isabel only smoked at the university or when Uncle Donaciano visited, with his

English cigarettes in their tempting pastel-tinted papers. The settee she lounged upon was of teak and rattan, an elegant piece brought back from her father's tour of India years ago, and not very comfortable, though padded with sequinned cushions of black and purple and pink. "Perhaps," she said, extending her impudence, "you have used her too hard. You should make her an honest woman, as a reward for her years of service."

Donaciano blinked his weary eyes and touched his hair, tousling it further. He had accepted Isabel, conversationally, as one more of those adult women whose affection took the form of harassment. "Aunt Luna is still my wife," he said. "When you are naughty like this," he added, "you remind me of your mother. It is heartbreaking."

"Did my mother break your heart?" Isabel had long wondered if her uncle had loved his brother's wife. On his bedroom dresser, along with the requisite studio portrait and vacation snapshots of Aunt Luna, had stood a framed photograph of Cordélia—slightly blurred, standing on some rocks, beneath a single pine, a picnic site, where a breeze was spreading her wide white ruffled skirt and full gauzy sleeves, pressing her blouse against a full bosom, the white muslin emphasizing her mother's lovely tan, that drop of darkness which makes a true Brazilian beauty, the blurred face joyous in a half-smile, her glossy cheeks rounded, her eyelids lowered seemingly against some glare. Isabel had often stealthily studied the photograph, in Uncle Donaciano's absence, wondering where her father had been, how far or near the rim of the camera's field of vision. Who was making her mother laugh and lower her eyes flirtatiously? What had the voices in the air been saying? The very blurring in the photograph seemed a trace of her mother's breath, warm on the lens.

But these mysteries, these old romances, fade, and in the end are as depressing to youth as the photographs of old Rio with its trolley cars and passé fashions that hang on the walls of restaurants sentimental about themselves.

"She broke the hearts of all that looked upon her," Uncle Donaciano said. "Look at your father. He has never remarried. He is but a walking casket for the memory of your mother. Do not you, Isabel, imitate him in this folly, which has made him old before his time. Embrace life. Love many men before you die. This beach brat was but a beginning. Go to Europe. Become an opera singer."

"But I have no voice."

"Neither does Callas. What she has is *presence*."

He had, by kindness or accident, breached the forbidden, and mentioned her lover. "Speaking of beach brats, Uncle," she lazily ventured, "what do you hear from São Paulo? Has any harm come to that poor boy whom I so wantonly invited into our shared home? Ah, I do miss our apartment. Brasília is Hell, only duller than Hell must be. The city has been dropped on this hot plain like an egg to be fried."

His refined face, harrowed by decades of pleasure-seeking and obstinate selfishness, turned solemn. "My dearest, I hear nothing from São Paulo. It is a hell of another sort, the monstrously ugly demonstration of our futile desire to become an industrial nation, a nation like the soulless bullies north of the Equator. The world, once so green and charming—a literal paradise—is becoming infinitely ugly, Isabel; I am not sorry I will live to see little more of it." Tugging a snuffed stub of a cigarette from his holder to replace it with another, he managed a small fatal cough, though he was little older than forty. He did look faintly dingy and frazzled, for the first time in her vision of him—the cuffs of his ice-cream pants were soiled, and a button was missing from a jacket sleeve. His lack of a wife was beginning to tell.

It was curious for Isabel to see the two Leme brothers together; Uncle Donaciano made her father seem smaller and more gnomishly misshapen than ever, and more ruthlessly, pointlessly busy and official. Nevertheless, there was a fraternal likeness, and companionable murmurings in the library after dinner, over brandy or tall conical glasses of Cerma beer, while Isabel leafed through an album of Quattrocento paintings, all those deadly stiff madonnas and wizened baby Jesuses with buttonlike peepees—how tedious and dry what passed for learning was, how *past tense*, compared with what happened to her when she was with Tristão, or listening to one of those songs by Chico Buarque that slyly smuggled through the censorship lyrical hints of revolution against the military bosses, or watching one of the soap operas on television featuring actors and actresses as young as herself. This was present tense, carbonated by the future, a vague time of infinitely expansive possibilities. It was curious to look at her father and uncle together and to wonder if they had ever made a woman feel as Tristão did her. It seemed impossible, and yet there were moments when the two men abruptly broke into a cackle together, a flash of conspiratorial hilarity like a fissure reaching down to their shared boyhood, and she comprehended their fraternal maleness, their venerable complicity.

One evening after a visit by her uncle had ended in a flight back to Rio, her father, about to fly off himself, to Bogotá for a four-day economic conference, asked her into his study. Uneasily he offered her a choice of brandy, white-wine spritzer, *suco*, or Tab.

"No *cachaça*?" she asked, thinking of Ursula's shack with its sweet stink of fermented cane and pungent inchoate womanliness.

Her father permitted himself a snobbish shudder.

"Brandy, then."

Reluctantly he poured the French elixir. When the neck of the Cognac bottle had ceased its polite expostulations, he cleared his own throat and said, "Isabel, my paternal duty compels me to raise a delicate issue." The lights in his study were set at a low level, for reading, and his forehead seemed to topple forward in the raking shadows. "It concerns my brother. I cannot help but notice that an exceptional state of affection and familiarity exists between the two of you."

Isabel winced at the harsh taste of the brandy, and pointed out, "Ever since my mother died and you drowned your grief in a torrent of work and travel, my uncle has stood in the place of a father to me."

"Yes. I regret that it had to be so. To you I tender my belated and futile but sincere apologies. How can I justify myself? Your presence, perhaps, pained me, reminded me as it did of your mother, or of the procreative urge which had led to her miserable dying."

Isabel shrugged. "You did your best, Father, I am sure. The arrangement had its psychological advantages. It placed you beyond the reach of disillusion on my part. Each flying visit on your way through Rio, each week of shared vacation in Petrópolis or Patagonia or Miami Beach was magical to me, and had you been more available the magic would have worn thin. Children need physical affection, but are not choosy as to the source. Aunt Luna was friendly when not distracted by her social schedule, or rendered half-insane by one of her crash diets, and there were maids, cooks, nuns at school who all spared me a caress, or a smile, or a meaningful word. I was seen, I felt, as a precious child, well-favored. Always, in the background, like a massive sheltering wall, stood your high reputation."

Her father again allowed himself a shudder. When he closed his eyelids, the fine vein-webbed skin just below them twitched, like the nictitating membrane of a frog. "A sad childhood, as you describe it."

"It takes a sad childhood," she offered, "to make us eager to be adult."

"My brother—" he resumed, and interrupted himself.

"Speak frankly to me, even if I have never earned your trust. Did my brother, as you remember, ever abuse the closeness in which your mother's death and my ambition placed the two of you? Did he ever, I mean to say"—more hesitation, more facial quivering in the shadows—"trespass beyond the bounds of an uncle in his physical relation with you?"

He had touched her in her one remaining site of innocence.

Isabel was sickened by the question, it demanded so great a shift in her conception of her rearing and her sexual progress. She blushed, and a rosy veil seemed simultaneously to have suffused her childhood, obscuring its details. All she could see was the apartment, the view from its windows of similar windows and apartment houses and a sparkling slice of ocean, and not the inhabitants within, those many years she lived with her uncle. "He gave me avuncular hugs," she graspingly recalled, "and the quality of these became more courtly and gingerly once I—once I had matured. At times, he would come into my bedroom to kiss me good night, though no longer with a book of Babar or Tintin to read aloud, which he used to do, when I was a child, with a wonderful expressiveness and animation. Now he would merely sit, on the chair beside my bed; he would be silent, and seemed weary, and I sometimes felt, girlish though I was, that I was providing him something that Aunt Luna could not, though I did nothing. And then of course they separated, and Uncle would be out at strange hours, often several nights at a time, and I was enrolled with the nuns, so our contacts became rarer, and less comfortable when they did occur. Yes, I loved him, and he me, but I think you underrate, Father, the quality of the Leme blood, if you imagine your own brother capable of any physical trespass. He was totally honorable in his fulfillment of the guardianship your personal ambition and distraction placed upon him."

And yet, even as she enunciated her uncle's stout defense, sealing off the issue forever, she felt something stir amid the rosy vagueness of her early memories—some touch, or probe, or quickening, that memory would not allow her to recover. How frightening, she thought, that one does not merely grow and enlarge one's experience, but one loses earlier selves. We move forward into darkness, and darkness closes behind.

Her father's face in the warping light seemed to melt with sadness, becoming ever more shapeless and sluglike as he contemplated his daughter with gray-blue eyes several shades lighter than her own. He was thinking, Isabel could not know, of a certain *rapariga*, a black girl who sold sex and loved *cachaça*, a self-destructive girl with a small oval head and slender shameless body, to whom he used to resort chronically, in the gay Rio days before he married, and who became pregnant, by what man among her multitudes it could not be known. She disappeared from his life to bear the child, and now gazing at Isabel he wondered if his daughter had not somewhere in Brazil a gray-eyed brother, carrying in him to no purpose the proud Leme blood.

xi. *The Factory*

MEANWHILE, Tristão had acquired, thanks to diplomatic pressure from above, a job at a *fusca* factory. The cars, little Volkswagen "beetles" painted the shades of tan and brown that gave them the name *fusca* in Brazil, were manufactured in a giant shed whose northern end, like a hungry mouth, took in Volkswagen parts and whose southern end, like a tireless anus, emitted the completed *fuscas*. Inside, beneath a heaven consisting of a flat steel roof underpinned by diagonal braces and clattering, squealing tracks for the transport of heavy constituents like engines and chassis, the racket of assembly was so incessant and loud that Tristão feared he would lose not only his ear for forró music but all capacity for the enjoyment of life. The machines made machines of men.

His first assigned task had been the sweeping up of loose screws, Styrofoam food containers, slivers of metal, and oil spills—the sticky secretions of a giant industrial beast. Then he was promoted to the position of right-handed bolter—at first, of the bearing-retaining bolts for the rear brake plates (sixteen millimeters, tightening to a foot-pound torque of forty-three), and then, at the beginning of his second year, of engine-mounting bolts, which were seventeen millimeters in diameter but were tightened to a torque of only twenty-two. Their lesser torque and a more accessible angle reduced the ache at the base of his neck and beneath his right shoulder blade at the end of an eight-hour day. At night, lying down to sleep, he felt as if someone were probing this spot with an awl; slowly the necessary muscles compensated and the ache sealed over. He marvelled at the look of his hands, each little muscle overdeveloped to bulging, and a slab of callus across the palm where the torque wrench was gripped.

His bolting partner, the second year, was a good-natured, left-handed *cafuzo* from Maranhão named Oscar. As they functioned all day in symmetry, turning and tightening the six bolts (four major and two minor) that held the plucky little engine to the *fusca*'s compartment brace, Oscar's broad flat face, in which genes fetched by slaving ship from Africa met Asian genes transported on foot from Siberia to the sweltering Amazon, became more familiar to Tristão than his own. When he looked into the clouded mirror in the workers' washroom, the face there seemed a mirage, a mistake—too dark, too high-browed, too thick-lipped, too intensely staring. Oscar had a wide space between his two front teeth, so that in the mirror Tristão's two incisors looked painfully wedged together, so accustomed had he grown to the gap in Oscar's mischievous, companionable smile.

Sometimes, to relieve their boredom, they would bolt in an engine upside down, and if the workers further along the line, who made the cable and hose connections, coöperated in the jest, the hardy little automobile, at the far southern end of the factory, would actually propel itself and its driver the few hundred yards to the parking lot where shipping was staged. The Volkswagen was a great-hearted machine, Oscar explained, designed by a famous sorcerer called Hitler to take the German masses to a place called Valhalla.

Had their prank been discovered, Tristão and Oscar would have been fired and jailed for sabotage. Under the military government, the vocabulary of wartime colored the language of the state. Tristão would have welcomed release from his job but dreaded prison, as removing him still further from Isabel. He had not yet surrendered his dream of love. Nor had he lived utterly chaste: Chiquinho's neighborhood, interconnected by wandering children, provided a number of willing big sisters, and even at the plant, for all the tyrannical rigor of the regulations which the government and the *sindicatos* in collusion perpetrated, contacts could be made, and even consummated, in the coffee breaks and during trips to the washroom. Nevertheless, he had remained chaste in his soul, that spiritual organ where his life cried out for its eternal shape.

Virgílio, the leaner and younger of the gunmen, had guarded Tristão closely at first, greeting him at the factory gate after work, accompanying him throughout the evening's little recreations, and sleeping in the same room, his cot barring the door. But during the long hours while Tristão was at the factory, Virgílio had become involved with a soccer team in Moóca, the Tiradentes. Their practice sessions sometimes stretched into the late afternoons, and their away games would absent him well into the evening, and then overnight, and then for several nights at a time. Chiquinho, Polidora, and Tristão speculated that he had become involved with a woman—for there were many girls shamelessly eager to attach themselves to a soccer star, let alone one who packed a gun—or else that he had been reassigned to a more urgent case by the shadowy *poderosos*, the Big Boys.

But Chiquinho warned, "Do not think, brother, that because Virgílio has become delinquent you can therefore escape in pursuit of your romantic madness. The Big Boys know where I live, and if you escape their vigilance they will take vengeance upon me and my innocent family. Little Esperança or Pacheco could be dumped with her or his throat slit in my front yard. Polidora might be kidnapped and gang-raped. I do not speak of myself—I appeal to your decency as an uncle, and as a brother-in-law."

"Where was your decency as a brother, my brother, when you betrayed me into the hands of my enemies?"

Chiquinho's chalky-brown arms flopped about awkwardly, disavowingly. "Any enemy of your folly is my friend. I acted to save you from your sexual obsession, at the request of our blessed mother."

Tristão laughed at this absurd lie. "My mother took a shine to Isabel."

"Not so—she detests her, as one of the oppressor class, and condescending besides. The shine runs only one way, for reasons of perverse upper-class psychology. I observed the girl when she was here—she was fearless, as only the unreachably rich can be. The reactionaries, at least, respect the poor enough to fear them. But forget this blond piece of fluff, just as she no doubt has forgotten you. Have not Polidora and I fed you, day after day? Are you not now better off than when you came to us, two years ago? You have a marketable skill, and savings in the bank, in an economy enjoying unprecedented growth—over ten percent a year!"

Tristão marvelled that his brother, like him the son of a black mother, could mouth so earnestly the pap of the white establishment. We enslave ourselves for crumbs—for the mere image and rumor of crumbs. Tristão, even while submitting to his brother's *abraço* of repledged fraternity, was resolving to escape.

He went to his bank and withdrew his cruzeiros— enough to last him several weeks, if he lived modestly, and travelled on the cheapest conveyances. One night, with Virgílio safely off in Espírito Santo playing in some intra-regional semi-finals, he waited for the noises of the cranky, sleep-resisting children to die down behind the wall of his barred cell of a bedroom, and for the murmur of Chiquinho and Polidora processing the

102

day's events—her neighborhood gossip, his professional difficulties as head of the lab-cleaning team—to give way to an intertwined sighing and snoring. It had been interesting for Tristão, after the *cachaça*-soaked chaos and squalor of his mother's shack, to observe an aspiring lower-middle-class marriage. Chiquinho and Polidora seemed to him a couple crouching as they moved down a narrow corridor, with flaking paint and leaking walls, bumping their heads every time they tried to straighten up, never coming to the large room they envisioned, with its airy high ceiling and its tall windows open to a view of the world. Instead, they had this long apprehensive creep together under flickering light bulbs, while their bones turned brittle, their skin shrivelled, and their hair fell out. Tristão, once he rejoined himself with Isabel, would be exempt forever from such a living death. She was his eternal life.

The wall near his head now vibrated with the sound of oblivious breathing. The neighborhood about the little ranch house was still but for the yowling of mating cats and the humming of stolen electricity in the illegally installed transformers. Stealthily, barefoot on the tile, wearing some old swimming shorts and his LONE STAR T-shirt, which did him for pajamas, he packed the bulk of his wardrobe and his paltry few possessions in a new bag, a knapsack of luminous orange canvas, which he had purchased and smuggled underneath his bed. His plan was to hide the bag beneath a stunted jelly palm that grew in the corner of Chiquinho's tiny lot. The palm's orange fruit and low broad branches made it an ideally secretive accomplice. He would leave for the *fusca* factory early in the morning, while the children were still badgering Polidora for breakfast, like tiny sharks taking bites out of a larger, dying shark, and while Chiquinho was having his compulsory morning shower, since even a fleck of human dander could play havoc with the computer chips. Unseen, Tristão would retrieve the knapsack at the corner and slip it onto his back and be off to Brasília. The money he had withdrawn from his bank was bundled and tucked into the knapsack; now in the dead of night he stepped outside to hide its orange bulk beneath the little jelly palm.

But his brother was not asleep, for no sooner had the aluminum screen door, with its stamped waffle pattern in imitation of woven cane, clicked shut behind Tristão, than Chiquinho, a gray shadow naked but for boxer shorts, was beside him on the small cement porch. He had come around from the back door. His hand on Tristão's arm was like one of the metal hands that lifted large parts in the *fusca* factory. "You cannot leave."

"Why not?"

"Polidora and I need the rent the Big Boys pay for you. Your departure will disgrace us."

"You have already disgraced yourself, by taking money from your brother's abductors."

"Where else, in Brazil, will money come from but from the *poderosos*? They will kill you, for going against them."

"To die is not the worst thing a man can do. To live

defeated, that is the worst. Life without Isabel to me is no life."

"She will have forgotten you."

"If so, then I will be the wiser for knowing it."

"The Big Boys will blame me. They will take their revenge on my family."

"We have had this conversation before."

Their voices were urgent, but soft, out here among the yowling of the cats. To avoid waking the family asleep inside the house, the brothers had moved to the little yard, with its threadbare grass and packed red earth, littered with Esperança's and Pacheco's cheap plastic toys. Chiquinho's hand stayed on Tristão's arm like a shackle. Tristão moved to shake it off, but gently as yet. "Tell them you could not help but let me go," he told his brother. "It is the truth. It was not your job to hold me, it was Virgílio's."

"The truth is no help to men like us. People are killed in Brazil for telling the truth." In the streetlight his brother's face, thrust unnaturally close to make its whispers heard, seemed the color of buffed metal, bolted tight upon its own fanatic self-interest. But such grand talk of "men like us," what did it have to do with Tristão and his need for Isabel—her white beauty that slipped through a darkened room like a viscid oil, the lubricated two valves that welcomed his aching yam below? He tried to pull his arm free, harder. The two brothers began to wrestle, with silenced grunts, there on the little plot of scratchy grass, on the empty blue-lit street. The stuffed knapsack was an encumbrance, and

Chiquinho in his financial panic had the bony strength of a demon. But Tristão's own muscles, hardened by two years of bolt-tightening in a repetitive pattern that forced itself upon him even in the rhythms of sleep, like a template, tensed and twisted his brother's brittle arm with his free hand until Chiquinho whimpered and backed away. Still Chiquinho held a position of combat, his long arms out like those of a beach crab standing on its tail in self-defense, and would have flung himself again upon his brother had not the one-edged razor blade, emblazoned *Gem*, materialized in Tristão's fingers. He kept it in his shorts at night, in case Virgílio returned from soccer—as had happened once or twice, after a losing match—in a drunken, petulant, assaultive mood. It was the work of a split second for two thin quick fingers to fish Gem out. The blade made him a new creature, with a single waving tentacle. "Careful," he warned, waving his tentacle slowly in the light, so his brother could see the glinting edge. He felt magically concentrated in that merciless honed edge, much as, two years ago, the gray guns of the two hirelings had refocused the ranch-house living room, redrawn its lines.

He dropped his knapsack with its array of straps to the ground. While Chiquinho's eyes were focused on the glinting, gently waving little blade, Tristão's other hand gripped his brother's skinny throat to hold his head still. He rested the edge of the blade on Chiquinho's cheek. His movements tense and calibrated, he let the blade's upper corner puncture the skin and then drew the edge down the chalky flesh into where day-old whiskers made their prickly shadow. The gash, five or so centimeters long, leaped up smoothly, emitting a thin sheet of red; something rasped in the dryness of Chiquinho's throat. His Adam's apple tried to work its way around Tristão's stern grip. Tristão moved the blade across his brother's hypnotized gaze as if to transfer it to the other cheek, but read a glaze of pacification in Chiquinho's eyes.

"Show that to the Big Boys, to prove how you struggled," Tristão suggested. "See, I have done you a kindness, in return for the many you have shown me."

xii. *The Bus Terminal*

THUS TRISTÃO made his escape, though barefoot and in swimming shorts, and the T-shirt so tattered and faded that its advertisement for a restaurant in Leblon was all but illegible. He did not feel that the rhythm of this bloody fraternal encounter permitted a return to his room to retrieve the clothes in which he had planned to set off to work—the slacks and the flowing silk shirt Isabel had bought for him on their honeymoon. Chiquinho might recover from the shock of his wound and set up an obstructing cry. Better to abandon the clothes to their next wearer and trot smoothly down the street, taking care not to cut his feet on the abundant broken glass.

He counted the cross-streets and after ten of them he slowed to a walk, panting, his back sweating beneath the straps of the knapsack. Tonight was already tomorrow. The buses had stopped running. The sidewalks abraded the soles of his feet, which had grown soft after two years in shoes; and São Paulo cement was not the sand of Rio's beaches. He threaded his way out of

Moóca north into middle-class neighborhoods where the suspicious gaze of block watchmen urged him to move on, even when they spared him insults. The intenser glow of the sky in the west told him where the heart of the city lay. On a high overpass, vaulting the ravine of the Rio Anhangabahu and approaching the Avenida do Estado, Tristão walked above the green acreage of the Parque Dom Pedro Segundo, the treetops frozen and scrabbled like hardened wax. Crossing into the Sé district, he was greeted by a quickened pace of life: *boîtes* and bars emitted the monotonous bliss of pulsating music.

As he moved north, toward the Estação da Luz, girls in high white boots and very small shorts stood chattering with men whose glances kept darting here and there, alert for any crack in the wall of life where a weed of opportunity might bloom. One of the booted *raparigas*, her color that of sanded and oiled cedar wood, approached him, poor as he must appear; so great and cheerful was her shamelessness, the tops of her breasts bared in their taut blouse to the dark gooseflesh of her areolae, that his poor yam made a start at stiffening. Usually at this hour his consciousness was buried in a chronic nightmare of turning bolts that would not turn, while fragments of Oscar grinned at him as in a broken mirror.

"You like me, I know," the girl said. "My name is Odete."

"I like you, but my heart is pledged to another, whom I am on my way to rescue from the Big Boys."

109

"If she loves you in turn, she would not mind if you let me blow you, for a mere ten new cruzeiros."

The sum was about the price of a small shrimp pie, an *empadinha de camarão*, which he also craved. "But where would we go together?" he asked.

"A block from here is a clean hotel, where they know me and charge an honest rate, for working men." This girl sensed that there was more to him than bare feet and a torn T-shirt. In the hotel, she said he was too big for her mouth, so he must fuck her, for only ten more new cruzeiros, plus the price of the condom. Tristão puritanically resisted the condom, but Odete said it was for his good and not hers, since bad girls like her did not have long lives. There were many diseases, and drug addiction went with the late hours and the stress, and furthermore there were sick men who killed whores for sport.

"Then why . . . ?" he began to ask.

"Live my life at all?" When she smiled, her lips peeled back upon her teeth like a fruit splitting to reveal its little round seeds. "Better a short life than none. Even the longest life feels too short on the deathbed."

"My mother," Tristão felt compelled to tell her, "is a whore."

Odete's plucked eyebrows made perfect arcs of surprise above her cinnamon-brown eyes. "And do you hate her for that?"

With no love proclaimed between them, this girl was easier to talk to than Isabel. "I feel nothing about that," he confessed. "That is what she has taught me—to feel nothing for her."

"Ah, we always feel something for our mothers," Odete said. "We fool ourselves, that it is nothing."

He wanted to describe to her how Isabel had pretended to feel love for his unlovable mother, but this seemed too complicated to explain, and an imposition and defilement all around. But now, even though he had not yet fucked her, Tristão felt a little bored by this encounter. These girls who kept appearing in his life, willing to fuck, suggested to him how precarious and arbitrary was the perfect love he and Isabel shared. Love was everywhere, he perceived, and it solved no problems. In fact, it created problems. The men who strode the noon streets of São Paulo excitedly conducting business were not awake at three in the morning conducting love. Tristão trembled within, to see how tenuous was his life's grip on any pattern, beyond that of a steady decay from birth to death; he clung to Isabel's image, as the one shining thread in his dark future.

Nevertheless, he fucked Odete, at first with her on all fours, at her suggestion, her buttocks raised like smooth oiled arcs of cedar wood, and then with her riding him, he half-propped up on pillows against the padded headboard—stained by many greasy heads—so his lips grazed her left nipple in its circle of dark gooseflesh each time her breast bounced past; she rose and fell, cylinder to his piston. He was slow to come in the clammy embrace of the condom, and when he did, writhing and whimpering, she smiled in professional satisfaction. As she lifted herself from his detumescing prick, there came a small sucking sound from around a corner of dense curly hair dusted with red, as was the hair of his head.

Unlike Isabel, Odete was built close to the ground, with thick legs and an abdomen that in a few years would sway like a hammock. Her smile of satisfaction was swallowed now by determined efficiency; if she got back outside, on the Avenida Cásper Libero, she might land another customer before dawn.

As he paid her, he asked, "Could you tell me, before we part, where I might buy a pair of shoes at this hour? As you can see, I can afford them—I merely left my former residence in haste. And a small shrimp pie—the hour is approaching for my usual breakfast." Why did Tristão feel shy with this stocky whore, now that they were dressed? He felt she needed fewer illusions than he to live—that in this dirty world she was streamlined, a fish in water, where he had to make his way cumbersomely knobbed and hobbled by a sense of mission, of superior destiny.

"Shrimp pie, I can point you toward a little place, off the Jardim da Luz, but for shoes, you may have to wait until morning. Do you still like me? Do you think the one you love would mind, that you fucked me and played with my nipples?"

"She would keep it in proportion," Tristão estimated. "Like you, she is a realist."

After Tristão and Odete parted forever, and he found a bright-lit triangular store where the sleepy clerk had

no *empadinhas de camarão* but *empadinhas de galinha*
instead, and stale at that, he carried his knapsack north,
through the district of Bom Retiro, with its shuttered
shops illegibly lettered in a crumbling, fading alphabet
of letters shaped like flames, to the bus terminal in front
of the Sorocabana Train Station. Its portals poured
sickly electric light out into the dawn. Within, hundreds
of sleepers lay stretched on the floor with their bundles,
their caged parrots and pigs muzzled with strips of
checkered cloth. The terminal was like a snout, smelling
of the vast back country, thrust to the edge of the metropolis. The musty dankness of human sleep rose heavily from the floor. Loose chickens roosted on the backs
of molded-plastic chairs where drunkards nodded off,
their heads doing a twitchy dance. The *caipiras*, the
hicks, had filled the nooks behind stairways and banks
of lockers and lined the terminal's walls with impro-
vised shelters; what looked at a glance like corners full
of trash turned out to be people sleeping in a huddle,
layered over with cardboard and plastic garbage bags to
give a semblance of shelter from the glaring, flickering
lights. Now, as morning light crept into the terminal,
caged roosters began to crow and small children, clad in
rags that came no lower than the inverted navels of their
swollen bellies, toddled back and forth looking for
places to peepee, blinking in bewilderment as to why
they had been born.

Tristão at last found, in the maze of the building, the
place to buy a ticket to Brasília. The counter would
open in two hours and the line was already long. In the

line, travelling salesmen in rumpled suits and students in sandals and ponytails and Che Guevara sweatshirts mingled with poor *caboclos* and *sertanejos* from the hinterland, dressed in what seemed pajamas stiff with yellow dust, who had been attracted to São Paulo like starving dogs to the depleted carcass of an ox. Even these looked down upon the black boy in bare feet and old swimming shorts, and several cut ahead of him in line, until Tristão flashed, with a curt word or two, his warrior mettle.

He tucked the ticket to Brasília into the inner pocket with his razor blade, and found a sports shop just opening on another floor of the terminal where, for three times what it had cost to sleep with Odete, he bought a pair of white canvas tennis sneakers. They looked on the stems of his slender ankles like clumsy levers, like glaring boats, but were blessedly comfortable, with spongy soles. The bus trip to Brasília took fifteen hours, and he had to stand in the aisle as far as Belo Horizonte.

xiii. *The Ice-Cream Parlor*

Iالس ABEL AND HER FRIENDS would often spend evenings at an ice-cream parlor, the Sorveteria Jânio Quadros, named after a President who had melted away. Some Brazilian Presidents quit in a huff, some shot themselves to show their love for their country, some were replaced by the military to please the United States— only Kubitschek, in Isabel's lifetime, had served a full term, and he had saddled the country with Brasília and inflation as his memorial. Posters of Brigitte Bardot and Fidel Castro were up on the walls of the ice-cream parlor; tall booths gave each group of four or five or (squeezed) six or seven in a booth the feeling of conspiratorial privacy. The blue smoke of cigarettes— Continental, Hollywood, Luís XV were the common brands—hung as thick as the smell of sleep and urine in the bus terminal that Tristão had traversed eighteen hours ago. A marble counter up front bristled with the chrome apparatus—the nozzles and pumps, the knobs and flexible tubing—needed for the production of sodas, sundaes, and espresso coffee, tarry and bitter as Brazilians like it.

"Sartre is a one-eyed clown and pedophile," one of Isabel's university friends, Sylvio, was saying this night, "but Cohn-Bendit will bring de Gaulle down, just as Jerry Rubin brought Johnson down, and Dubček will destroy Brezhnev." The globe was in turmoil, beyond the borders of Brazil, and it seemed youth was taking over, and Isabel's circle of the sons and daughters of the elite were as excited as soccer fans in the stands as the tide on the field turned. Sylvio, whose father was a great *fazendeiro* in Bahia, showed his radicalism by having shifted his brand of cigarettes from the costly Minister to Mistura Fina, the rasping cigarettes of the workers.

"Brezhnev will never permit Socialism to have a human face," argued Nestor Villar from his side of the smoky booth. Thin and ascetic, he was the son of a colonel, and claimed to be an anarchist, far beyond the futile pieties of the left wing. "If Socialism were to take on a human face, it would vanish—*hup, poof!* The dictatorship of the proletariat cannot afford to have its subjects be human—it must have robots on the bottom, and monsters on top." Saliva welled in the corners of his lips as he spoke, making disgusting white bubbles. Isabel had slept with Nestor a few times, several terms ago, but his penis was thin, with sad blue veins and an alarming bright-pink scrotum, and needed from her too much undignified labor to make it stand. She had broken the relationship off, on the excuse of his political views. For he had imbibed more of his father's fascism than he knew, and his supposed anarchy lay adjacent to militaristic crackdown. Anarchy, Isabel had told him, merely means for you doing away with the feeble restraints to exploitation and pillage that already exist; if there is one nation on earth that does not need an ideal of anarchy, it is anarchic Brazil, whose national flag so wistfully inscribes order and progress across the southern sky.

"In the United States," Sylvio went on, studying Isabel's face through the haze of smoke, the fumes of coffee, and the sour-milk scent of ice cream melting in heavy glass dishes shaped like caravels, "the blacks have reduced Washington to rubble in the wake of Martin King's assassination. In Chicago and Baltimore, too. The end is near for the lily-white imperialists of the North."

He knew she liked to hear good things of blacks. She had not yet slept with him, but negotiations were under way. In the torchlit darkness of an anti-imperialist march, he would be at her side, his hand seeking the hand of hers that was not upholding a fiery placard or a candle of protest. In the warm muddle of a pot passaround, while the bossa nova of Elis Regina or the *tropicalismo* of Gilberto Gil or, from a greater distance, the jazz of Coltrane or plangent Spanish of Joan Baez trickled through Isabel's slackening brain, the lips that she found pressing on hers, while a fumbling hand parted the crevices of her clothing, belonged to Sylvio. He had greasy curly hair to his shoulders and was shorter than she, but his shortness did not preclude her sleeping with him; the moment had simply not arrived, and she did not wish it to arrive. As long as she had not slept with Sylvio, there was something in reserve, something to savor or anticipate. She had just turned twenty-one, and her life seemed to be emptying out rather than filling in. Her father had taken up his post in Afghanistan, and Uncle Donaciano came less and less to Brasília. Now that she was a complete legal woman, she interested him less; it had been only her embodiment of innocence that had fascinated him, with its possibility of violation. It was May, and winter was setting in, here on the *planalto*, with its starry nights that had compelled her, for the first time in her life, to add wool sweaters to her wardrobe. This term, she had shifted her field of concentration from art history to botany; still, she felt adrift, unsatisfied by her education. The acts of learning and reading—all those nagging gray rows of type, scratching her eyes, demanding she go back and forth until some kind of meaning tumbled forth in a gush like an ugly baby—did not please her; the future did not belong to written words. It belonged to music and to flowing pictures, one image sliding colorfully into another, the soap operas and football matches and reruns of last February's Carnaval; she had installed a television set in her dormitory room, and her roommates worried about her. She was living in a dream, she would flunk out.

Yet she lit another Hollywood cigarette and told Sylvio snappily, "The blacks will never revolt, there or here. They are too happy and good. They are too beautiful. Always it was so. The Indians died of slavery; the blacks rose above it, of their own great natures. Because they are superior, they let themselves be treated as inferior. Like the Jews, they are able to live in our hideous twentieth century—*live*, and not merely survive." The mention of Jews was perhaps flirtation with Sylvio, an imperceptible bringing closer of the moment they would sleep together, for he was descended from the "new Christians" who migrated with the first Portuguese colonists, to thrive in the sugar economy, blending in without prejudice, it seemed. Yet the Jewishness was never quite forgotten, the contrast between "new" and "old" diminishing as Catholicism faded through the generations but never quite vanishing, like the stain in a threadbare tablecloth that persists through any number of launderings, albeit as a fainter and fainter shadow.

Clarice, Isabel's roommate, who had slept with Sylvio and wanted to sleep with Nestor, even though Isabel in a fit of giggling indiscretion had described what it was like, drew with lazy ease on a Continental and said to her hostilely, "I think you romanticize them, darling. We all do, to spare ourselves guilt over their abysmal condition. And they conspire with us, is the insidious thing, by being so damned picturesque."

The other co-ed present, pedantic Ana Vitória, with her astonishing hair cut in rough clumps and dyed burnt sienna, and her tiny wire-rim eyeglasses perched on the end of her button of a nose, intervened: "So does contemporary sociology romanticize, following after Gilberto

Freyre, that master of self-congratulation. If Brazilians did not romanticize, they would have to awaken to their realities, and the realities of Karl Marx."

"Marx himself is a romantic fool," Nestor scoffed. "He thinks the proletariat is one big superman when in fact it is a collection of snivelling, petty-minded connivers and freeloaders. Like the capitalists, the Communists seek to paper over the oppressions and cruelties of their societies with glamorous myths. What are Castro and Mao and Ho Chi Minh but our movie stars, our Mickey Mouses and Gary Coopers on their posters? All governments seek to hide from us the truths about ourselves. Only in a state of anarchy does the truth about men emerge. We are beasts, killers, savages, whores."

Ana Vitória protested, "Why set 'whores' in such a string of pejorative terms? The whore is a woman, trading a woman's assets in a certain type of market situation. Your queens of society, your Princess Graces of Monaco, trade under different conditions. There is no sexual morality. The phrase is an oxymoron. Women must survive."

"Exactly!" cried Nestor, in a tone of triumph, like the military seizing upon chaos to impose itself.

"Exactly, exactly," echoed Clarice across the table, a single broad plank of purpleheart, or *pau roxo*, sticky with ice cream rubbed into the grain, and striped all along the edges with cigarette burns. She spoke in a throaty voice to Nestor: "As you say, anarchy is the only honest condition—the human race without romanticism, without capitalism, without Marxist bullshit."

Nestor looked foolish at the compliment, his acne-dotted jaw going slack, as if his prick were being sucked. Isabel closed her eyes and pictured his wormy white organ and shuddered.

"And Isabel—do you agree?" Sylvio asked her, thinking perhaps that such reëvaluation of all values brought his conquest of her closer.

"Ana says only 'survive.' I say 'live,' " said Isabel, sounding naïve to herself, and blushing a little. There was a fever in her veins she could not bring these others to share.

Sylvio, his broad face eager and wary like that of Tristão's brother Euclides on the beach that day, had an announcement to make, in a voice so hushed and charged that even the cigarette smoke seemed to freeze in attention. "This Thursday. A university-wide student protest. Scheduled for noon. We will march up the Eixo Rodoviário to the cathedral and continue toward the presidential palace until the police open fire. We want casualties, to the point of international scandal. Television cameramen will be there, we have been promised. It is timed to coincide with worker strikes in all the textile and paper-products plants. It will be beautiful—we will slay the beast with our deaths. Those who survive will rally afterwards on the golf course."

Ana Vitória's pinched, determined voice was saying, with the dryness of pages turning, "Student protest is the opposite of worker protest: it is the attempt of the ruling class's younger generation to maintain power, disguised as revolution."

121

"Brazil is not too romantic but not romantic enough," Nestor was expounding, under the goad of Clarice's longing for him. "It is the most pragmatic nation on the continent. Who have our revolutionaries been? A dentist who wrote bad poems, and an Emperor's regent son looking to keep his job!"

"Isabel," yet another voice was pronouncing, in a tone both shy and demanding. "Isabel."

She opened her eyes and saw Tristão standing there, at the end of the plank of scarred purpleheart, a tall black boy saddled with an orange knapsack and wearing a T-shirt so faded and tattered its legend could scarcely be read. For a flashlit moment, in the glare of her friends' startled stares, she doubted that she knew him. Her first emotion was fright. "How did you find me?" she asked him.

Her accusatory tone made him smile. In the slow ease with which he bared his perfect teeth, the strong square taken-for-granted teeth of youth, she knew him again, as an amplifier of her best and deepest self. His brow, also square-cut, was taller than she had remembered, like a rampart erected above the deep-set eyes swimming sadly in their own inky darkness. "I smelled you out," he explained in a voice whose sombre clothy texture, with its Carioca softness, exerted a spell of silence upon her sharply talkative companions. The lovable shape of his nose, flattened as if to give its nostrils a greater grip on the air and its fragrances, made his hyperbole plausible.

His voice had set off vibrations within her: she felt

transposed—harpsichord music now scored for string quartet. His smile went diminuendo, turning grave as he explained, "Virgílio heard from César that you were a student at the university here. When I got off the bus, after a journey of fifteen hours, I asked where the students might gather. This is the twelfth place I have searched. You do not seem pleased to see me. You are no longer a girl of eighteen."

"I *am* pleased," Isabel told him. "Excuse me," she said to Sylvio, who sat between her and freedom, on the outside of the booth.

He asked her, "Are you in trouble? Who is this riff-raff?"

To Isabel's ears, Sylvio's voice sounded blanched. She heard the fear tightening it, pitching it high, though he had just boasted of marching into the guns of the military, to make a splash of news with his and their blood. She steeled herself, explaining firmly, "He is my friend." She could not quite bring herself to say, *He is my husband.*

Clarice was exchanging conspiratorial glances with Nestor across the table, and beside him Ana Vitória stared stiffly ahead, as if waiting for Marxism to tell her what to do. Sylvio, petulantly declining to rise, turned his thighs sideways so Isabel could ease past him, her ass in its denim miniskirt an inch from his face. Nestor's acne-dotted cheeks looked slapped, so reddened had they been by this sudden embarrassment, this irruption into their student life.

"*Ciao*, guys," Isabel said to them all.

"*Ciao,*" they said back, in a limp, jarring chord.

"*Adeus,*" Tristão pronounced, more formally, with a dismissive bow.

Cradling her heavy botany text against her taut breasts, she followed him through walls of blue smoke to the out-of-doors. The fresh air, the night sky, his muscular dark presence—this was ice cream of another kind, a deliciousness in the dimension not of the mouth and tongue and throat but of the organs lower down, intimately linked to the soul and its aura. A rip in his T-shirt at his shoulder revealed a triangular patch darker than varnished purpleheart, and she remembered how touchingly susceptible to scars was black skin, which unlike white skin never forgives, remembering each scratch and blister with a forever dulled gray like that of chalk on an imperfectly washed blackboard.

xiv. *Under the Stars*

O UTSIDE ON THE SIDEWALK, Brasília's urban il-
luminations pushed back against the overarching emptiness. Restaurants serving watery *canja de
galinha* and bars emitting the harsh judgmental laughter
of youth threw squares of light onto the sidewalk;
overhead, lit rectangular windows mounted as if to out-
swarm and smother the stars. Isabel wore a little rose-
colored short-sleeved jersey and had tied around her
waist, in case the night turned cool, a sweatshirt imprinted with the Catedral Nacional's crown of thorns; as
she quickened her steps to match Tristão's stride, the
swinging sweatshirt gave her hips a heedless, challenging sway. His raw white tennis sneakers flickered ahead
of them, in and out of puddles of electric light. Other
pedestrians glanced briefly in their direction; they were
a mismatched couple but Brazil had been populated by
mismatched couples.

Beginning to breathe hard, she dared touch his arm,
as if to slow his pace; her hand jumped back, startled by
the iron hardness of his biceps. Yes, he was older, his

muscles more knotted, his face a bit leaner, with, she noticed from the side, the faintest crease at the corner of his lips, where none had existed before. She felt lifted up, exalted, but also hurried, as if time had turned a corner and was rolling downhill.

"Yes, I have been working," he told her. "For two years they had me turning engine-brace bolts in the *fusca* factory, until I was turning them in my dreams. I wanted to dream of you, Isabel, but I was losing your face, your voice, day by day, night after night. I rebelled, and cut my brother's face to get away."

"And now you see me," Isabel said, feigning a jaunty gaiety, resting her white hand on his iron arm and turning him, with his orange knapsack behind him like a hump, to walk more slowly toward where the lights were thinning, as the Eixo Rodoviário Norte gently turned. "You still like me?"

Her dear convex monkey face, bright with the pallor of student sleeplessness, had a certain faint fragility now, as if the sadness of life were slowly draining it of juice. "Touch me and see," he told her.

"Here on the street? You are crazy, Tristão." Yet the idea moistened the crotch of her bikini underpants, beneath her denim skirt.

"Are you ashamed to be with me? I fled my brother's house in the clothes I generally sleep in. That accounts for my shabbiness. Actually, I have resources—two years' worth of savings in my knapsack."

"Never will I not love being with you," she said, and as they strolled side by side she brushed her other hand across the fly of his shorts, where his yam had awakened.

"We must fuck, and talk," he told her.

"Yes. Keep walking, my husband. Soon there will be a place."

They were beyond most of the city lights and were passing knots of workers waiting for the buses that would take them back to their shantytowns miles into the bush; their pale shirts fell away in the darkness like whitecaps in the night ocean. Now when no headlights passed there was only the flicker of his sneakers and the sideways tossing of her imprinted sweatshirt, her long platinum hair. The sidewalk gave out. The double highway had a middle strip of grass as wide as a city block. When they walked on it she could feel through her sandals small prickings of dew descended from the inverted bowl of night ever clearer and more crystalline above them. Their pace together turned languid and halting as they paused to kiss and to stroke one another and to reach under each other's thin clothes to seize and caress yielding skin.

Here and there in the great central highway strip were plantings, virtual groves; as they drew near to one, her botany training enabled her to recognize *pacovas*, wild banana trees, with their huge sheltering leaves, interspersed with Spanish bayonet in glowing lilylike blossom. The growth was dense enough for Tristão and Isabel to feel hidden, on the floor of bark mulch and dried *pacova* fronds. As the lovers lay there they could see far above them the black sky strewn with stars, thicker in some places than others, like desert shrubs spaced closer together in dried streambeds that had once held water. From within the grove, away from Brasília's willed lights, the stars shone with an intensity that overruled their disorder: surely some vast miracle was being proclaimed. It needed only for her to slip the bikini panties out from under the small rough skirt and for him to discard his swimming shorts for them to become lovers once more. Her cunt was to him like cream poured upon two years of aching.

"Let us never be parted again," he sighed, his throbs still ebbing within her.

"We will not," she promised.

"Where can we go? Your father's wrath will follow us everywhere."

"It is not wrath, it is distaste, bred of his cultural conditioning. Look above us, Tristão. Vast as that sky is, so is Brazil's hinterland. We will go west, and lose ourselves in it."

As these two lay hidden in the ornamental planting—rendered junglelike by the irrepressible wild banana plant, whose green and pointed fruit mingled its faint sweet scent with Isabel's stirred-up musk and Tristão's *bodum*, which was strong after his day's ordeal of travel—Brasília's traffic rushed along both halves of the superhighway; winged angels of headlight glare visited them blindly in the undergrowth, engendering jagged, wheeling leaf-and-stem shadows and exposing to the concealed lovers' own eyes their bare limbs and exposed soft bellies. In these washes of brightness their faces looked, each to the other, frightened. Each was trying to imagine the hinterland.

"We can live for a while on my money," he told her, "but inflation eats at it, it will not last long."

"I have spending money only, but I can steal some things from my father's apartment, to sell as we go. I still have the candlestick I did not give your mother, and Uncle Donaciano's cigarette box and little cross. I can steal what my father has kept of my mother's jewels. They are in effect mine anyway."

"Do not take anything of your father's that has sentimental value," Tristão commanded. "I hope some day to be his friend."

She made an involuntary noise that told him this was a hopeless vision. Fright, dark and extensive like the territory to which they had committed themselves, coldly invaded his stomach; yet being with her halved the terror. Bits of Brazilian-pine bark, laid down to mulch the planting when it was new and now rotting back into nature, had stuck to her bottom during their fucking; he asked her to get up on all fours, like Odete yesterday, and brushed the embedded bits from the twin pillows of her white, white ass. He kissed the left buttock, then the right, and stuck his tongue into the tight small hole between. He had never done this before, even in the Hotel Amour. She reflexively pulled away, then, feeling serious intent in the grip of his hands on her hips, settled back into his face with its boneless prong, not wishing to sully their love with any stain of shame. What was hers was his. This was new ground for them. He inhaled, with those round apprehensive nostrils she had freshly admired tonight, the basic mystery of her shit, matter that was hers yet not her. Thus he put Odete behind him and relaxed into his fate, rejoined to Isabel's.

When the couple emerged from the *pacova* grove, Brasília's abstract lights seemed dim on the horizon—tattered punch-cards dwarfed by the stars' voluptuous spillage. Walking toward the capital on the dark median strip, Isabel and Tristão agreed to meet at the bus terminal at seven, to catch a bus to Goiânia.

xv. *Goiás*

THE BUS was a lumbering, creaking box whose lime-green paint was all but covered by red dust and dried mud. It was full at first, but emptied rapidly as they slipped away from Brasília's fragile modernity and the ring of shantytowns that had grown up during its pellmell construction and had never—contrary to the plans—dispersed. Soon the passengers were few and they had left the Federal District and were in true country, *campo cerrado*, rolling ranchland broken by scraggly low forests and fields turning brown in this second month of the dry season. Isabel with her new botanical knowledge identified tobacco and beans, cotton and corn. The harvested stalks looked desolate; there is a melancholy, a stupidity to rural landscape that numbed the citified hearts of the young couple—a yawning repetitiveness, as of a man who knows only a few words but will not stop talking. Where there were no fields, scatterings of black cattle scarcely distinguishable from clumps of thorny bush dotted an unfenced parched savanna stretching toward bluish mountain ridges. The land had once been more productive, perhaps; the road passed through towns emptied like cracked jugs, with collapsed mansions of whose walled gardens the wild scrub had reclaimed possession.

The couple held hands stickily in the growing heat, dozing alternately. Tristão had spent the night stretched on a bench in the bus terminal, fearful of being robbed, his arms entwined with his knapsack straps, his bundle of cruzeiros tucked against his lower belly, behind the pocket of his bathing shorts where the razor blade waited to be unsheathed. The terminal lights were bright and a small local group seemed to use it as a gaming club, slapping down domino tiles and shrieking as they rolled the dice, playing *bozó*. He had slept for ten minutes at a time and kept waking as the straps cut off circulation in his arms. Isabel had lain awake, in her bleak room at the end of the gently curved hall, listening to the tall thin manservant and his fat wife slowly settle to sleep. She stared at the angles of the room she had adorned with a college student's posters and records and books, books whose broad spines stared back at her in the moonlight, reproaching her with desertion. At five she rose and stealthily packed in two blue suitcases, made her way down the hall, and trusted that the security man in the lobby would be stretched out behind his desk asleep. With her heavy two suitcases on the streets she looked like one more hopeful immigrant to the capital, come to find government work, rather than a fleeing child of privilege. She took a taxi to the bus terminal, where she shared with Tristão a cheap breakfast of coffee and *pupunha* and bread and cheese. This time as a couple, they promised each other, they would be more economical than in São Paulo.

The bus would jerk them both awake when it creaked and wallowed to a stop in a town where the single church wore its lonely stark cross atop a scrolling false front upon whose shoulders chipped stone saints gesticulated. The patchy storefront beside the bus stop bore no new posters, only a pastel quilt of faded old ones; the only sign of commerce came from a crone selling ears of baked corn from a charcoal brazier in a hot angle of sun by a whitewashed wall. Her dirty dress sported a lace halter but on her head perched a plastic hat with a sun-bill and the name of a beer, Brahma. The clay roof tiles of this town looked cracked and knocked askew by the weight of the indifferent sky above, its blue as crude as freshly applied paint.

Moving inland, they seemed to move backwards in time. Fewer automobiles contended with the bus for the narrowing road. Men and women bounced along the shoulder on donkeys with giant eyelashes like those of dolls. The automobiles presented the square silhouettes, the running board and arched two-dimensional fender, of an earlier era, before Brazil had its own industries, when cars, already much travelled and often repaired, came second-hand from North America. In the middle distance a slat-sided truck spearheaded a widening plume of ochre dust, and cowboys, *vaqueiros* dressed all in leather, dustily blended with their horses and herds. The landscape itself, where wire-fenced fields did not interrupt the onrolling dry uplands, was itself like a tawny hide, repellent to scratches and water, full of scars and pale scuff-marks. Tristão and Isabel looked eagerly out at the monotonous sights of Goiás, but after a while, their eyes stinging, they returned their attention to each other. Their stomachs growled, with hunger and with fear of what they had taken upon themselves.

"It is all owned, by cattle and their owners," Tristão observed. "I see no place for us, vast as this land is."

"We have only travelled a few miles," Isabel reassured him. "Brazil is endless, with endless opportunities."

Yet in the city of Goiânia, which they reached in six hours, a remorseless geometry of street plan—circular streets, numbered and unnamed—kept delivering them back to the bus terminal on the Avenida Anhanguera. Erratic sleep and meals were catching up to Tristão. Isabel had packed many of her clothes and treasures in the two blue suitcases, and his back beneath the orange knapsack ached; she seemed a heavy jewel hung around his neck. Copper-colored ranch-hands dazed by *cachaça* stared on the street at a girl so white with a man so black. Indian blood strengthened away from the coast. Tristão felt conspicuous, and Goiânia felt enough like Brasília—another abstract design imposed by planners upon an unresisting emptiness—for Isabel's father to seem dangerously close. The young couple was starving, yet the restaurants they approached frightened them off with bursts of rough male laughter from within, and the gnashing of spurs on wooden floors, and gusts of the strong smells of barbecued beef and cheap *pinga*. At last they found, on the Avenida Presidente Vargas, a restaurant, Restaurante Dourado, specializing in fish of the nearby rivers and lakes. The proprietor was a Ukrainian, with a bald head and several steel teeth. He took a shine to his newest customers, exotics like himself. The *dourado* is especially tasty, he told them, with a sauce of puréed banana mixed with grated onion and lemon peel. For dessert, he recommended the rare fruit called *marimari*, and sat down at their table long enough to explain how he had come here. It was a tangled tale, involving an ancient war: he had been captured when the Germans invaded, and been compelled to enlist in the special troops that manned some prison camps of obscure purpose. He had fled when the Russians invaded Poland, knowing they would execute him as a traitor and war criminal. "I had witnessed too much history," he said. He had found his way to Brazil. "It is a happy country," he told them. "It has deep pockets and a short memory." When he laughed, his old-fashioned teeth flashed like a drawerful of knives.

No longer hungry, their vitality reasserted, Tristão and Isabel wandered into a store on a curved street called Rua 82 and bought themselves both some cowboy boots, with pointed toes and elaborate stitching. Taking the hospitable restaurant as an omen, they boarded a night bus north, toward Goiás Velho and the Dourada Range.

The lovers awoke from a tormented, jostled sleep to find themselves in a screaming gear. The bus was climbing, on a road that had become a wide dirt track, in the feeble first light of morning; branches of thorny brush raked the bus on both sides. The land was no longer fenced, so that the bus had to stop for wandering zebus, with their drooping ears and absurd humps. For one stretch the bus was trapped behind an ox-cart heaped high with unshucked corn cobs and guided by a barefoot boy of perhaps ten, equipped with a switch and a hat of disintegrating straw. Dawn revealed here and there the white walls of one-story *ranchos* tucked into the hillside, and unpainted shacks still higher up, where only the smallest cleared patch, dotted with irregular plantings of manioc and beans, indicated human effort pitched against the palms, creeping vines, and thorny quipás and opuntias. Up and down, but more up than down, the bus rocked, and Isabel's head rested with despair's leaden heaviness on Tristão's shoulder. Before noon they came to a town by a mountain creek; it consisted of little more than a tavern, a store, and a church with a sealed door.

"Where are we?" Tristão asked the driver as the passengers all, as if at a signal only he had failed to hear, filed out of the bus onto the slippery blue cobbles of the tilted town plaza.

"Curva do Francês," replied the driver. "There is no more road from here."

The other passengers were melting away. Some had been met, and reconstituted couples, having embraced and shared out the mountain of bundles which one of the pairing had brought from afar, receded together down a path half-heartedly sketched on the wilderness, to an unseen home. Isabel, groggy and nauseated from the long ride, felt stunned by the abyss of their situation. Tristão's heart had clamped shut on the necessity that he be brave on behalf of them both. He must protect the stolen luxuries concealed in their luggage, and his packet of cruzeiros. Perhaps, this far into the hinterland, inflation would not reach.

The rushing, chuckling sound of the curving mountain creek pervaded the air, dimmed by the encroaching forest and a cloud cover that made the sun as dim as the moon—a mere fuzzy sore in the sky. The open doorway of the tavern, whose name was Flor da Vida, beckoned them to the only place of shelter and liveliness. When they entered, the handful of other customers stopped their jabber in the loud accent of the backlands, which twanged out as if to be heard above an incessant wind. A female child, with a face as round as a plate, her hair pulled so tight into braids it shone on the top of her head like a coating of lacquer, came toward them timorously.

"My wife and I are hungry," Tristão said, even in this humble setting relishing the honor of calling Isabel his wife. It was as if his body had sprouted another, and the composite creature was clumsy but awesome, possessed of a monstrous dignity.

"What do you have for us to eat?" Isabel asked, in a woman's voice now, graver than a girl's, and with a determined gentleness aimed at coaxing a response from their timid waitress.

"Rice and black beans," the child brought out, "and *farinha*."

"And what are the other choices?" Tristão asked.

"Sir, there are no other choices." The little girl then added, "There may be some dried goat meat."

"Yes, we would like that very much," Isabel told her. When their waitress had disappeared through a rattling swinging door beside the bar, Isabel cupped her white hand over Tristão's on the rough table, saying, "We have come to a realm of few choices."

"Starve or eat dried goat," he said, with a bitter relish.

But when the food came, on plates thick as a finger, it was steaming, and surprisingly delicious. Even the stringy goat's meat melted in their mouths. As they ate, a man approached them—a heavy short man whose red beard blended closely into the coppery red of his face. He had hair high on his cheeks and even a tuft on the tip of his nose. Without asking, the little waitress had brought them tumblers of clear *pinga*, and now this friendly stranger added his third glass to the table. "What brings you to Curva do Francês, in the foothills of the Douradas?" His speech was rough in timbre yet turned with care, like a ponderous country copy of baroque joinery.

"The bus stopped here," Tristão said, touching the little metal rectangle at the belt of his shorts, for reassurance. "We had no choice, my friend."

The all-red man smiled, his teeth uneven and rotting within his gingery beard. "The track goes on, the driver is a rogue. He has a woman in the suburbs, with whom he spends the night. The road goes on for miles, believe me."

"There are suburbs?" Isabel asked, in her girl's voice now; a silvery laugh escaped her.

The all-red man, blearily fixing his eyes upon her, stated, "The suburbs are extensive. Once, the parish held twenty thousand souls, not counting Tupi and Chacriabá Indians."

"What happened?" Tristão asked.

Beneath the man's fiery eyebrows his eyes with their pink whites rolled back and forth, as if what he revealed must not be overheard within the Flor da Vida. "The gold gave out, in less than a century." He paused, dramatically; he wore a leather vest over a coarse shirt, both of them ruddy in color, whether through the action of dye or of local dust was not easy to discriminate. "But Curva do Francês will be a metropolis again," he assured them. "All the plans are intact. Concentric avenues, symmetrical parks, a handsome medical commissary, to be run by the Jesuits. There is even—forgive me for tainting your ears with this, *senhora*—a district set aside for brothels, with entryways arranged for the privacy of the patrons." His rolling eye rested an uncomfortably long time on Isabel, awaiting her response.

"It sounds very nice," she said, "for those who need such services."

Tristão touched his razor blade again and asked bluntly, "Is there any work in this region for a man?"

The all-red man seemed astonished by the question. "*Senhor*, I beg you—look around you. What do you see at present? Shacks and thornbushes, memories and hopes. The gold, as I said, is gone. It has gone elsewhere." Now it was Tristão to whom he gave his quiz-zical, eager eye.

The young hero took the bait. "Where has it gone?"

"Ah . . . up *there*." Their informant gestured vaguely, through the drink-shop walls, toward the mountains still above them. "At Serra do Buraco. There are thousands of men, my young friend, getting rich, on the labor of their backs alone. Every day they pick up nuggets as big as my fist"—he displayed the fist, a formidable clump, sprouting hairs like rootlets on a reddish-brown tree burl—"or at least as big as the seal on the lady's ring." He had noticed, in the dim light of the place, the glinting oval face of the DAR ring. "Even a few nuggets the size of a match-head will buy the pretty lady dresses to last ten years. I cannot help but notice, you carry very full suitcases."

"We are seeking a new home," Tristão told him, glancing at Isabel to see if this had been too much to say.

"Why would that be?" asked the all-red man, glowing with his pleasure in this conversation. "From the look of your lady, and the fine dress she is wearing, her last home was a comfortable one."

"There is more than one type of comfort, *senhor*," Isabel told him, her womanly voice stiffened to force its way into the conversation. Tristão was grateful, fearful that he alone might botch the shadowy negotiation afoot.

The man smiled so agreeably that his red lips showed their wet pink inner sides within his frothy beard. He addressed her as if challenged: "And you have found an unsurpassable kind of comfort in the arms of your black buck, yes?"

To Tristão's surprise, she coolly said, "Yes."

It alarmed him, to see the womanliness he had given her now part of her, hers to bestow on other men if she wished.

"I rejoice for you, *senhora*," came the level answer, as the stranger's shaggy brows lowered over his glittering bloodshot eyes. "In Curva do Francês, we do not underrate the body and its needs."

Tristão intervened: "How does one apply for work in this mine? In São Paulo, I worked assembling *fuscas*—my responsibility was to bolt the left side of the engine support into place."

"Ah," said the man, impressed; his bristling red eyebrows lifted and doubled the number of furrows in his coppery forehead. "I have heard they make carriages in São Paulo. The Paulistas are a clever race, but ruthless. You did well to escape them, my black friend. They think of nothing but acquiring slaves. At Serra do Buraco, you will not be working for others; you will be a *garimpeiro*—a self-employed miner, an independent entrepreneur. All the gold you find within your claim will be yours, minus a mere eight percent to the government, and reasonable fees to the miners' coöperative, which maintains order, keeps impeccable records, and operates the sluices and pulverizing mechanisms. You must not imagine that gold walks directly from the earth onto your lady's fingers. There are many steps, many stages and challenges to the Brazilian genius for organization. The bits of gold are like lice in Mother Earth's tangled hair—they hide, they wriggle away! But gold's heaviness betrays him; when you swirl away the lighter minerals, the dirt and mere silica, there the little critters are, still stuck in the bottom of the pan! You must have a miner's pan, a *batea*, for the cooperative allows each *garimpeiro* to take back to his shack the most promising lumps of ore, and there in the evening, my friend, as you squat your aching muscles down in the mud beside that babbling witch of a mountain creek, they emerge like glowworms—they can't climb over the *batea*'s riffles, the little devils, the precious gold-mites! Again and again, I have seen a poor *camarada*, owning nothing more than the rags on his back, become overnight as rich as one of Dom Pedro Segundo's appointed lords!"

It seemed strange, to hear of Dom Pedro's lords as if they were living. Still, Tristão asked, "And how does one apply for this work?"

The red eyebrows shot up again, so far they revealed rings of pallor around the man's weary, *pinga*-fuddled eyes. "One does not apply—stop thinking like a slave! One goes and claims! All one needs to become rich is a pickax, a hammer, a shovel, a *batea*, and a claim."

"How does one make a claim?" Isabel asked. For she had learned, in the years of watching Uncle Donaciano languidly manage his wealth, that nothing comes without a price, and there are few things that have no price.

"Why, one *buys* it!" came the answer. "One buys a claim from a *garimpeiro* who, like myself, has made his fortune and, ere the woes of old age close over him, wishes to enjoy it. But be confident that, though with a few turns of the shovel I have secured all my comforts

142

right up to a burnished coffin of purpleheart and brass, there is plenty left in this claim, enough to support a prince and princess of Araby! There is no claim at Serra do Buraco like it; it happens to fall where an ancient volcano caused a vein of lead and a gust of the purest blue fire to come together, creating a veritable fountain of gold, a frozen throat in the earth like that of the Earth-Mother singing her most exalted note! Here. Behold."

And from the back of his tall right boot he took a folded paper, bent like a shoehorn to the curve of his heel and smelling of leather-cloistered feet. It was a map, brown and brittle and smudged, so often folded and unfolded that its creases, when the paper was spread on the table, admitted a grid of light. The map showed a vast checkerboard of numbered squares, with one of them so often indicated by a stabbing finger that its number had been rubbed out. "There she is—my lovely. As giving as a cunt, pardon the expression."

The claims all measured five feet by five feet, he told them, and extended infinitely—to the center of the earth, if a man could dig that far. When they asked his price, he named a sum twice that of the cruzeiros still remaining of Tristão's bundle.

Tristão looked toward Isabel, and she saw the eagerness in his opaque and shining eyes, and in the rampart of his forehead the pride keen to test his strength and cunning against the obduracy of the earth. Lest his eagerness betray them, she hastily informed the all-red man, in the firm, full, crisp voice of her new maturity, that though his price must be a jest they would spend the afternoon and evening in inquiries and reflection, and would consult again with him in the morning.

"By morning, another may have seized this heaven-sent opportunity," the *garimpeiro* warned, but with a wink, and left them to negotiate the price of a room upstairs in the inn, with the pregnant mother of the round-faced girl. Tristão was beginning to like the feeling of the backlands, and of having a wife as a business partner.

xvi. *The Mine*

THEY DECIDED, whispering together till after midnight, to purchase the claim. From the time their eyes first met on the beach they had been in God's hands and the idea of so rash a gamble appealed to both of them. Having found each other, they believed in their luck. They would become rich and at the same time hide from her father and his minions, in the remote reaches of Goiás. The all-red man accepted all that remained of Tristão's packet of cruzeiros, plus the crystal candlestick whose mate Isabel had impulsively given two years ago to Tristão's ungrateful mother. When this still seemed less than enough, the man's pink eyes threatened to turn away in the cold morning light of the inn, squinting as if to close again upon the fond vision of his "lovely," Isabel offered him a medal she had stolen from her father's bedroom bureau, a medal bestowed upon him by the King of Thailand for his services when he had been Brazilian Vice-Consul there. The heavy beribboned disk depicted a crowned elephant and the inscription was in a curious alphabet, which suggested magic power. The callused thumb with its spray of red hairs caressed the pleasingly contoured silken metal—a coppery color like his own—and the deal was closed. The claim, produced from the other boot, consisted of several sheets of paper folded together and hardened and yellowed in proximity to his heel. It gave Tristão a headache to try to read it, but for the sake of form he stared for a number of minutes at its portentous litter of government seals, tiny print, and dashing official signatures.

The bus that had brought them to Curva do Francês from Goiânia was returning to the city, now that the driver had had his pleasure with his lady in the leafy suburbs. Tristão and Isabel hitched a ride to Serra do Buraco in the back of an ox-cart, open to the sky but with tall slatted sides. Four emaciated oxen pulled it along the grassy track scarcely faster than a man could walk. Their progress was generally uphill, but with a number of dips into small valleys where the track crossed dry, pebbly rivers on bridges of bending planks.

For some hours they shared the rocking vehicle, its hard floor softened by a strewing of old sugar canes, with three other passengers, mestizo *garimpeiros* or parasites upon the *garimpeiros*, who marvelled at Isabel's bright white hair and her two blue suitcases, as weighty with her clothes as if loaded with stones. They assumed she was going to work on the mountain as a prostitute and that Tristão was a curious cross between her slave and her protector. They joked about her price, speculating that the arrival of such luxuries betokened an upturn in the luck of Serra do Buraco. Their advances became sufficiently physical—a dark hand reaching to caress the shimmering faint fur on her forearm—that Tristão seized the nearest of the three and struck him a blow in the face, as calmly as if tightening a bolt on a *fusca* engine support. The man mumblingly called him nigger and cur but slumped back among his two companions, caressing the bloody gum above a tooth the blow had loosened. He had lost several front teeth already, to combat or decay. "We are going to test our luck with the gods of gold," Tristão explained, as if to apologize. He showed them the folded papers of the claim.

The man took his revenge in words, grinning, displaying the black gaps in his mouth. "Such papers are printed by the hundreds in Goiânia and Cuiabá; they are worthless," he said. "When you get there, you will find you have no claim. The mountain is an ant-heap, crawling with rascals."

Isabel, hearing these words, was pierced by a cold dagger of realization: her girlhood was a thing of the past, she was heading into the unknown, and, if there was a legitimate claim, a process had started which might consume the prime of her life. She pushed closer to Tristão, for nebulous comfort. Though his being was focused upon proving himself to the other men, he allowed his hard-muscled arm to find its way around her waist and absent-mindedly to tighten its protection.

As it turned out, the claim was real: the all-red man's unworked plot stood out among the others like a square pillar, high with neglect. Under the onslaught of digging, what had been a mountain was becoming a giant hole; not hundreds but thousands of men, in a bowl a half-mile across, trundled sacks of mud and pickaxed rock up crude wooden ladders leaning against the cliffs hacked out in a quarry of descending terraces. Almost every day, loose rock and eroding earth slid down upon the slaving men; every day, a *garimpeiro* or two died, of avalanche, disease, exhaustion, or knife-fight. Robbery and murder occurred right in the pit, as well as in the dozens of shack towns that had sprung up on the surrounding slopes—strings of hovels mixed with a few shops, mortuaries, and, incongruously, manicurists' parlors, with numerous small cubicles for the manicure. There were no bars; alcohol was forbidden in a ten-mile region around Serra do Buraco, or the mayhem would have been far worse. The men, hardened by hauling sixty-pound sacks of stone up ladders and narrow ledges forty times a day, were possibly the best-conditioned men on earth, with chests like weight-lifters' and legs like soccer players'. Brawling was their only pleasure, but for the lucky few whom God allowed to find a gold nugget. They had flocked to this terraced abyss of opportunity from the parched, starving north-east, the threadbare fishing villages of Bahia and Maranhão, the slums of Fortaleza and Recife, and the torpid, pestilential villages of the Amazon and its tributaries. A mining company in far-off São Paulo, with a Brazilian name but controlled by Arab and gringo money, legally owned the land, amid enormous tracts of the parched Dourada Range, but a federal judge in

Brasília had ruled that no Brazilian should be deprived of the right to prospect for gold. It was a national right going back to the year 1500, when Brazil's green shore was first sighted. The miners had established a coöperative which operated a sluice-works, a preliminary refinery polluting with mercury all the local rivers, a weighing station, and a bank.

Once he learned the ropes, and had acquired from the coöperative commissary his pickax and shovel and sledgehammer and sacks, to add to the battered, well-worn, yet still refulgent batea that the all-red man had sold them along with the claim, Tristão was happy. In the *fusca* plant, shorn from Isabel, he had felt crushed to the floor of an overarching clatter, a cog within the giant works, an insignificant economic integer inserted between the *proprietários* of the factory and the *chefes* of the union. Locked into place opposite Oscar's gaptoothed flat face, he had tightened bolts until his back and shoulder muscles screamed. As each *fusca* moved down the belt it seemed to carry off some of his own blood in its oily, beetlelike body. Here, in the hollow mountain, atop his personal pillar of stone, breaking its stone into fragments, any one of which might contain the glint of a fortune for himself and Isabel, he felt exalted and free, a heroic figure silhouetted against the sky, contesting the elements while yet their companion.

But as the first year became the second year, and a third and fourth year followed, his pillar of unprospected stone drew level, beneath his exertions, with the terrace of worked claims around it. Then, as the workers of these other claims fell away, through death or injury or despair of ever making a strike, his five-by-five claim became a pit, gouged and hammered inch by inch into the adamant, inscrutable rock, and his once-high hopes sank to a groggy, fanatic faith in the nearly impossible.

Not that he did, in all these days of patient working, fail ever to see the glint of gold. Tristão and Isabel had occupied an empty shanty with its back to a mercury-polluted creek—perhaps the very shelter the all-red man had abandoned. Each night, Tristão would bring back home a sack of the most promising rocks the day's labor had uncovered—the palest with quartz, the most glittering with scales of pyrite, the "fool's gold" that is sometimes true gold's companion. These hopeful lumps he would pulverize with a hammer and steel-tipped stake while Isabel within the shack prepared the evening's black beans and rice. At the creek's edge he would squat, swirling the fragments in water and watching for the heavy fragments to adhere to the batea's gentle corrugations, which radiated out from the center like the rays of a haze-entrapped sun. It was a process that never ceased to be fascinating, this waiting, beside that "babbling witch of a creek," for "the little devils, the precious gold-mites," to appear. As a man betranced sometimes gazes into a fire to read therein a hint of his fate—a fluttering face, a demon hand—so Tristão, evening after evening, until his eyes wept in the darkness, stared into the swirling batea. The biggest crumb of gold he ever recovered was smaller than a matchhead, but even on the strength of this meagre strike they bought some dried meat, *xarque*, at the commissary, to fortify their monotonous diet, and made love for the first time in weeks.

Tristão was too bone-weary, generally, to minister to Isabel. His passion now was all directed toward the imagined contours of the precious metal hidden in the maddeningly obdurate matrix of stone. The light of his adoration had left his wife's body. Here on the sloping outskirts of Serra do Buraco, a fine dust had worked itself into her skin, accenting the creases that had appeared on her forehead, at the corners of her eyes and lips, even at the base of her throat, which had once been smooth as a flow of milk. Her youthful monkey face now exhibited a determined set to the mouth, a shadowed weariness about the eyes. When she took off her clothes to get into bed, there was still a burst of supple white glory in the cabin darkness; though his heart could still rise to it, as to the sight of a thunderhead mounting into sunlight above the mountain's profile, his body rarely could.

"You don't love me as before," she naturally complained.

"I do," he protested. "My love is like Mother Gold, immutable, though it momentarily hides."

"Gold has become not just your mother but your wife. You work even on Sundays, and still we almost starve. What miserable flecks and grains you do find, the coöperative officials cheat you in the weighing, and you drink up half on the way home."

It was true, *cachaça* was smuggled onto the mountain, and sold at an inflated price, and Tristão in his desire to be like the other *garimpeiros* did not always decline a glass or two. His mother's old weakness, which he had despised, was awakening in him. When the brain was enough dulled, a luminous cave opened in life's implacable cliff, and one could crawl in. His proud and independent spirit, which had demanded on the beach that he claim this dolly for his own, prying her loose from the matrix of other bodies, was rotting away, as his LONE STAR T-shirt had been rotted away by sun and sweat, as the pillar of his claim had slowly been chipped into nothingness by the backbreaking days.

Isabel, seeing her words whip up pain on her husband's face, and the shadow of defeat and cowardice flit across the rampart of his brow, felt pain of her own; but she had decided that she must put distance between them, if she was to remain a person in her own right. In her first months as his bride here she had been slavish, thinking only of ministering to his comfort and pride as he adjusted to the ordeal of the pit, falling into a kind of doze when he left her alone in the shack, with the babbling of the poisoned creek behind, and the dangers of the desolate sunstruck street outside, with its single-octane gas station, its busy mortuary, its commissary selling overpriced essentials, its multiplying manicurists' shops. She had thought of finding work, but her skills—her rich-girl social graces, her student smatterings of knowledge—were of no value here. She had but one asset, which the men of the street noisily appraised whenever she stepped outside the shack, into the blinding open, where thunderheads above the shaggy profiles of the mountains glowed brilliantly but rarely produced rain. When the sky did come to rain, it was vicious rain, numbing, blinding sheets of it that left gulleys in the broad dirt street and brought the edges of the creek lashing and tumbling up to the sill of the back door.

Isabel had stayed inside, sleeping or reading—reading aimlessly, to satisfy a ravenous thirst for some world other than this one. Mining tools and supplies came wrapped from the coastal factories in pages of old magazines or newspapers, which held fragments of stories years out of date, with illustrations of heroines in outmoded fashions and gossipy references to popular singers and soccer stars now middle-aged or dead of debauchery. Yet the stories, which she could rarely follow to a conclusion, on the scraps of creased and wadded paper, were timeless—the same five or six basic facts of human existence endlessly revolved, like arrows the wounded animals bring back to the hunter's hand in their corpses. Love, pregnancy, infidelity, vengeance, parting. Death—always death in these stories.

Her clothes began to give out. The two heavy blue suitcases were now limp with vacuity; the larger of them held only the begemmed old-fashioned cross she had stolen from Uncle Donaciano's apartment, the monogrammed cigarette case, and a fuzzy toy capybara she had loved as a very little girl, calling him Azor and holding him against her breastless chest as she slept.

Now this toy was stiff and dull with the ubiquitous si-
liceous dust from the incessantly stirred mine hole. The
dresses and blouses and tight smart jeans she had not
worn into rags she had sold to the manicurists, to put
rice and black beans and *farinha* upon their table. For
Tristão in her eyes had become an engine of muscle she
must keep fed or their progress through life would grind
to a halt.

By the time there were no more clothes to sell, she
had become friends enough with the manicurists for
them to show her how to earn money. It was surprisingly easy, once you learned to keep a part of yourself
out of the way, high on a mental shelf. The little male
drama of rise and fall was touching, despite the men's
ability to kill you with their hands, if the evil mood
took them. But hers was the woman's power to forestall
the evil mood. Hers was the power to take all they
could give, between her legs.

When Tristão came home and found on the table not
simply rice and beans but bacon and a sizzling pan of
that succulent freshwater fish called *dourado*, with
pineapple and *pitanga* for dessert, he looked at her for
a long minute—the whites of his shining onyx eyes
chafed pink by quarry dust like those of the all-red
man—and deliberately did not ask what vein of gold
she had struck. She despised him for this, this mute acceptance, but also loved him for his realism, his stoic
tact. Romanticism is what brings a couple together, but
realism is what sees them through. He dropped his sack
of promising ore to the earth floor unpanned this eve-

ning and sat himself at the unusually loaded table with the constrained formality of a king whose sceptre is hollow. All evening, it seemed to her, he moved around her with a wary delicacy, as if her flesh had been changed to a crystalline substance. As she drifted off to sleep on their pallet of maize husks she felt him touch her back and shoulders with the experimental lightness owed to a virgin's body.

He became more affectionate, in an impotent way. Isabel frequently sensed him glancing at her in the candlelight of their shack at night, and heard a careful slow melody in his voice, as he recounted the details of his day in the mine-pit. It seemed to her now that there were more people in the room than the two of them. Or was it that her memories were thronged with other men—their cries, their grips, their bodies in so many different tints of skin, tones of muscle, smells, kinds of hair, forms of orgasm muffled within her? With her unexplained surplus of cruzeiros she bought a long zinc bathtub, and Tristão each night, in what became a ceremony, would fetch buckets of water from the creek, which they would heat on their kerosene stove. She would descend into the long trough of steaming water and stay until it felt cool around her, and the sight of her immersed body, her skin tinted pewter and her pubic hair lifting and drifting like seaweed, numbed her memory; then her husband, gray with stone dust, would rewarm the tub with a fresh bucket and bathe himself back to shining blackness in the water she had dirtied. In that way they made themselves clean and languorous for bed; they drifted off with feeble fond touches like two drowning persons parting in the sea.

Even in the days when their lovemaking had been vigorous and incessant, Isabel had not become pregnant. In their second year at the Serra do Boraco, she was, and the shack shook and trembled with nature's miraculous upheaval. She vomited at dawn each day for weeks, and then grew big and torpid, so swollen and taut and shiny in her belly that Tristão felt dizzy with love of her, this inexorable doubling of her. The baby came (her waters broke at midnight, and the first squall came just as dawn's gray revealed, in the shack, the edges of things) and was a boy, with wrinkled blue palms like flowers just unfolded and genitals like a bud still packed tight. She timidly suggested naming him Salomão, after her father, but Tristão, roused from his gold-betranced passivity, objected with passionate gestures, saying that her father was his deadly enemy. Since he had no known father, he accepted her second suggestion, the name Azor, after the toy stuffed capybara she had loved as a girl.

"Our baby seems very pale," he observed one day.

"All babies begin pale," she told him. "The midwife says their melanin is all in a little pocket at the base of their spines. Then it travels out, to the rest of their skin."

But as the days went by, and the infant grew fat on Isabel's milk, and his rubbery limbs began to strengthen, his skin did not significantly darken in color. Tristão held the blameless blob of flesh in his arms and gazed down—Azor gurgled upward, reaching a slobbered star-shaped hand toward the familiar black face—and tried to glimpse a shadow of Africa, the faintest drop of dark blood tincturing Isabel's whiteness. He failed. Isabel pointed to the child's flattened nose, the small cupped ears, the square and rather stern little forehead, and claimed to see Tristão there. Her next child, a girl born fourteen months after Azor's birth, was darker, but dark, it appeared to Tristão, with an Indian redness. The child's hair, though black like his own, was utterly straight. He had no objection to Isabel's naming the baby Cordélia, after her mother, whom she scarcely remembered. Isabel's surviving two parturitions was in a sense a triumph over her mother, who had died of her second.

The arrivals filled the shack with the innocent intensity of their own needs, their tantrums and tumbles, their colic and spit-up, their hunger and excrement, affording the adults little time to doubt the course fate had chosen for them. Nature now told them why they had come together. The manicurists' coöperative found an old woman, a toothless Tupi severed from her tribe, to take care of the children for some hours of the day, so Isabel could go back to work. The name of this addition to their household, who came at noon and left at night and would not reveal where she slept, was Kupehaki.

xvii. *The Nugget*

THE THUNDEROUS HUM of the mine—the click of the picks, the hammering as deeper ladders and stouter shoring walls were assembled; the desultory conversation and singing as the men trudged in single file up the slanting muddy ledges toward the sluices and the slag heaps that spilled down the sides of Serra do Boraco like a second mountain growing beside the gutted first; the occasional flare of outcries as a fight broke out or an avalanche spilled across the terraced claims— the hum had become Tristão's element. Away from this great inverted beehive, even to be with Isabel and the two children, he felt a bit attenuated, lopsided, and guilty, as if he were betraying his true wife, the temptress gold. This sensation, at the mine, of his true self closing around him strengthened when he was actually in his shaft, the deep neat hole, five feet square, which he had picked and shovelled into the rock of the mountain.

The claim adjacent to his on the left, idle for a year, had been taken over by a set of brothers and cousins from the state of Alagoas, the Gonzagas, and the team they formed was rapidly digging down, overtaking Tristão's solitary progress, exposing his shaft to air and sun. But there were still seven or eight vertical feet of enclosed rock in which he could lose himself, where the hum dwindled to a faraway murmur and the sky shrank to a tidy blue square overhead, crossed by clouds like actors in a drama seen through a gap in the curtains. His privacy suggested the terrible solitude of the grave yet had something erotic about it; it was not cooler in the depths of his claim but slightly warmer, as if he were slowly approaching one of nature's hotly guarded secrets.

For some days he had been following a twisting stretch of pallor down the leftward wall, a ruddy pallor of the type thought most promising, for gold was generally found in association with her brothers, copper and lead. When the earth blushes, the miners said, gold was about to bare herself, gold in her naked shining.

His pick attacked the rock, solid blow after blow. Its two points were equally dull, polished by wear; he had worn out three such picks in his three years here. With an awkward effort Tristão was swinging sideways, since the vein of ruddy pallor was turning inward, away from him; it felt as if the point of his pick were pursuing the curve of a woman's body around a kind of corner, into her semi-seen, furry, rousing cranny. He was getting an erection, as sometimes happened in the privacy of his claim. The sexual energy he could not muster at night, with Isabel, overtook him in the middle of the day, as he plied his pick against the rock. Sometimes he even masturbated, with the sky's square eye staring above him, imagining always, however, the body of his wife— yet himself with his spurting yam not her husband but one of her brutal customers, spitting upon her breasts when he was done.

His pick, slashing inward, bared a glint, or so his eyes, tormented by the dimness and by stone dust, seemed to tell him. He got down on his knees and attacked the cranny of rock, broadening the glint. Clouds, trailing gray wisps like fists loosening and unloosening, passed overhead; the hum of the vast quarry outside filtered over the rim of his private mine. When the sun slipped into the square of sky and threw its beams straight down, the captive air felt as hot as Isabel's bathwater. But he could see better. Within an hour, while the fury of his attack piled up rubble behind him and left the skin around his scrabbling fingernails bloody, he had lifted the glinting area into low relief. The lump had a sullen reddish lustre, not silvery-scaly like pyrite, the deceiver.

In another two hours, squinting as if into a furnace, Tristão had carved away enough matrix above and below to pick the nugget free. For a nugget it was, a rough yet silky chunk of gold, the essence of wealth, in his palm, far heavier than a comparable piece of stone. Perhaps ten centimeters by four, and eighty grams by weight, it had the beginnings of a shape—a kind of belly, a division of what might have become legs, a faceless head. It was an idol; it was sacred. It had little craters, like the moon. He moved it from one hand to the other, agitated; he tried to hide its glittering from even the square of the sky above. If any of the thousands of men humming around him knew of this, he would be killed for it. His head buzzed; his breathing was as rapid and shallow as that of a bird; he sank to his knees and thanked God and His spirits. The hand that shapes destinies had again reached down and touched his life.

The work uniform of Serra do Buraco consisted of shorts, T-shirt, sunhat of straw or polyester, and high-topped basketball shoes, for all the climbing up and down that had to be done—Tristão's new cowboy boots had proved to be impractical, as too slippery-soled and chafing, and his tennis shoes from the bus terminal too flimsy. Also, the men wore pouches cinched around their waists, in which flecks of gold accumulated until there were enough to be melted down and converted to money and deposited in the coöperative bank. Tristão feared that his nugget would bulge his pouch too much; instead he jumbled it with other rocks in his sixty-pound sack and trudged home under the load as if toward one more night of pulverizing, panning, eating rice and beans, putting the children to sleep, bathing in Isabel's dirty water, and collapsing.

When he dumped open the sack in Isabel's sight, for an annihilating second he feared the nugget had vanished. It had sunk to the bottom, by dint of its weight, and looked much like the other, valueless fragments of the mountain. But its weight betrayed it, and he brought it forth. A few vigorous rubs of his thumb removed enough silica dust to reveal the raw gold's lustre.

"We are rich," he told his wife. "You no longer need to leave our home in the day to be with the manicurists. Perhaps we can buy a farm in Paraná, or a small house by the sea in Espírito Santo."

"My father might find us then," she said.

"What do we care? We have given him grandchildren. Have I not proved these years to be a loyal husband?"

She smiled at his naïveté. Just as she had insisted on loving his worthless mother, so he harbored, between fits of hatred, a pathetic hope that her ruthlesss father would relent and become the father he had never had. "He is not so easily assuaged, Tristão. The notion that he is acting as a parent, not only for himself but for my dead mother, makes him fanatic. He wants the best for me. You are the best, but he cannot see it; he sees with the old eyes, the eyes of the white *poderosos*, the eyes of the old slavers and plantation masters."

"How drearily you talk, Isabelinha—as if the past is still the present. The manicurists have made you cynical; they have made you sour. When God bestows a gift, it is blasphemous to regard it with suspicion. Embrace me: our years here have borne their fruit, their treasure!"

In his exuberance, wishing to embrace Isabel, he gave the nugget to little Azor to hold. The toddler dropped it on his own bare toes, and burst into wails that set his sister to sobbing sympathetically in her crib—an old crate for pickax handles, lifted up on bricks, away from snakes and fire ants.

Isabel held her sobbing son in her arms and said to Tristão, "These have been hard years, and something of our love has suffered, but we have been safe here, and hidden. I fear this nugget will drag us into the light."

"You worry too much, my darling; it is your bourgeois blood. Tomorrow, I will take the nugget to the coöperative assayer. If his price seems to me too modest, there are independent gold traders who rove the workings—they are able to offer more, since they evade the government's eight percent by smuggling the gold across the Bolivian border, with the connivance of the Indians." Such lore was commonplace in the human beehive of the Serra do Buraco: as gold lived in minute flecks and veins within the vast mass of stone, so it lived in the talk and thought of the miners.

But Isabel's forebodings were correct. Though Tristão managed to carry his nugget undetected to the assayer's office, from there word spread quickly of the magnificent find. The office, with the coöperative bank and the government taxation office, occupied the only cement-block structure in the sprawling wooden town. Topped by the starry Brazilian flag, it stood directly adjacent to the mortuary, which was freshly supplied each day with the products of knife-fights, mining accidents, pulmonary disease, and the banditry that plagued the roads in and out of the Serra do Boraco. The assayer, a thin yellow man wearing a black suit and a celluloid collar and speaking Portuguese with the effete lisp of the old country, clucked his tongue appreciatively and, after consulting his scales and explaining that an exact valuation could be given only after melting and purification, lisped a sum in hundreds of thousands of new cruzeiros. "What ith more, thir, the value will go up, ath that of the crutheiro fallth." Tristão pondered the nugget; its physical aspect overnight had changed from that of a humanoid idol to that of a craggy potato, its eyes the little pockmarks that suggested a rock from the moon. He left it in the care of the bank, accepting the receipt with a suspicion that he would never see the heavenly nugget, his message from beyond, again.

It had poured during the night; the slopes and foot-worn ledges of the quarry were melting underfoot. As he approached the area of his claim, he saw a cluster of men gathered; the neglected claims around his were being suddenly worked. Brown backs bent busily into the ore made potent by rumor, and two of the Gonzaga brothers were climbing out of Tristão's own claim. Before he could challenge them, they challenged him.

"You bandit!" the older, shorter of the two, named Aquiles, cried. "We have looked and measured, and you had burrowed and dug over into our claim! That nugget is ours!"

"Poachers like you," said the younger and taller, Ismael, "should be strung up and dismembered as an example to all *garimpeiros*!"

"I was well within the walls of my own claim," Tristão insisted, though, recalling the glint, the frantic sideways picking, and the sensation of reaching into an unchaste intimacy, he wondered if in truth he had trespassed. The evidence was indeterminate, for not even he could now say from what exact spot in the gouged earth the nugget had come.

"We will summon surveyors," Aquiles frantically threatened, "and policemen, and lawyers!"

They did sue him, and the suit, which dragged on for months, attracted the attention of the national press. The nugget, repeatedly fetched from its place in the bank's safe to be photographed, was the biggest and purest ever unearthed in the Serra do Buraco, though not so large as some of the golden boulders found in the Australian hinterland in 1851. A new surge of greed and hope excited Brazil, through its news media. A reporter from *O Globo* came and photographed Tristão and Isabel in their shack: Isabel bathing in her zinc tub, billowing suds concealing all but her naked shoulders and arms and a gleaming length of calf and her coyly arched bare foot; Tristão holding his pale plump son and redtinted infant daughter in his arms, his eyes gleaming like bubbles of black glass beneath his nobly high forehead as he warily stared into the camera's depths.

The photographer, a squat and rumpled middle-aged man with several spare cameras hung about his neck and many quips designed to induce a smile, and the reporter, an intelligent and progressive young woman with net-stockinged legs as slim as switches, had been so disarming and companionable it would have violated all rules of backlands hospitality not to have entertained them and posed as they wished. The invaders seemed, for the hour they were in the shack, family—citified kin impulsively come to Goiás to bestow the largesse of urban charm—rather than the tip of a widening wedge of impersonal exposure. Isabel, true, did have the wit to evade the reporter's direct questions about her parentage, and Tristão's street-boy cunning led him to lie about his family, of whom he was ashamed; but the photographs, in black and white, spoke worlds. Tristão and Isabel, staring out from within their flashlit hovel on page three of *O Globo*, became one more of those couples whose stunned, wizened physiognomies and pathetically shabby surroundings are lifted by some curious stroke of fortune up from the mass of untold poverty into the light, like hooked fish. *Miners Dispute Discovery of Huge Nugget*, the headlines ran. *Vagrant Couple Balked on Verge of Riches*. Other newspaper reporters followed, and Tristão was courteous to them all; this invasion might bring danger, his hopeful spirit reasoned, or it might bring breakthrough.

One day he returned from work in the dusk and found a silvery shadow, a man in a gray suit, sitting in one of the shack's two chairs. His first thought, shameful, was that Isabel was doing her business in their home now; but then he saw that the man, with his sad expression and grizzled temples and carefully trimmed mustache, was César. Isabel was standing, frightened, by the stove, with fat Azor on her hip, and her hair loose to her waist. Cordélia was in her crib, sobbing in her sleep. "My friend, I have found you again," César said, casually displaying his gray gun, pointing it not at Tristão but, more politely, to one side. "In the bosom of another family—one of your own engendering, this time. My heartiest congratulations."

"And where is Virgílio?" Tristão asked. "Does he still play right forward for the Moóca Tiradentes?"

César wearily smiled. "Since you gave him the slip, Virgílio has been . . . reassigned."

"Why do you persecute us? We do not disturb anyone, here."

"That is not exactly true, my friend. For all its lamentable lack of discipline, Brazil is not yet altogether without standards, without traditions, without order. You disturb my excellent employer, for one."

César, who fancied himself a courtier in the service of Isabel's family, must have been chatting, in his falsefatherly tone, with her for some time, for he was unduly relaxed—a little languid and foppish, his gun idly pointing toward the clay floor. He did not expect that Tristão would hurl, with the strength acquired of backbreaking daily labor, the sixty-pound sack of ore straight at him, striking him in the face and toppling him backward in the chair, a fragile construction of primavera wood.

In a lunge, while Isabel screamed and Azor laughed at the excitement, Tristão was kneeling on César's chest and had, with a decisive staccato stroke, smashed the side of his head with the largest of the rocks that had spilled. The older man's grimacing face relaxed, and his eyelids quiveringly closed. His gray temple was now bloodied. He had grown too old for his line of work.

Tristão gave Isabel César's gun and told her, "We must leave. You gather our possessions and ready our children; I will hide the body."

"He is still alive," Isabel protested.

"Yes," Tristão said merely, with some of the silenced César's melancholy, the superior melancholy of those who have the upper hand. The man was heavy, heavier than three sacks of stone put together, but Tristão, in contact again with his veering fate, feeling the exalted calm of an adrenal rush, lifted the body easily onto his shoulders.

It had become night outside, with as yet no moon and few stars. Cicadas shrilled. Across the little creek, a few yards upstream from their shack, a bridge of slippery stepping-stones had been created; on the other side, in the thicket of riverside vegetation, lay a snaky path where, as the darkness thickened, a man could walk unobserved. The *garimpeiros* and their dependents came here to do their natural business, and more than once Tristão's foot slipped on a soft unseen human turd, whose hardened skin, thus broken, released a pungence that followed him for many strides. Along with the slithery caresses of palm fronds and wands, the shiny round leaves of a bush whose name he did not know brushed his skin with a gently slicing touch. When he blundered off the path, thorns scratched him. He became afraid that César would awake and condemn him to another tussle. His shoulder muscles, hardened as they were, began to throb; but the greenery thinned, the moon had come out, and his environment was more visible. Now Tristão could see, in illumined silhouette, like a distant castle, the coöperative crushing mills where the bags of ore were pulverized and amalgamated with mercury, and then with cyanide, chemically sucking up the atoms of gold. Tons and tons of slag had formed, on the hollow back of Serra do Buraco, a second mountain, and it was down the powdery gray slopes of that avalanche of waste, of digested and excreted stone, that Tristão carried the unconscious César. No one came here, into the precipitous valleys of this man-made wilderness. Even serpents and fire ants shunned it.

In a remote hollow whitened by the strengthened moonlight, Tristão dumped down his burden; in his coma César groaned, even this groan conveying, uncannily, the man's personal accent, the half-humorous paternal dignity with which he masked his enforcer's bite. Tristão gently twisted the ponderous, dignified skull, using the mass of gray hair as a handle, so the bulge of César's jugular vein cast a shadow in the moonlight, in the soft place behind the jaw, under the crescent of shadow cast by the earlobe. Beneath the vein, Tristão knew, crept its brighter, redder brother, the carotid artery. Removing his single-edge razor, the faithful Gem, from the pocket inside his shorts where it slept, just under his belt, he slit, as deep as the blade would go, the bulge horizontally, and then, since the flow of blood, though great, was not as great as he had pictured, he added a vertical stroke above it, not realizing until afterwards that he had signed his crime with a T.

His plan had been to bury the body in the powdery

mining refuse, but as long as the blood was pumping, the heart was functioning, and it seemed an obscenity to bury César alive. Like a dog frantically shovelling with its forefeet, Tristão covered the gray suit with gray dust, but he let the head remain in the air, sticking up on the slope like a boulder or like a shattered statue's handsome head.

xviii. *The Mato Grosso*

RETURNING to the shack, wearied to his bones by the guilt and labor of his deed, Tristão found instead of rest an atmosphere of necessary action. His family stood ready to depart, their few portable belongings bundled at their feet. His orange knapsack had been stuffed with spare clothes, and their lighter cooking utensils wrapped in blankets and mosquito netting. In the fluttering light of the shack's kerosene lamp, even the baby was wide-eyed and solemn, her cries hushed by the danger in the air. The old Tupi woman, Kupe-haki, had got wind of their departure and had appeared; speaking harshly and rapidly, they sought to argue her out of accompanying them, but she gave no sign of hearing. She remained an arm's length from Isabel's shoulder, moving when she did, swaying when she swayed, even sympathetically slumping when Isabel slumped in fear and despair. She had attached herself to them and could not be detached. The old Tupi had brought with her a long wickerwork basket, a tubular creel, worn down her back and supported by a thick band across her forehead, and in fact would be useful, they decided, even if she only travelled with them a little way at the start.

The five set off at last in single file across the polluted stream, and down the path away from the crusher and the slag heap, into a valley uninhabited except by the bandits who preyed on the gold traders and the supply caravans of loaded oxen and mules. The mechanical hum of the mountain, which persisted until midnight, faded behind them; the sounds of the mining town died but for the howl of a dog and a burst of especially loud laughter or expostulation. To Tristão it seemed that their path, widening and narrowing among the jagged black shadows of vegetation, glowed blue underfoot, as his eyes adjusted to the night. In the blue light César's blood had sprung out purple. Isabel carried little sleeping Cordélia, with her bobbing bald head, in a striped sling, at her breasts. Tristão at first carried Azor on his shoulders, the child's hands feebly but tenaciously gripping his bearer's head of stiff, stone-dust-impregnated hair. When Tristão felt the grip relax and the child topple into sleep, he took him into his arms, marvelling at how heavy he had become, in less than two years' time. In his knapsack he carried, along with spare clothes, César's revolver, loaded with its six bullets, and the cowboy boots, and the folded belt-bag with a crumb or two of gold in its seams; his heavy mining tools, rounded with use, had been left behind, without regret. We shed skins in life, to keep living.

Kupehaki, her head bent forward against the pull of the *tipóia*, the headband, carried in her creel a few cooking pots, a tin box of matches, some hooks and lines for fishing, the bejewelled Portuguese cross, and, snatched from the shack's larder, three days' meagre supply of powdered milk, dried beans, *xarque*, *maté* leaves, and sour, hardened cakes of manioc pulp. She and Isabel alternated carrying on their heads the bulky but not heavy bundle of netting and blankets, with an old ox-hide that, spread on the ground, suppressed biting ants and poisonous, earth-dwelling spiders.

They camped that first terrified night on a ledge not two miles from the mine, the adults taking turns keeping awake, while their fire sputtered and the darkness around them crackled and seethed with unknown creatures or spirits. Even the trees seemed to have voices, and a predatory purpose in the reach of their limbs. All night, anguished voices cried out, as murder threaded its way through the darkness. Yet the mist-colored dawn discovered the homeless travellers intact, free to clear their throats and eyes of sleep's phlegmy residue and to shoulder the burden of survival. Avoiding the travelled trails, they made their way down through the scree-strewn valleys of the Dourados, travelling always from the sunrise toward the sunset, toward the interminable rolling plateau of the Mato Grosso. The sky became enormous, as if God had breathed a sigh of relief and given up the intense labor of Creation, contenting Himself with a few tangles of low thorns, mixtures of cactus and brush, and tall grass, and occasionally an unimpressive forest. The most conspicuous tree of the *mato* was the Brazilian pine, shaped like an upside-down cone, each dark branch reaching out over the lower until a precisely layered pyramid seemed to be standing on its point. Kupehaki showed them how, in the rotting bark of these giants when they fell, succulent white worms called *coró* could be dug out, and, if no fire was convenient, eaten unroasted and wriggling; once squeamishness was overcome, they tasted like coconut butter.

It was Kupehaki who, in the days and weeks of their travel westward through the Mato Grosso, showed them how to catch bats and skinks and toads, spiders and grubs and grasshoppers, how to milk the bombax tree of its water, which berries to pick and which to beware as poisonous, what seeds and nuts were worth the harvesting and the shelling, and where to find the honey stored by the stingless little bees, called "eye-lickers," that delight in human sweat and furiously flock to the nostrils and tear ducts and moist corners of the lips. They were worse than the blood-sucking flies and *maribondo* wasps, these tiny bees who would die ecstatic within the fluids of the human face rather than fly away.

Nature had been turned inside out on the Serra do Buraco—gouged and uplifted and pulverized by man's passion for gold. Here, in the endless monotonous scrub forests and spotty savanna, the dry rises of *chapadão* alternating with trickling brown rivers, man resumed his lowly place in the churning struggle, the ocean of hungry protein, the frothy delirium of predation. Kupehaki showed them how, with Tristão's razor, to cut out the gray parasites that with an insidious painlessness burrowed into their legs, and how to strip in an instant when an innocent-appearing leaf would, brushed against, release a mass of tiny orange ticks that spread beneath their clothes like a species of fire; these invaders unless instantly brushed and beaten off would burrow in a minute beneath their skins. It was Kupehaki who showed Tristão how to gather deadwood from the brush and how, when their matches had given out, to ignite the night's fire with two sticks twirled in a pocket of dry grass, and who showed Isabel how to throw together a lean-to of green palm fronds that gave the illusion of shelter if not the reality. When, just beyond the shrinking circle of their campfire, a jaguar loosed its roar, it was Kupehaki who calmed Azor with tales of a mischievous jaguar-god. She set soothing limits to the dangers around them, describing the wilderness creatures as their brothers and sisters. When the howler monkeys screamed overhead and showered excrement upon them, she interpreted this as a humorous greeting; the bite of the little vampire bats, when they fastened upon the exposed hand of a sleeper in the night, she described as a kind of kiss, that purges the blood, in moderation. By day, she gestured rapturously toward the wealth of birds—the green parakeets, the white ibis and plover, the roseate spoonbills, the jabiru storks as tall as men, the yellow-bellied *bem-te-vi* kingbirds and the showy troupials whose nests crowded among the violet orchids that flourished on the stately *uauaçu* palms. In the distance, where a marshy pond glimmered like a mirage, colored clots, pink and white islands, of flamingos and egrets shimmered in the heat. Hearing the unaccustomed sound of human voices, the great birds took wing in a soft explosion, and as they poured past overhead the air thrillingly thrummed.

Tristão was fearful of wasting the six cartridges in César's gun. Once he fired at a heron on the wing and missed; another time he shot a sluggishly waddling anteater whose roasted oily flesh made them all sick; a third time he wounded a deer that on three legs scrambled beyond pursuit into the reaches of the savanna, there to fail and fall victim to the rapacious wild hogs, the white-lipped peccaries. The remaining three bullets he resolved to keep for a human enemy, if any should appear. Kupehaki showed them clearings, with a dusting of ash on the coffee-colored earth, where Indians had cultivated manioc, maize, and tobacco, and left a few calabash vines as souvenirs of their stay of a season or two. Of whiter men—questing *mamelucos* born of Portuguese men and Indian mothers—there were harsher traces, the overgrown tummocks and tunnels of aborted mining, and the rotting huts of vanished towns. Sometimes the ruins were centuries old and barely recognizable as human remnants—a row of stones that had once been a wall, a depression in the earth that had been a storeroom. Men had greedily flitted across this vastness but found nothing to root them. Many had died, and left beneath the giant sky mounded graves marked by nameless rock pyramids or wooden crosses eaten into papery husks by termites. Where the wood had been painted, the termites ate around the letters, leaving them on the earth as illegible crumbs of paint. A man's name did not last long in the Mato Grosso.

The mood of the newest explorers, even as they moved on the edge of starvation, was not without hope. A populated town must someday appear on the horizon, or a river that would take them to a place where their labor could be useful, where their persons could be woven into a social fabric. They seemed under their loads to be moving backward in time, away from the furies that excessive population had brought to their century, into a chaste space where pairs of willing human hands would still be valuable. Isabel remembered from the maps the nuns had showed her at school that Brazil had an end in the west; it became Bolivia, or Peru. There would be white-capped mountains, and Indians wearing blankets and bowler hats, and Maoist revolutionaries who might take them in and turn them into soldiers in the war against the men in silvery-gray suits.

In the meantime, their progress through the monotonous scrub offered the daily urgency of finding food, of staying alive, of staving off the demons of illness that besieged the blood. Azor, who had been plump as a grub at the start, had grown thin limbs and a hollow-eyed stare; he had learned to walk with them, for hours at a time, uncomplainingly, though his face was passing, it seemed to Isabel, into a mummified old age. Cordélia, still suckling, had fared better, though Isabel's milk was drying up. Isabel had lost her female round-ness, and was as lean as Kupehaki, even if her skin did not hang in such loose wrinkled folds from her arms, like the throbbing flap that falls from an iguana's throat. Isabel's ribs became as distinct and delicate as the ribs of a palm leaf, and her calves bulged with muscle as hard as Tristão's. Whereas she had turned a glowing brown in the daily sun, her hair bleached in dazzling contrast, he had turned dusty, his black shoulders faded like the once brilliantly orange knapsack he wore, which had become a faint, uneven pink, a rectangular banner leading the way through the aisles of grass, of scrub, of forest, as one changed into the other and back again in the endlessly repeating distances of the Mato Grosso. A kind of dullness had crept into Tristão's skin—pale splotches like a ghostly map, on his cheek and forearms—and a few tiny circlets of gray had appeared in his dense springy mat of head-wool. He had given up shaving, to preserve the edge of his razor blade, and his beard had come in thin, finer and softer than his head-hair, and grew out an inch, and then stopped.

Isabel's love for him was taking a new shape, an elongated shape like a great loop spinning off into the sky, the tireless vastness above and below, and then looping back, surprising her with its force, a sleeping force aroused by some sudden, seldom-seen angle of his face—from above, say, so the high square serious brow hid those eyes like windows into blackness, and the foreshortened curve of his jaw nestled in the hollow of his muscular shoulder—or by the sight of his gaunt body bent and folded, its lean outline curved into the task of building a fire, the knobs of his spine visible like the gleaming humps of a rapidly tumbling current. Sometimes, when he squatted by the fire, hunkering on his long pale heels to inspect Azor's wasted, patient little body for ticks, lice, leeches, and worms, or when in the dead of night he would bring the sobbing Cordélia to her to suckle—since even her milkless teats consoled the infant—Isabel would all but cry out in her odd joy, joy that he had chosen her, that he had come up to her in the blinding light of the beach and stamped himself on her eyes, on her soft young fibres, and given her life definition. He had chosen her, and had taken and accepted her, and was accepting even now these children as his and as his the fate of being hunted by her father. When she looked at him as he moved about unawares, she felt him treading on her insides, so they wobbled within her watery and fearful and painfully, ecstatically stretched. And when she, with the others at last quiet— Azor and Cordélia sleeping in a tangle with old Kupehaki, underneath a single piece of netting held up by stakes—would slide across the sandy soil of the campsite to remind him of their love, he would with obliging quickness grow his yam. The impotence of his mining days had been banished, but his potency, once fruit of their closeness like a seed sprouting in a damp crevice, now came from a distance like a mutter of thunder that disdains to make rain. In the wilderness, the only man among them, Tristão had become elusively large—a moon that appears the same size as a button held close to the eye.

"Tristão," she softly asked him one night. "Suppose we die out here?"

His hard muscles underwent the quick contraction of a shrug. "Then the vultures will clean us up and your father will never find us."

"Do you think he still pursues?"

"More than ever since I killed his agent, I feel your father at our backs."

"It is not my father that hunts us," she said defensively. "It is the system."

"Dear Isabel, I should never have come into your life. You would be a plump society wife in Rio by now, living on the Avenida Vieira Souto."

She put her fingertips on his lips. "You are my fate. You are what I have always wanted. I dreamed you, and then you appeared. I am truly happy, Tristão."

Mornings, they would rise, throw dry wood into the fire's embers, reheat what was left of last night's meal, scout about for food to fuel the day's trek, and move on. If there was a stream nearby, or a lake not too brackish, they would bathe, quickly, before parasites and poisonous fish became alerted to their splashing presence. Quickly lifting one of her children's naked glazed bodies out of the night-chilled water, Isabel gazed upward and the dome of sky seemed to swing on a pivot; there was a quality in the landscape and its towering sky, where the bleached clouds stood transparently erect or else thickened to crouching masses hurry-

ing east with their simultaneously leaden and
diaphanous centers—east toward the remote coast, the
remote present century—a quality of motionless movement, a gentle cruelty, a brimming absence, a haughti-
ness of far-flung matter that yet held a tenderness
around her as an eggshell holds the nutrient albumen
around the burgeoning yolk.

Travelling day after day, they seemed to be on a
treadmill that, failing to budge space, had become
geared to time. There was a taste to the *planalto* air, a
faint smoky spiciness, that Isabel thought must be the
smell of Brazil which had wafted out to Cabral and his
ships that April day in 1500, the smell of Tupi cooking
and of the red dyewood that was the vast hidden land's
initial single treasure. She felt increasingly at home,
rocked within the repeating rhythm of their journey—
the rising from their entwined sleep, discovering that
they all had moved for warmth into the fire of the ashes
and were filthy; the bathing in the pearly, guileless
morning light; the circling search for food, for berries
and nuts and wild pineapples, for small animals to stun
with sticks or stones, lizards and moles and orange-
bellied squirrels with flagrant orange tails, a search
never so fruitless that they starved or so successful that
they felt full, hunger like a gas they all kept inhaling,
making their heads dizzy; the loading up, amid gay and
mendacious promises to fretful little Azor that soon
their journey would be over; the burdened plod, single
file, across the tawny distances to that western target, to
that far clump of dark-green araucarias, that rosy cliff,

that notch in the blue-brown horizon; and then the evening encampment. Under the trembling red gaze of the setting sun—like a glowing coal, a *brasa*—they made a new home, and did the gathering, the reconnoitering, and set their fire to twinkle under the first stars, as a feeble child of the sun that had set.

Isabel felt safe and snug within this recurring routine but Kupehaki noticed ever more recent signs of cultivation in the savanna. In a shallow valley they shunned, they saw a herd not of bush deer, but of horses—the mammoth, wild-eyed, servile beasts that European intruders had brought to the continent.

"Guaicuru," the old Tupi said, but could not be made to explain what the word meant. Kupehaki merely rolled her eyes and bared her teeth, which had been filed into points when she was a girl. Her newly nervous manner infected the children, whose cries and complaints and unmeetable demands in turn irritated the weary adults.

They came to a brown river, too wide and rapid to wade across. A few rotting stakes in the water, X-shaped to support a walkway, remained of a crude Indian bridge that had been swept away. They would make a raft tomorrow, of balsa logs lashed together with lianas. Sandy terraces had built up along the river's edge, and on the highest of these, near a dense fringe of *uauaçu* palms and taller, slender *carandá* palms, they settled for the night.

xix. *The Raid*

A N ANIMATED TRICKLING and splashing at the edges
of the river, and the scraping cry of the frogs there,
kept Isabel from sinking deeply into sleep, so it was as
an extension of half-formed dreams that tall naked men,
painted like playing cards, materialized in the dim light
mixed of moonlight and the glow cast by their campfire's dying embers. The language the men used with
each other was harsh and rapid but not loud, even as the
raid reached its quick crisis. They must have been spying, for their actions were planned. Two shadows seized
Kupehaki and lifted the old woman up; while one
pinned her arms the other held her hair and, sawing at
her throat with the white curve of a sharp-toothed jaw-
bone, twirled her head and pulled it loose; there was a
plume, a black feather, of blood, as the body dropped.
A disbelieving scream rose in Isabel's throat and
jammed. The severed head, it seemed to her then and
ever after in nightmare, gazed at her with heavy-lidded
calm, as if to say she had done all she could and now
awaited a word of dismissal from her mistress.

Two other tall shadows lifted up the children, still curled asleep in their cocoons of mosquito netting, and disappeared with a clatter of their tongues back into the fringe of palms. Azor tried to cry but a hand must have clamped shut his mouth. Another shadow had inverted Kupehaki's long basket and was searching among the spilled scraps for treasures, on the sandy earth beside the headless body.

Tristão had scrambled to his feet and thus the Indian assigned to approach them halted. The disturbance had fanned the dying fire into a flare of life and by its flare they saw each other. The Indian was naked but for his conical penis-sheath and the bracelets of shells and teeth on his wrists and ankles. His face, plucked hairless, so that his lashless eyes had a red and wounded look, was covered with lacelike designs of red and blue dye, and like slender white tusks three wands of bone thrust from his pierced lower lip. His hair was short and rigid with some sort of wax; when he bared his teeth, they were crooked and black. He bared them because in the same muddled light by which he was seen he saw a man darker and a woman paler than he had ever beheld and the sight was terrible and holy to him. He carried a lance of sharpened and no doubt poison-tipped bamboo but held it aloft a fatal second, as a fisher hesitates in calculating the angle by which his spear must pierce the deceptive water. Isabel smelled the sharp resinous stench that came off the stiff hair and saw that where the Indian's ears should have been there were bird's wings; then Tristão shot him, with César's gun.

The attacker dropped his spear and, uttering a guttural cry of astonishment, clawed at his side, as if at a bee-sting. He tried to run, but this injury to his mechanism made his legs asymmetrical, so he ran in a circle, and then fell inward, toward the fire, still pedalling, his feet digging the sand. The other Indians, with the unembarrassed cowardice of savages, had vanished at the sound of the shot. In Isabel's ears it had sounded like a slap, waking her at last. When had she leaped to her feet, to stand beside Tristão in their final second? She had no memory. Instead, the resinous smell had reminded her of the violin lessons that Uncle Donaciano had once arranged for her. Like all such lessons—in drawing and dance and embroidery—they had failed to take; her only aptitude had been for love.

Tristão walked to the Indian's kicking body and pointed the pistol but failed to fire it. Instead, he fished from his shorts what must have been the razor blade and squatted to do something that his bent back prevented her from seeing. When he stood again, the murderous numbness of his expression fell on her face like dew. To be still alive was strange and humid.

He explained, "I must keep two bullets. Perhaps for you and me, if they return."

The thought of being killed by him had a beautiful rightness that made Isabel's loins clench. Then against the shining cliff of fantasy the bitter dull waves of their reality broke. Kupehaki's body lay at her feet, detritus smelling of the excrement released in the death paroxysm. "They've stolen our children!" Isabel wailed, the possessive pronoun a lie.

"The Indians have horses," Tristão told her. "Listen. You can hear the hoofbeats departing. We can never catch them on foot." He was panting, the rampart of his brow was knotted in a scowl. He was angry, it seemed, at her.

"Oh my little babies," she said, and fainted. The sandy earth came up to meet her as the powdery mattress of her childhood bed would float upward to her body when, in the days before her mother died in childbirth and her father became a wounded monster, he would carry her asleep in his arms from some bright exciting place they had all been together, and for just a flicker of wakefulness she would be aware of his strong arms, of the white sheets and fuzzy covers turned back, of her weariness and trust as she felt herself ladled from the deep bucket of one dream into another.

xx. *Alone Together*

WHEN HER CONSCIOUSNESS RETURNED, morning light sparkled on the river's gliding brown skin and Tristão sat staring into the fire he had rekindled. She went into the bushes to answer the call of nature and saw by the broken vegetation and troughs in the sand where Kupehaki's body had been dragged away. Ants and vultures would soon reduce the faithful Tupi to nothing. Isabel's mouth was dry, her stomach empty. "What shall we do?" she asked Tristão.

"Live, as long as we can," he said. "We must cross the river. We must keep moving west. Behind us, there is nothing but grief and danger."

"But Azor and Cordélia . . ." Tears flowed as she pictured their little pliant limbs and the trust shining in their moist wide gazes, like cups being held up to be filled. Even as hunger and weariness had poured down upon their unprotected frail bodies, they had looked to her with faith.

"We have no strength," he said, "no power to recover

them. Even if we did, how would we protect them against the hazards of this wilderness? They are perhaps better, dearest Isabel, with those who know how to survive. Had the savages meant to slay them, they would have done it on the spot."

The rage of her helplessness surfaced. He seemed so complacent, stating their desperate situation so bleakly, so reasonably. "Why should we ourselves trouble to live?" she asked him. "What is it to the world"—her gesture reached to include even those stretches beyond the Mato Grosso—"if we die now or later? Why struggle on even for a day, Tristão?"

He looked at her warily—his head tilted slightly to one side, his eyes half-lidded—as he had when he was a mere thievish beach boy, though since those days his face had grown its first creases. "It is a sin even to ask," he told her. "Our plain duty is to live."

"There is no one there," she screamed, her gesture expanded to include the sky, "to care what your duty is! There is no God, our lives are a terrible accident! We are born in a mess of pain, and pain and hunger and lust and fear drive us on for no purpose whatsoever!"

He looked grave, and spoke softly as if to pull back her outcry from the vastness of scandalized silence. "You disappoint me, Isabel," he said. "Why is the world so elaborate, if it has no purpose? Think of the care that goes into the least little insect and weed around us. You say you love me; then you must love life. Life is a gift, for which we must give something back. I believe in spirits," he told her, "and in destiny.

You were my destiny, and I yours. If we die without a struggle now, we will never reach our fates. Perhaps our fates include rescuing your children, perhaps not. I know this, Isabel: you and I were brought together not to feed children into the world's maw, but to prove love—to make for the world an example of love. I felt this even in the *fusca* factory, when it seemed I might never see you again."

And it was true that she, submitting to his judgment, and enduring with him the coming weeks of wandering and slow starvation, felt more love than ever. Her need to make love to him had never been stronger, not even back in the hotel in São Paulo. In their desperate isolation fucking was a claim upon him, and a comforting of him, and a reminder to herself that she was still there beneath the sky, and a begging for his forgiveness, and a perverse triumph of failing strength. Since they had little food, fucking became their food. Since they were lost, their bodies became their mutual destination, their only home. They were not as skilled at gleaning the bush as Kupehaki had been, so several times they mistakenly ate poison berries, or dug up poison roots and boiled them. Fevers and hallucinations nearly carried them off; diarrhea emptied their bowels to the cleanliness of scoured marble. Emaciated, nauseated, shivering with fever so that her teeth kept clicking, yet she wanted to toy with his yam, and trace its swollen veins with the tip of her tongue, and sip the little transparent drop of nectar from its single small slit, before feeling then its rush of friction between her legs, and his back hard as a knobbed board beneath her clutching hands. If her last strength were to be yielded up in such an embrace, her life would be shaped like a flower, its soft bell open to the light of life.

And he, wondering at her passion, as superfluous and extravagant as a convolute orchid that feeds on air, allowed her to arouse him even when his vitality had sunk so low his own skeleton felt to him like heavy stones he was dragging in a thin sack of skin across the thorny *chapadões* and dizzily letting drop at the night's hard resting-place. Too weak to rise from the earth, he would dreamily watch naked Isabel straddle his hips and lower herself onto his rod. Her hips and belly and her transparently furred mound of Venus were even in her emaciation rounded, her last sliver of female fat. Her cleft would slip its clasp upon him, first dry and hurtful, then moist and gluey, down to his oily black froth of pubic fur, and back up, and back down, her shrunken breasts twittering on her white chest with its ribs like the ribs of a palm leaf.

Hunger is a pain at first, a growling, gnawing interloper, and then a narcotic, an accustomed daze and dimness in which consciousness unprotestingly floats. Even the howler monkeys, in the patches of forest, drew back respectfully into the green canopy, to let their ghosts past. Damp sandy spots held fresh paca and tapir tracks, but they never saw these animals, and would have been too weak and slow to catch them. Isabel's classes in botany enabled her to distinguish between the buriti palm, with its stiff fanlike fronds, the bacaba palm, with its very long, curving fronds and dishevelled look, the low-growing nacurý palm, the thorny, slender-stemmed boritana palm, which loves wet ground, and the even more slender accashy palm, its bole as straight as an arrow; but there was nothing of these trees to eat in this season, not nuts or palm hearts. The thriving life about them was the tormenting wallpaper of a barren cell. Once they came to an entire petrified forest, half-erect and half-collapsed in great shards like those of a vandalized temple, the shattered columns calcified in tints of mossy green and muddy rose, dead white and aloof blue. What god had been ardently worshipped here, and nevertheless had died?

When the couple was on the point of collapse, iridescent hummingbirds, called flower-kissers, with emerald backs and yellow chests and wings in a blur, would hover in the air before them, fruit begging to be plucked; Tristão and Isabel learned to reach out and seize the small birds, suppressing the churning of the frantic wings in their palms and with a flick of the thumb breaking their necks. Six or eight of them, painstakingly plucked of their exquisite metallic feathers and roasted on sticks fine as needles, yielded up a few bites of tough, bittersweet flesh. At other moments, Tristão and Isabel would find themselves surrounded by a circle of ripe cashew trees, a plantation left by some flitting, vanished agriculturalists, and would ravenously consume all they could reach, nut and thick skin both. In this way, from one evanescent feast to the next, the couple wandered on, in a thickening forest where it was difficult to see the westering sun, and where daylight was often a mere icy sparkle above the highest tier of vegetation.

They had begun their time alone together by swimming the brown river beside their fatal encampment. Each took as float a fat and fallen palm trunk, but the rotten logs absorbed water like sponges and quickly sank; Isabel had to be dragged through the last hundred yards, her white hand resting on Tristão's gleaming shoulder like a leech on a gleaming black sturgeon. Luckily, the piranhas that nibbled their kicking ankles were not accustomed to human flesh and movements, and no random snap of their jaws elicited the drops of blood that would have tripped them into a frenzy. At his strength's end, Tristão found sandy shallows beneath his feet; he and Isabel were able to wade, gasping, to the far bank of the river. Unbeknownst to them, they had crossed on the *planalto* from the region where the rivers flow south, into the Paraguay, over to the land of the Paressi, where the streams are tributary to, a thousand miles to the north, the Amazon.

xxi. *The Rescue*

WEEKS had passed. They had lain down to die. A little grove of wild wax palms offered a shifting, pleasant shade; through their slender undulant trunks Tristão and Isabel could gaze together down a grassy, scrubby slope toward yet another river, this side of yet another slope in the seemingly endless *chapadão*. It was late afternoon; the thin shadows were weaving their soft net tighter, and the mosquitoes and tiny sand-flies were beginning to inflict those bites to which Tristão and Isabel had long grown impervious.

The lovers held hands and turned their faces to the sky; he heard her breathing sink into a rasping, slower pace, and turned once more to see her profile—the sunburnt brow where her blond hairline feathered back shimmeringly from the temples, and the outward curve of her lower face that signalled sensuality and a capacity for mischief, as he had guessed at first sight. His fingers encountered, loose on her emaciated finger, the hard circlet of the DAR ring he had once given her, and his eyes, almost as numbly, encountered the presence of, beyond Isabel's profile, high leather boots, much battered by wear and weather. There were other boots, men's boots with the mute, deeply used look of animals' feet, and above them torn breeches of coarse baize in a variety of faded colors.

Tristão sat up, and felt the point of a rapier at the pit of his throat. "Stay, nigger," a deep voice said, not unpleasantly, in a quaint and courteous accent Tristão had never heard before. A brass-colored face, plump but not soft, fully bearded, and framed by a wide leather hat, loomed beyond the embossed cup hilt of the rapier. "From thy gaunt looks, thou hast long been in search of a meal. It would take no deep prick to come out t'other side. And what vision sleeps next to thee? A fair princess, it would appear, far wandered from the court of good João Quinto. Two squares of the chessboard, come to give us a game!" And from the jubilant quality of the man's laughter, and that of his companions as they crowded curiously around, Tristão could not doubt that some sort of fun would follow. Even when they fitted heavy, rusty shackles around his wrists, and an iron collar with a dangling chain around his throat, he felt, in his passivity and fatigue, that it was being done for his own good.

Isabel awoke with a soft cry transported, it seemed, from the disintegrating theatre of her dreams. "Tristão," she said, "if we have died, Heaven has rough angels!"

These ruffians, of whom there were six or seven, were all bearded and clad in scuffed and tattered patchworks of leather and cloth; all wore a curious kind of chest armor, a carapace of rawhide padded inside with cotton—soft enough for comfort, she judged, and yet hard enough to withstand arrows. Their clothes showed years of weather and wear; some men wore hats of woven palms instead of leather, and some had tied kerchiefs on their heads instead of hats. Some were missing a limb or two. A number carried muskets and blunderbusses. They murmured with enchantment to hear Isabel speak, as if a tinkling, singing harpsichord had been transported from Venice or Antwerp to this remotest point of the advance of civilization. Ages had passed since they had heard the voice of a white woman. Their number was augmented by twenty or so Indians, whose costumes ranged from stark nudity to the baggy trousers and blouse of a field-hand. One scowling savage wore crossed parrot feathers inserted through his septum; others had decorated their nakedness with armlets of monkey-skin and many-stranded necklaces of pearly river-shells; but all, including the several women, who held babes in their arms or in their stomachs, appeared to be harmonized within this motley troop, and all, as persistently as eye-licking bees, gathered about Tristão, touching him clingingly, shamelessly, inspecting his parts as if he were a curious mechanism.

They were more reluctant to touch Isabel, and she attempted to use her authority to interpose her body in front of Tristão's; but the roughness with which she was thrust aside marked a limit to the awe in which her pale beauty was held. She felt a limit, too, in the extent that her light feminine voice and Carioca accent penetrated the thick eardrums of these leather-swaddled adventurers. However, in a curious piece of deference, the leader of the band, the man with the rapier, let her hold the chain on Tristão's neck-shackle, as if acknowledging her prior ownership.

"I am frightened, Tristão," she confided in a whisper.

"Why? These are your people." He hurt her by sounding hostile and bitter. A gulf had abruptly opened between them, after the long journey in which their dwindling bodies had all but merged. His voice relented a little. "At least we will be fed. These rogues are fat as pigs."

The party walked downhill, on a broadening path, toward the river. Cleared fields and tended plantations of manioc and beans prepared them for the sight of the settlement, a straggling array of round palm-roofed huts, some open-sided in the Indian style, and others walled with logs and mud to suit a European sense of enclosure. Along the river, there were scaffoldings for drying fish, and arcs of stakes set out to hold nets. Several dugout shells lay about in a state of incompletion, surrounded by chips and a few rusting iron tools. A sun-rotted *bandeira*, with a cross and scrolling escutcheon visible in its faded folds, drooped from a bamboo pole fixed to the roof-tree of the largest encampment structure, an open longhouse where the entire population could gather. Here the captives, after an hour of being fed and bathed by deft, insistent Indian hands, were taken before an assembly. Their discoverer led them through the excited crowd to another brass-faced man, similar but older and leaner; he sat in a basket chair whose high wicker back, ornamented with a dappled jaguar pelt that included the snarling skull, echoed the splendor of a throne.

"I have the honor to be the captain of this *bandeira* of brave and pious Paulistas," he explained, introducing himself with an ironic sonority: "Antônio Álvares Lanhas Peixoto. Thou hast already met my younger brother, José de Alvarenga Peixoto." Antônio's beard was shaped to a long point, and in his face the yellow-brown of the familial racial mix was almost golden, a swarthy gold that gleamed on his cheekbones and along the curve of his prominent arched nose. He fancied he saw Isabel's eye on his nose, laid his finger beside it, and said, "My mother was a Carijó and my father a new Christian, that is, a former son of Abraham, as are half the residents of São Paulo. The Holy Office of the Inquisition in Bahia never extended its blessed services so far into the south—not," he hastened to add, "that the priests would have found us lacking in fervent orthodoxy. By God's wounds, have we not risked our very lives and sanity for the salvation of heathen souls? Have we not roved for years beyond counting this damnèd inferno of cactuses and anthills, tormented by every manner of sharp-toothed fish and whining insect that the Maker of All saw fit to invent? Have we not been beset without mercy on every side by the very savages we seek to save, savages armed and maddened by the

Spanish Jesuits, who are black-robed traitors to their race and religion both?"

The exhortatory questions seemed addressed not so much to Isabel—though even at the height of oratorical fury he kept a glinting small eye, the amorous color of amber, fastened upon her—as to the ragged band of warriors assembled at the captives' backs.

"The robed blasphemers harbor the infidels," he told her, of the Jesuits, "in so-called reductions, for their own profit and lechery, keeping them in idleness and nakedness, when it is *we* who would truly reduce them, in our settlements and the King's *aldeias*, to divinely inspired religion, useful labor, and civilized decorum."

"I have heard of kings," Isabel said timidly, "but they ruled long ago."

"Aye," interrupted the round-faced José. "Long we have been in these backlands, having vowed never to return without Indians or gold. If we outlast a king or two, and find in our absence we have miraculously fathered a babe or three, what will it signify when as rich men we return to our estates, with troops of willing servants to employ and to barter for more land still? White gold is the goal, red gold is the gain!"

His brother lifted a long forefinger to silence such rapacious enthusiasm. "We enlist the heathen for their own salvation," he reminded the company, while speaking to Isabel. "Though they strike us on one cheek, we turn the other, and merely make them captive, where they would heedlessly slay. In the dark of their Godlessness, they eat of their enemies' brains and inner organs

198

to gain prowess in combat. We correct such deluded customs, teaching them proper science and useful employments instead. Thus, amid the cruelties of battle, even as they repay us with poisoned arrows, we introduce them to the mercies of our Saviour!"

The laughter at these rotund avowals could not be suppressed; as the other *bandeirantes* indulged in mirthful hubbub, José confided to Isabel and Tristão, with the slyness of long acquaintance, "Unless of course they be too feeble or young to work, or the women too old to warm a man's bed."

"These natives around us," Isabel asked Antônio— "are they all slaves, then?"

"Pray, child, say not 'slaves.' Enslavement of indigenes is forbidden by firm royal instruction, and condemned by a reiterated papal bull. 'Administration' is all that we intend. Those thou seest about us are our allies, Tupi and Guarani and Caduveo persuaded to our cause and therefore become our guides and loving companions. We were many of us born of Indian mothers, and conceive in the same strain. Some others, yes, would escape our service if they could. But God has not yet favored our expedition with an ample harvest of converted souls, and many of those we won to Jesus have been called, alas, to His heavenly home by fever and pox. Our chaplain has exhausted his store of precious wine, with the giving of last Communions."

"The rascals escape," José burst in, "they escape by dying! They are so little grateful for our protection they villainously will their hearts to cease! That is why thy nigger, my lady, is a welcome treasure here; in São Paulo itself not many can afford the luxury of pure-blooded blacks. They are a race God made to enrich their betters: the sons of Ham to serve the sons of Shem and Japheth. They do not die. They mourn their pestilential homeland and hack themselves idols and drums, and if enough collect into a pack they rebel and flee and in the wilderness form *quilombos* where all is license and anarchy; but they do not die on our hands, in such traitorous numbers."

"He is no slave!" Isabel exclaimed.

Antônio's baroque eyebrows, in which curving gray wands were mixed with brassy strands, lifted in gentle surprise. "What is he, then?"

"He is my man—my companion, my husband," Isabel said. She braced herself to withstand a wave of mockery, since it seemed absurd to speak so of a stubbornly unspeaking creature held in collar and chain like a dog or monkey; but her words fell into an astonished silence. "I love him," she said, into the silence, in a small voice that faltered, so many miles had she carried this love, like a piece of Dresden china, across the breadth of Brazil.

Antônio leaned forward, still gentle, his amber eyes intent. "Tell us thy story," he commanded.

"We have been travelling west for more weeks than we can count," she explained, "escaping my father's displeasure at our match and searching for a place where we can settle and perform useful work. A fortnight or more ago, our little party was attacked by painted savages; they killed our faithful Tupi woman and kidnapped our two children, and rode away on gigantic horses." At this brief recounting, the sum of her burdens bore upon her emaciated spirit, and tears spilled down her cheeks, while her throat ached with the suppression of sobs.

"Ah, those were Guaicuru—devils incarnate," said José eagerly. "They have taken to Arabian horses like magicians, using neither saddles nor stirrups; they mount up in a single leap. Their women, to keep the tribe mobile, exterminate their children in their bellies, with violent self-injuries that leave them forever infertile; to make up their shortage of children, they steal them where they can, to raise as their own, in the ways of Satan. So unnatural these buggers are, they keep some men in women's dress, men who piss squatting down and once a month suppose they have a flow of blood. Their sacrileges know no bounds!"

Isabel addressed Antônio. "Sir, might my children"— her voice broke in her aching throat—"might you and your stalwarts rescue my children?"

The captain of the *bandeira* leaned forward toward her in the manner of a loving father. "The Guaicuru are many, and ferocious," he sadly said. "We were three times our present number, before our battles with the Guaicuru."

"And their brothers in deviltry the Paiaguá," José busily interposed, sweating indignantly in his thick leather carapace. "They have not horses but canoes, in which they skim the water like birds! They swim like fish, with cutlasses in their mouths!"

"Did not," Antônio asked Isabel, his amber gaze and his pointed grizzled beard bearing upon her with a pressure that reminded her of her father's lumpy, leaning forehead, "he whom thou pretend is thy husband strive to protect the children that were his as well as thine?"

This was scarcely the moment to explain that the children were not beyond doubt Tristão's. The confusion of the raid—the children wrapped in the netting like larvae, the Guaicuru in his red and blue paint, the thin white bones raying from his lips—returned to her horrified vision, as she explained, "He did. He shot one of them, but there were too many, and the children were already carried away."

"Shot, thou sayest?"

José interposed, "We found this mechanism among their belongings, sire. It appears marvellously made, and we took it for a Dutch toy or an Italian snuffbox until scrutiny showed it to be a pistol, but squared off and cleverly shrunk, and lacking a wheel-lock."

He handed over César's gun. Antônio inspected its silky-smooth machined surfaces and, with a debonair gesture befitting an old-fashioned musketeer, aimed it over their heads, but not far over, and squeezed the trigger. The acrid slap of its report and the singing flight of the bullet transfixed the longhouse, without leaving a visible hole in the roof thatch; amused, the captain fired again, and then produced a click. Those had been the two bullets Tristão had been saving for Isabel and himself. Now they must live.

"As thou sayest, brother, a children's toy. Its barrel wouldn't hold enough shot to bring down a *beija-flor*."

Antônio spoke then to Isabel, in a tone of concluding disposition. "This black slave is no longer thy husband, my dear child. Slaves do not marry. Do not despair. I am a lonely man, and not as ancient in my faculties, thou shalt discover, as has first appeared to thee."

Tristão's stubborn silence at her side was a kind of thunder, like the beating of her own amazed, persistent heart.

xxii. *The Encampment*

THE OLD *bandeira* chieftain took Isabel as his wife—his third wife, since two aborigine women, Takwame and Ianopamoko, already catered to his needs. They did not appear to resent her addition to his household; her hands lightened their own work, and for her first year they were greatly spared service in Antônio's bed. She became pregnant, and in the second year produced an amber-eyed son, whom she named Salomão, in the hopes he would grow to become wise, and to honor her father; perhaps thus his pursuing fury would be placated. When she smuggled word of her decision to Tristão, by way of Ianopamoko—the younger of the Indian concubines, younger even than Isabel; a dainty Tupi-Kawahib beauty with cylindrical, waistless torso and slender, graceful limbs—Tristão sneered, and cursed his wife. "May the child devour her heart," he said, and Ianopamoko's dainty face, as she endeavored to imitate the black man's full-lipped sneer, was so ferociously contorted as to be comical. A lacy pattern of indigo paint covered Ianopamoko's rather flat features, the dotted lines and fishhook-shapes full of meaning known only to the wrinkled crone who renewed the designs when they faded, and who was herself near the great forgetting, or immense remembering, of death.

Perhaps Tristão's curse took hold, for her new baby was curiously quiet and limp in her arms, where Azor had kicked and pushed with his fat little muscles from his first weeks.

Tristão, wearing a leg-manacle to prevent his escape, had been set to work in the fields at first, the burned-over fields planted in manioc and maize, sweet potatoes and groundnuts, tobacco and gourds and black beans—but then, as the mechanical skills he had developed in the *fusca* plant and in the gold mine became apparent, he was reassigned to carving the canoes for the *bandeira*'s eventual move downriver. The canoes must be substantial and wide, to discourage Paiaguá warriors swimming underwater from capsizing them, and needed the biggest of chestnut, mahogany, and araucaria trees, to be painstakingly hollowed and shaped by the encampment's single, rusting iron adze. The Peixoto brothers hoped this river would lead to the Madeira, where Indian villages, earlier expeditions had reported, were as thick as grapes on a vine, begging to be plucked, and thence to the Amazon and by sea back home to a paradisiacal old age in the province of São Paulo, surrounded by domesticated, grateful former heathen.

Lying beside Antônio, on the bed beneath his tall, fascinatingly detailed crucifix—every fingernail and

toenail and nailhead and rivulet of blood realer than
real—Isabel heard the tale of the *bandeirantes'* long
journey: How they had set out with high hearts and ample supplies, wives and children and banker-backers
cheering and waving them through the first miles of
well-trampled roadway; how they had arrived forty days
later, their ranks thinned and bedraggled but hardened,
at the Paranapanema and the Guairá Missions, only to
discover that the missions, with their docile Christian-
ized tribes gathered like corralled sheep, had been so
plundered by previous *bandeira* raids that the dastardly
Spanish Jesuits had moved on, with the survivors, to the
south and west, beyond the Iguaçu Falls, on the Paraná;
and how they reached and crossed the Paraná, after
months of hardship, only to face several terrible battles,
since the Spanish authorities had at last permitted the
Jesuits to arm the Indians with guns. The easy triumphs,
yielding thousands of captives, of the famous Antônio
Raposo Tavares and André Fernandes belonged to a
more innocent past. The Peixoto *bandeira* retreated
west and north, into the swampy Pantanal, where the
pickings were thin. Slaughter, disease, and plagues of
jaguars and caimans feasting upon the enfeebled Indians
had preceded them. Starveling remnants, a mere family
or two, would no sooner become captive than, one by
one, with much obnoxious farting and coughing, they
would die. "Arriving at a village, we would encourage
the inhabitants to complete the harvest of their plantation, and ourselves demonstrate a patience equal to the
task; when harvest at last eventuated, I, having permit-

ted my men a night of feasting and debauchery, would give the command to move on, carrying the remainder of the victuals, in this way intriguing the Indians to follow and swell our party. As José told thee, my dearest Isabel, the heathen tended to perish, if not of agues to which their spirits made no resistance, or of the excesses of *pinga* which the men mischievously pushed upon them, then of sheer bewilderment—sheer savage incomprehension of what it was we were trying to achieve. When we mentioned gold, they conjured up cities of the stuff, beyond the next mountain range, as if to hurry us out of sight, and cities of diamonds likewise, when these gems were described. Never, though, did we come to an end of wilderness. Wet season followed dry season, blue river followed brown river, and still our band failed to arrive, as under the Southern Cross we travelled toward the North Star."

"How long ago was this, my lord? How many seasons have you been travelling?"

"There is no telling, dear child. My brain has taken into itself the white fog of distances."

However long they had been mired in this encampment, the hope of moving on still burned in her master's brain, and stirred his waggling chin-whiskers to an excitement that sometimes spread to his gnarled and delicate loins—the hope of reaching that Madeira River which would spill its healthy inhabitants, anxious for conversion to the Brazilian way of life, into his possession, and transform his *fazenda* back on the *terra roxa* of São Paulo into Heaven on Earth.

Holding her unresponsive son in her arms, and finding in his bloodless face barely the strength or wit to suckle, Isabel would weep, and weep doubly at the thought of Tristão, her proud lover, chained to the interminable task of hollowing out a fleet of broad-bottomed canoes with swings of a dull adze. For the Indians, who before his arrival had desultorily worked on the canoes, now thought it beneath them, and their duty to consist only of whipping the black slave to faster labor.

Ianopamoko pitied Isabel; a sisterly love had grown up between them, and a mutual language woven of Ianopamoko's sparse Portuguese and those phrases of her native language—a tongue whose words ended with the sharply accented syllables *zip, zep, pep, set, tap*, and *kat*—that Isabel gradually acquired.

"You know," Ianopamoko one day told her, when the listless child of Antônio's delicate loins was over a year old, "magic still exists. The invaders have not yet destroyed every shred of our old compact with the spirits. There remain far places where the"—and she used a word, ending with *zep*, which derogatively designated the Portuguese as "eaters of armadillo entrails"—"have not placed their polluting step. A shaman exists, seventeen days' walk to the west, who might—"

"Free Tristão?" Isabel eagerly asked.

Ianopamoko hesitated; a small twitch of a frown moved beneath the blue lace of her facial adornment. "I was going to say, who might give your baby the brains other babies have."

"Oh, yes?" Isabel tried to sound interested, as a

mother should. But as a former Brasília University student, who had taken courses in psychology, she knew that a brain could not be so easily bestowed, in its billions of interconnected neurons. And Salomão's feeblemindedness, his refusal to crawl or begin even the rudiments of utterance, had deflected affection back onto her husband; Tristão's curse had proved to be stronger than her father's name and her captor's seed, and so the child's defects served as a secret link with the African slave whose tireless, angry adze-swinging filled the encampment, dawn to dusk, with the sound of percussion.

"Magic," Ianopamoko explained carefully, as if to bridge the gap she felt between their priorities, "has its rules and limits, like the nature from which it derives. To take, we must give. If your baby were to become intelligent, it is possible that you might have to give up some of your own intelligence, just as his body in your womb ate food your mouth had chewed."

"I am prepared to sacrifice myself in part," said Isabel, with a frankness and care matching the other woman's. "But I cannot conceive of myself as less intelligent, without ceasing to be myself."

"It will be a long trip to the shaman, not without danger. Nor is he immortal. He is very old, and very sad, as he sees and foresees the fate of his people."

"If he has authentic power," Isabel asked, "why has he not reversed the tide of death and defeat that came with the Europeans?"

"Magic cannot be general," Ianopamoko explained,

not in the least impatiently. "It cannot be"—and this long word ended in *tap*—"political. Its arena is the personal soul, not a nation or a people. There must be a personal petition, and procedures, and a consequence to which must cling some ambiguity. As in nature, you do not get something for nothing. Among many Indians"— the word, ending in *kat*, literally meant "decent people; those who are not indecent or unclean"—"magic has become too exhausting. The shaman is shunned, and receives little business. But for you, whose arrival among us had the quality of an apparition, and whose sorrow has the tranquil depth of an enchantment, I thought a magical solution might be in order."

"You would come with me, Ianopamoko?"

"Yes. I would have to. You would never get there otherwise."

"But, darling, why?"

The slender young woman averted her face, as if to avoid a glancing blow of possible indecency. Her short-ish hair was stiffened with a mixture of ashes and resin into the shape of an inverted bowl. "I love you," she said, approximately, in her intricate, snappy tongue.

The casual touches, as soft as thin anthers brushing bees' golden-haired legs with velvety cocoa-colored pollen, with which the prior wife had welcomed Isabel into the *bandeira* chieftain's household, had evolved, through the many nights, into more prolonged and purposeful caresses, carried on in view of the others, in the innocent style of a race to whom nudity was full dress. If at moments the playful cuddling produced a secret

shudder, a dew of happiness upon the petals of femininity and a fluttering wish to reciprocate as far as the
mysteries of flesh permitted, what shame could attach to
Isabel's heart, suspended awkwardly as it was between
an elderly lover and a shackled one? Yes, the two wives
loved each other, and made love.

"And Salomão?" she asked. "Must we take him with
us? The journey might kill the poor weakling."

Ianopamoko's answer was solemn: "That is true. He
must stay. Just you and I will go. Takwame and her
daughters will care for Salomão, feeding him a nutri-
tious gruel of manioc and banana. I have noticed your
flow of milk has been ceasing, and in any case your son
never thrived upon it." Did Isabel hear a hint of re-
proach in the other woman's voice? What did this little
sepia female, no bigger than a child, know of mothering, its dead patches and natural callousness? Though
for a time Antônio's favorite, she had remained barren,
at her deepest level impervious to male charm.

xxiii. *The Mesa*

T HE FOREST to the west, across the river (which they
traversed, on the dawn of their escape, by means
of one of the small dugout canoes the encampment fishermen kept tied to the bank), could fairly be called
jungle—*selva*, or *mata*. From the sun-parched, masculine scrub of the great *mato* they passed into a lusher,
dimmer, feminine world. Thin paths that Isabel's eyes
could never have followed wound through a world of
green shadow heavy with flowers and fruits. The
trumpet-note of the *jacu* and the screeching and skit-
tering of unseen spider monkeys accompanied their
flickering passage through this dense tapestry, whose
topmost canopy of branches admitted only slender
shafts of sunlight, swirling with a dust of insects. Between the monotonous smooth gray trunks of trees
stretching skyward, festooned with vines and buttressed
by uplifted roots, the growth underfoot was sparse; for
miles the two women walked upon a brown pavement
of dead seed husks and palm fronds, as upon the uneven
tombstones of some dim deserted cathedral redolent of

rot's sweetish incense. Chestnuts and Brazil nuts rained down upon them when Ianopamoko prettily skinned up a trunk and shook the branches; gliding barefoot from dawn to dusk, the travellers feasted upon the purplish, cherry-sized fruit of the *araçá*, which smells of turpentine and makes the saliva in one's mouth fizz, and the pods of the *ingá*, which are stuffed with sweet-tasting down, and wild pineapples whose flesh abounds in big black seeds and tastes of raspberry, and the pears called *bacuri* and that even greater delicacy named the *açai*, which overnight curdles into a fruity cheese. All these sweetmeats hung waiting for them, in an Eden without inhabitants. Creation felt young, and full of tentative, ornate forms; like many another artist, God had achieved His most elaborate and fantastic effects early.

At night the two women lay together in a single cocoon of mosquito netting, and in the morning unfolded themselves like damp butterflies. They clung ever more closely as the night chill sharpened its bite; for they were climbing gradually higher through this cloistered green world, and broke out on the sixteenth day into hillside fields of tall grasses, irregular terraces pulsating with the onrush of silvery wind-shadows and leading up to a rocky mesa down which a number of waterfalls threaded their glittering way. These tear-trails on Nature's face, at spots indistinguishable from frozen veins of quartz, were set in broad ribbons of algae and moss. Several Indians, speaking a language Ianopamoko understood with difficulty, warily greeted them in the tall grass. They stared at Isabel as if she were unhuman.

Ianopamoko's voice gently tapped and zipped on and on, explaining, pleading, demanding. At one point she lifted Isabel's long shining hair in both hands, as if weighing it, and at another she briskly rubbed her moistened fingers over Isabel's skin, demonstrating that its pallor was not painted on.

"They feel they are running great risk," Ianopamoko had at last explained, "and want a tribute."

"We have brought the cross and the cigarette box," Isabel said. "Save the cross. Offer the box."

Uncle Donaciano's ornate, engraved monogram disappeared beneath the creased umber thumb, broadened by the forest's patient manual crafts, of their chief welcomer. He kept clicking the box open and shut, and each time it opened he followed, with a slobbery rot-flecked grin and outright astonished laughter, the zigzag flight of something invisible he fancied to have been captured within it. The gift was accepted. After this long parley, Isabel and Ianopamoko were led up the steep cliff along a slippery hairpin path, which several times wound behind a falling stream's veil whose waywardmost spray pricked them with rainbows the size of dragonflies.

At the top, a few domed daub-and-wattle huts, built low against the wind, huddled amid a vegetation such as Isabel had never seen—stubby, prickly, knobbed, and bejewelled forms transplanted as if from coral gardens at the bottom of a shallow sea. They had rooted themselves in the crevices of a lava surface crisscrossed by cracks. Isabel trod on this surface as across ragged

214

stepping-stones, or loaves of bread placed on end; the stone was an ashen gray, baked in a fire more ancient than the ocean. When she lifted her eyes, she saw in the vast distance something new to her, except in books and magazines of fashion and travel: snow, a pure whiteness on the peaks of mountains rendered by distance as blue as the undersides of clouds. She had learned from the nuns enough of geography to know that these must be outriggers of the Andes, and that somewhere between them and herself Brazil at last ended.

Though she had dwelt three years among Indians, and learned some of their language and lore, they still presented to her the opacity of moody children, an unpredictability mixed of stubborn shyness and masked desire. To those at their mercy, it seemed a small distance, which a spark could suddenly leap, from ministration to murder; a whole other world, full of psychic electricity, hung behind their almond eyes and mutilated mouths. This settlement on the mesa top was some kind of cathedral close, victualled from the grassland and forest below and centered upon the shaman in his low oval hut. Isabel associated safety with religious places; yet it was here, where an invisible system had its pivot, that she might give fatal offense. She embarked fearfully upon her first audience with the shaman.

His hut was in texture and shape like an ovenbird's nest, and so small she had to crouch to enter. Smoke hurt and blurred her eyes. A torpid fire, built of spindly mesa-top twigs and chunks of a moss that burned with a blue flame, slowly revealed a small naked man lying in a hammock strung up just behind the fire. His body was smooth, with a swollen belly, but his head was remarkably withered or else diminished in apparent size by his high upright headdress of parrot's-tail feathers. His face had been plucked of hair, lashes and brows and temples, yet above his prominent ears long white wisps had been allowed to grow like fine, lank ancillary feathers. Around his ankles he wore bands of large triangular dried nuts, and in one hand he held an empty gourd the size of an ostrich egg, which he shook to emphasize points in his utterance.

As soon as the shaman saw her, he closed his eyes and shook his maraca as if to ward off the sight. Though she had grown accustomed to going naked like the Indians, for this occasion she had tucked around her waist a kind of sarong that she had earlier fashioned— to protect her legs from thorns and stinging insects when gathering food in the wild for Antônio's household—of the dress of navy-blue silk covered with small red flowers which she had once worn, in all innocence, to Chiquinho's ranch house, on another occasion when she had wished to present herself favorably.

"Maira," the shaman saluted her. "Who are you? Why do you disturb my peace?"

Ianopamoko translated his words into her and Isabel's hybrid language, and often had to ask the shaman to repeat, since besides speaking a strange dialect he was toothless and wore a number of polished jadeite plugs in his lower lip, muffling his pronunciation. "Maira," she explained to Isabel, "is their name for a prophet like the Jesus of the Portuguese. He has never seen anyone your color, with hair like sunlight. White men have not yet shown themselves in this part of the world."

Isabel remembered Tristão saying scornfully "your people," which may have marked the beginning of her attempt to seek a miracle. "I am not a prophet; I am a woman reduced to desperation, come to beg for your magic," she said.

Ianopamoko translated, and the shaman frowned, and mumbled, interrupting himself with angrily prolonged rattles of his maraca. "He says," Ianopamoko whispered, "magic is men's business. Women are dirt and water, men are air and fire. Women are—I am not sure of his word, I think it means 'unclean,' but also has a sense of 'tricky business.' "

Then she talked directly to the shaman, at some length, and explained to Isabel, "I have told him you are come for the sake of your boy-child, whose father was so old the baby was born without the heat of a normal person."

"No," Isabel protested to her friend—"I have not come for the sake of Salomão, but for the sake of Tristão, my husband!"

The shaman looked from one woman to the other, sensing their cross-purposes, and brandished his maraca indignantly, saliva gushing from one of the holes in his lip where a jade plug had fallen out. He spoke without raising his voice, compelling the women to bend forward toward his swaying hammock.

Ianopamoko, flustered, murmured to Isabel, "He does

not like me, because I am a woman of his own race. He does not say this, but I sense it. I think he says you are a man in spiritual form and so he is willing to talk with you, but only directly."

"Oh, but I cannot! Don't leave me with him!"

"Mistress, I must. I displease him. Magic cannot take place, if I am with you." Ianopamoko had already stood, on her lovely smooth legs, while the shaman gestured and orated on, his spittle flying, his marvellously made headdress of feathers shaking. "He is calling," Ianopamoko explained, "for *cauim* and *petum* and *yagé*."

Petum, Isabel discovered, was a strangely flavored tobacco, and *cauim* a kind of beer that tasted of cashews. The shaman was impressed by how manfully she, as if restored to her student days in Brasília, put away the beer, and inhaled the tobacco, from a long pipe he kept passing her. He took care, it seemed, to blow the smoke directly at her, and when it occurred to her that this was a courtesy she blew her smoke back at him. A glaze began to overlay her vision, a set of highlights shimmering here and there in the dried-mud womb of the hut, and it occurred to her that the pipe held more than tobacco. Perhaps the added ingredient was *yagé*. The old shaman, with his naked boyish body, his penis decorously dressed in a woven sheath, a straw thimble through which his foreskin had been pulled like a rumpled little ochre cactus-flower, said nothing, just contemplated her more and more contentedly. All this time she had been hunkering across the fire from him;

her ligaments, stretched by these years among savages and *bandeirantes*, were comfortable thus stretched. In this position her sarong could not cover her underparts, but then why should underparts be hid? Do they not give us our most glorious moments, and guide us through life to our fates? Perhaps this was a drunken reflection.

When the shaman at last did speak, she miraculously understood; certain of his mumbled words stood out like highlights, glimmering with meaning, and the sense of the sentence slitheringly moved through under the dark spaces between. Something in the smoke had eaten away at the boundary between their minds.

He told her she had the heart of a man.

"Oh, no!" she protested, and for lack of words cupped her hands beneath her naked breasts and lifted them slightly.

He flapped his hand through the fog of smoke and with the other hand gave a desultory shake of his maraca. He said she did not want to heal her child. How could this be?

She did not have the words to say the child repelled her, made her ashamed. Instead she imitated Salomão's pathetic slack expression, the eyes in which no spark lived. She said the word for "man"—full of sharp edges, ending in *zep*—and patted her chest with a flat hand and pronounced, "Tristão."

"Tristão fucks you," he said, in effect.

"Yes," she said, "but not for three years," and with her fingers prettily mimed a fetter about her bare ankle.

"He has been made a slave by evil men," she said, dizzily proud of the length of this utterance. "He is black." Fearing that this was not clear, she drew his tall outline in the air, and held up a piece of charcoal from the edge of the fire. In addition she pointed up through the hut's little smoke-hole, where a star or two glimmered in a circle of black. For it had become night. "His people come from across the great ocean, from another great island, greater than even Brazil, where the sun has made people black."

"Maira, what is it you want my magic to do?"

As she explained, the shaman's browless eyes widened and his toothless jaw opened, at first in incomprehension and then in comprehension.

He said, as far as she could understand, "Magic is a way of adjusting Nature. Nothing can be created, only Monan can create, and he long ago grew tired of creating, because he saw what a mess men had made of his world. Magic can merely transpose and substitute, as with the counters of a game. When something here is placed *there*, something there must be placed *here*. For every gain, there is a sacrifice, somewhere else. Do you understand?"

"I understand."

"Are you willing to sacrifice for this Tristão?"

"I already have. I have lost my world. I have lost my father."

"Are you willing to change yourself?"

"Yes, if he will still love me."

"He will still fuck you, but not in the same way.

When we disturb Nature with magic, nothing stays the same. Things shift." His eyes had narrowed again, and looked blazingly red, with the smoke and the *cauim*.

"I am willing. I am eager."

"Then we will begin tomorrow, Maira. What we do we must do in the daylight, over six days." His mouth seemed to be moving behind his meanings, which arrived in her mind while his mouth was still closed. "How will you pay me?" he asked.

"When I left my home, I gave up much property. All I have left is a little cross covered with jewels. A cross is the symbol of our God. It means both agonizing death and endless life. In this sign my people are conquering the world." With the charcoal she drew a cross in her white palm and held it for him to see. The shaman closed his tired sore eyes, as if shutting out bad luck. "It is worth many cruzeiros," Isabel told him.

"What is a cruzeiro?"

She could not explain. "Paper that we use for trading instead of shells and resin."

"I will take *that*." He pointed at her ring, the ring that said DAR.

"No, please—Tristão gave it to me, to pledge himself to me!"

"Then it is good. It holds both of your spirits." He reached out his hand, the hammock swaying in recoil, and made the clenching and unclenching gesture of a fist that needed no mediating drug to interpret as "give me."

Heartsick, she slipped off the inscribed ring and set it

in the shaman's cupped hand. His palm felt feverish, like that of her children when the germs of colds or measles or whooping cough had entered them, and the cells of their bodies were doing battle. As if a tooth had been knocked from her face, she knew she would never get back what she had just surrendered. Life robs us of ourselves, piece by small piece. What is eventually left is someone else.

"For the treatment to take hold, you must know my name. My name is Tejucupapo."

"Tejucupapo."

"The treatment will change you."

"I am in your hands, Tejucupapo."

"You have a man's big spirit. A warrior's fury to live. Not like that dirt with you. She will soon die."

"Oh, no—not dear Ianopamoko! She has been so beautifully kind to me!"

Tejucupapo said gruffly, his plugs jostling against his lower gums, "It gives her sensual pleasure, to be kind. To surrender herself to you. She is pleasing herself that way. She senses the man in you, and—" In effect, he told her, "You fuck her." And he spat, massively, so the sluggish fire whimpered and sang out a thin high note.

Yet Ianopamoko was enlisted in the magical treatments, which involved painting Isabel over her entire body with the black dye called *genipapo*. It could not be broadly scrubbed on but had to be painstakingly applied in those lacy designs, of dotted lines and S-curves, that only Indian women know how to inscribe, with the proper secret symmetry and in the propitious order. As Ianopamoko worked, covering Isabel's radiant white skin, young girls from the mesa community assisted her, using little brushes made from capybara bristles pinched in sticks of split bamboo. Tejucupapo blew warm *petum* smoke over the designs, sinking them deeper, giving them the indelible impress of Monan's creation. Isabel suppressed laughter, feeling the brushes caress her so meticulously, and feeling the warm clouds of Tejucupapo's smoky breath blow into even her most intimate crevices.

Thus tickled, she marvelled at seeing Ianopamoko's cheeks gleaming with tears, like the face of the mesa itself. Ianopamoko had loved her as she was. In the nights, Isabel tried to convey to her companion that she had not changed within, and made love more insistently than before, with a masculine roughness, for the dainty Indian woman was less easily led to a shudder than before. Isabel's uncanny whiteness had been part of her charm for Ianopamoko, she realized, and felt insulted. Only Tristão loved the self within her outward selves.

As she was fixed in the daze of being painted, smoking the blend of *petum* and *yagé* so she could understand the shaman's words, he told her, between long warm exhalations of smoke, of legendary times, times when the earth was almost empty, so freshly had Monan created it. Men moved like little packs of dung-mites across the beaten floor of a longhouse thatched with stars, which burned more brightly then. Generation succeeded generation, always moving toward fresh game, toward spaces where the earth was not yet tired. The game was mighty: herds of horses with beards beneath their chins and trees of bone on their heads, and of long-haired creatures who picked up prey with their noses and whose twisted teeth crossed in front of their mouths. Fleeing always toward the horizon, the game led men across narrow land with ocean on both sides— ocean, which Monan had not made, but which was left from the rain he had used to put out the great fire of his anger with men before Irin-Magé, the father of the first Maira. These men were not exactly men but we call them men. The fire was called Tatá. The waters were called Aman Atoupave. Monan had put men on earth to praise him and to be grateful for their existence, but all they wanted to do was drink *cauim* and fuck. The new land was vast, but men used it up, killing game and each other and forgetting Monan. They came to another narrow place between endless blue pieces of Aman Atoupave. Men crossed over, and no one came forward to fight them. There were many tall trees in this new place. There were sloths that slumbered upside down for a man's whole lifetime, and great armadillos with stones in their tails, and little fish in the rivers that could eat a cow before she could lift her voice in pain. Men filtered in among the trees. They hunted and fished. They hoed manioc, and brought medicine out of the trees, and wove clothes out of feathers. Here they had peace. Here they had space. Here men were happy. Monan had invented woman in an earlier place. Now in this place he bestowed his final blessing upon men: he invented the hammock. Only Tupan, thundering unseen in the sky, and Jurupari, scuttling unseen in the forest with his evil smell, reminded men of time, and of the fact that all things change.

Each forenoon, the process was repeated, always with different designs, to cover the dwindling intervals of pale skin. After each gruelling overlay, Isabel was covered more solidly with the color of *genipapo*; on the seventh day she was a blackish brown, darker than coffee beans but lighter than strong coffee, everywhere but on her palms, the soles of her feet, the skin beneath her nails, and the insides of her eyelids. Even the lips of her vagina, she was amazed to discover, had taken the purple tinge of *genipapo*. Her monkey face, with its thrust-out lips and depressed nose-bridge, now owned its sly joy more fully, more openly. Her platinum hair had been rubbed, strand by strand, with black gum so often it had thickened and tightly curled. Her body in its new ebony pelt showed the knotted muscularity her labors as Antônio's third wife had earned her—a length of curved thigh and a bulging tautness of buttock and calf and breast that pressed back against space, that wanted to stride and move, to roll. Naked, she looked less naked than before. She wore a glisten, a thin flexible layer as of metal darkened by the electroplating process. The hair that had once trailed limply down her back was now cut to make a cushion around her skull, upstanding like Tejucupapo's headdress of *papagaio* feathers. She looked now more like the warrior Tejucupapo had told her her sex concealed.

Her eyes were still gray-blue. The shaman told her, "Eyes are the window of the spirit. When your soul becomes black, then will your eyes also."

In parting, he warned her, "Now you must seek a protector. You are no longer Maira. Your skin is no longer magic."

"*Your* magic, Tejucupapo—are we sure it has worked . . . everywhere?"

She hesitated to speak, in Ianopamoko's presence, of the miracle she had asked for. The other woman, she knew, did not approve.

Tejucupapo read her mind. Wearily slung in a hammock, his breath fetid with stale *cauim* and tobacco, he shook his maraca. "I have told you—when something there is placed *here*, something here must be placed *there*." He seemed a sad old savage, idle and defeated.

"Before I leave you forever, Tejucupapo, hear my last question. Your people suffer. They are robbed and raped; whole tribes die. Eventually the white man's guns and diseases will reach even this mesa, bringing Christianity and slavery. Why does your magic, and that of all the other shamans, do nothing against this tide?"

The magician spoke to Ianopamoko, so rapidly that Isabel could not follow, and both Indians laughed, in their childish way, averting their faces to hide the membranes of their mouths.

Ianopamoko in her gentle voice interpreted: "He says the past cannot be changed, and the past and the future are like the roots and the branches of one solid tree. He

226

says magic is good only for the fruit, in the moment that it is falling."

Watching with his inflamed eyes the women's faces, Tejucupapo held aloft the maraca in his left hand, and let it drop, with a harsh clash of dry seeds within, into his right. So quickly, his gesture said, does life pass, in its momentary potential of being swerved by magic.

xxiv. *The Encampment Again*

DURING their seventeen days returning, through the *selva* that lavished its fruits and nuts upon them, and whose faint paths the two women traced in a green gloom amid the cries of monkeys and parrots, of barking toucans with their preposterously big beaks and hissing hoatzins with their curious clawed wings, the Indian maid was tremulously affectionate, clasping black, lithe Isabel to her with a new fury, a fury born of foreboding.

Ianopamoko seemed to have grown smaller, frailer, more wistfully feminine, with her graceful thin limbs and waistless brown torso. Isabel at times grew weary of playing the man with her, though there was an exhilaration in being distinctly the stronger, and in striding ahead, tireless in her new skin, swinging a long light spear the mesa tribesmen had given her in farewell, while Ianopamoko followed behind, carrying their few belongings and rations in a basket down her back.

When they came after the sixteenth day to their river, the *bandeirantes'* encampment on the far side seemed ominously quiet. Where there had been shelters, now only a few ruins could be seen through the foliage, their upright support posts charred. It was late afternoon, and soon dark. A single torch wobbled back and forth in the gloom, and a shout or two drifted across the silently sliding river. The little dugout canoe they had stolen to make their escape was still where they had hidden it, in a thicket of low-growing palms, and Ianopamoko, resuming leadership, insisted they drift in it downstream, beyond where the cultivated fields gave out, and only there cross over. Then, in the morning, she would creep through the fields and reconnoiter. Isabel must stay behind. "My people will protect me. They know me," she said, "and they no longer would know you."

"But Antônio will be furious with you, for running away. I had planned to protect you, to defend you from him." Her plan had been to explain their excursion to the shaman as an attempt to relieve the idiocy of their son, and to pretend to detect, in the days thereafter, signs of intelligence and energy.

Ianopamoko touched Isabel's upper arm, and ran her fingers down it, to remind her of her skin. "Dearest mistress, I fear now a defense from you would carry no weight. You forget how your exterior has been changed. Their first thought on seeing you will be to make you a slave, if not to slay you as a demon. What the eaters of armadillo entrails do not understand, they need to kill. It is the narrowness of their Christian universe that gives them their terrible heat and power. Tonight we will sleep together, and then, in early morning, I will

229

see what has happened to the encampment." The tenderness of the sepia maiden—her own interwoven patterns of painted lace faded during the long journey—drifted across Isabel's body all night, like a soft rain tapping among leaves.

When the dawn awoke her, she was covered with dew, and Ianopamoko was gone. When the sun stood at its mid-morning height, Ianopamoko had still not returned. Isabel crept forward cautiously, carrying her spear, along the edges of the fields of manioc and black beans, coming round to where the long hut had stood, and where now there were only ashes and char, scattered palm fronds and calabashes, and the hovering sweet stench of death. Several bodies of Indians, hacked by swords and torn by animals, had been lying on the ground long enough to seem scarcely human, dried-up like *xarque*; on the packed, swept earth between the long pavilion and Antônio's house, Isabel found the fresh corpse of Ianopamoko, her slender arms sliced from her torso. The lake of red in which the dismembered body lay was still partly liquid, an open-hearted hibiscus red empurpled by its reflection of the sky. Who would have thought Ianopamoko's little body had had so much blood in it? A swirling, churning cloud of sand-flies and eye-lickers, their massed triumphant buzzing loud as a chant, was feeding on the coagulating lake; the insects kept lifting and settling on Ianopamoko's dainty flat features, including the open eyes, in patterns like quickly shifting lace.

"Of all God's wonders, a nigger wench!" an archaic

baritone thundered behind her in Portuguese. Isabel turned to see José Peixoto, his hatless face frenzied and sunburned, approaching her with an uplifted broadsword. His padded escaupil seemed to be falling apart, spitting fragments of twilled cotton; he had lost enough weight, and been aged enough by recent experiences, to resemble his older brother. She lifted her spear but he flicked at it with the sword, cutting it in two, so close to her face she felt the stir of air.

"How came thee here?" he asked her. "Are thou yet another who conspires in my foul brother's treachery? Black as the milk of Hottentots, yet thine eyes an uncanny blue. Thou devil, there is something ladylike and familiar in thy gaze. Pity! *Merda!* The cursed Indians, we hack them and hack them, and still they come on—they've unleashed among us their friends the fiends of Hell, though we sought only their own eternal welfare, the God-damned *bugres!*" He was drunk, she realized, on fatigue and despair if not *cachaça*. The blood of his Carijó mother had not been enough to defend him against the terrors of the wilderness, faced alone. He mused aloud like a man for whom a spell has lifted, revealing a darker spell. He focused upon Isabel blearily, and decided, "*Negrinha*, ye might bring a milreis in Bahia, but everything living has become mine enemy. Before I clear my mind of thy riddle, though, thou'l't serve as well as any to ease an aching groin." Holding the ponderous sword still high in his right hand, with his left he fumbled at the buckle belting in his leather breeches.

Isabel tried to speak, but terror stopped her windpipe. A deathly stench blew from José's mouth as he drew closer and assured her, "By the sweet Mother of Christ, make a move and I'll cut off yer arms to calm ye, like I did that other witch. Thou'l't go to Hell with a brimming cunt at least, and bear a stout Christian to fart in Satan's face!"

Her heart pounding enough to break its frail cage, Isabel hung undecided between submitting and then seeking escape in the likely moment of relaxation afterwards, or trying to dart out from under the shadow of José's broadsword now. Heavy as a machete, it would take a moment to descend. The brute's buckle was undone and he had exposed a nub of dirty gray flesh, as pudgy and short as poor little Salomão's, and far from erect. A flicker of embarrassment crossed his murderous face. "Down on it, filth!" he said.

The smell of extremely stale cheese arose from his genitals. She willed herself to kneel; before her trembling knees could take up the command, a tall bearded white man appeared behind José and with a swift whistle of air and a crisp crunch of sliced bone buried a long-handled tool in the *bandeirante*'s skull. José fell at her feet, flipping in a last convulsion like a fish hooked onto the sand. The weapon that had slain him she recognized as the rusty adze used to hollow canoes, but her pale savior, with his slender frame, tall forehead, and melancholy brown eyes, was a stranger to her. Or was he? His beard was fleecy but the lips within it had a determined rueful set she knew well.

"Tristão," she softly cried. In the effort not to faint, Isabel now did drop to her knees.

The white man said, "You foul black whore—you were about to blow the bastard," and slapped her, hard, so that she fell to the sand beside the *bandeirante*'s body. Inches from her eyes, José's scarlet brains, lumpy like rice pudding soaked in beet juice, were leaking from the terrible rent in his skull. His pupils were rolled upward in the manner of the crucifix that had hung above Antônio's bed. Already, flies had begun to swarm. As soon as they settled, their little rotating heads busily bobbed, drinking the fresh corpse's undefended liquids.

Wracked by extremes of emotion—disgust, terror, amazement, relief—Isabel began to weep. She felt the other's gaze upon her, as last night she had felt Ianopamoko's caresses, like rain.

"How did you know my name?" Her lover's voice had become slightly higher, less granular and curvaceous, with the careless flatness of a white voice, which expects to be listened to. He tried to apologize for the slap. "Submitting to his vileness would have bought you a further five minutes of life at best. Better to die unpolluted. When are you people going to learn some pride? The Indian maid spat in his face, rather than submit."

She left off weeping and stared up at this man accusingly. "Tristão, how can you not know me? I let myself be made black so you could be white. A shaman did it,

233

far to the west, where one can see mountains whose tips are all ice."

He squatted down to her, his yam bulging the threadbare shorts between his legs, his old beach shorts, and touched her hair, her glossy shoulder, the dip of her waist, her long smooth flank, her muscled thighs. "Isabel? Is it you?" He explored with trembling fingertips her everted full lips, the strange double edges of them, and the vertical ridge in the center of the plump upper lip, with its yielding fat-buttons and violet tinge. "It is you. Your eyes."

She felt in the darkness within her skull—that theatre of spirit, a mere bloody rice pudding—the warm tears wanting to begin again. "Are my eyes all you have left to love? My old cold eyes. Then so be it, Tristão. Do not love me, merely use me. I will be your slave. Already, you have begun to beat me. Already, you are too proud, too fastidious, to give my mouth a kiss. When I was your color, and you were mine, I took you, a mere street boy, a miserable *moleque*, to my uncle's apartment, where there were more expensive things than you had ever seen, your eyes were like saucers, and gave you my virgin's blood, though it hurt me, hurt me horribly, I never *told* you how much it hurt that day. You were too big, and rough."

"I did not mean to be rough. It was the clumsiness of innocence."

This was so honest she was compelled to answer in kind: "Perhaps you were only as rough as you had to be."

"We gave each other our selves," he said. "We gave what we had to give. Where is the ring that says DAR?"

"It was the price the shaman wanted, so you could be white, and no longer a slave."

Selflessly as she had acted, she yet felt afraid, telling him this. He restated, as if incredulous, "You gave away the ring with which we pledged ourselves."

"I did not give it away; I exchanged it for your life. Your blackness had enslaved you here, and before then had roused my guardians' enmity."

He became thoughtful, touching his blond beard. "Indeed so, my dearest. You did beautifully." He extended his hand, helping her up from the sandy earth where José's head like a split gourd leaked its juicy contents, attracting hundreds, no, thousands, of buzzing little eye-lickers, *pium* flies, the winged blood-suckers called *borrachudos*, and sand-flies as small as grains of powder, *pólvora*. They moved away from this thirsty, stinging cloud, and sat together on what had been the porch of Antônio's house. "Let me tell you my story. It was very strange," he began, but her pride had been stung.

"Go ahead. Hit me again, for giving away your ring. Cut off my arms, like hideous José did to dear Ianopamoko, the only friend I ever had. You were never a friend, you were only a man. A man can never be a woman's friend, not really. She taught me what love was. You, you taught me what it was to be a slave. Beat me, leave me. I am sick of you, Tristão. Our love has put us through too much."

He smiled, in that confident thin-lipped way of white

235

men, and even laughed at her, lightly. "Nonsense, Isabel. You love me. We are fated to love one another; we hardly exist outside our love, we are just animals without it, with a birth and a death and constant fear between. Our love has lifted us up, out of the dreadfulness of merely living." He took her hand, and she felt her pulse slow, deliciously, within the careful rhythms of his voice. "Day by day, for seven days, the black went out of me, I did not know why. First I became gray, then white, as if I had never seen the sun. Your ancient fool of a so-called husband, Antônio Peixoto, ascribed it to one of the diseases that are always carrying off the slaves they capture. But then, when my health did not otherwise alter, and the other white killers superstitiously removed my shackles, he vaulted over them in superstition, and said my becoming a Christian like them was a sign from God, to pull up camp and move on. José objected that the manioc and sweet potatoes were not yet harvested, and the canoes were not all fashioned, but Antônio called him a heretic and a rebel to good King João for doubting this miraculous sign from above. My transfiguration was a sign that they would find the golden kingdom, ruled by the golden man, *o dourado*. The others sided with their leader and clamored to move on, and since there were canoes enough for only a few of their Indian escort, they killed the women and children, and burned the huts. During the slaughter, I pretended to join in, chasing a Caduveo girl into the forest, but then hid there, and kept watch at a distance. José had offended his brother with his doubt—perhaps trouble had been long brewing between them—for Antônio directed the other men to bind up José and abandon him in a place where there were many anthills. He came back, as you saw, as a madman. I have been watching him, these last days, forage and rage, wondering, since I am now his color, if we might strike up a partnership to escape the Mato Grosso, until today forced my hand. Something told me to save you, though from a distance you were only a struggling shadow."

"And my son, Salomão?" Isabel asked, unable to overcome a certain shyness with this white, and newly voluble, Tristão, though at the same time her own new self gave her, in an inner place she had not begun to explore, a fresh edge. Her former advantage in the outer realm had been replaced by an intimate wordless strength or sureness she could taste like a spice that makes a bland meal palatable.

The topic of Salomão clearly bored and discomfited this man, excited as he was by his recent deed of arms. There had always been distances behind Tristão's face but now they were the distances of the future, a future that related to this ruined, blood-soaked encampment as a mansion relates to a hut. "Antônio took him with him," he said. "In his fanaticism he believes the poor babe to be a kind of saint, who will lead him to Paradise for all of his sins. Salomão did not thrive under the care of Takwame and her daughters; nor did he die. But I fear for the fate of the entire expedition, Isabel. They will not get far on the river; the Indians had shown me how, in hollowing the canoes, to carve the bottom thin enough to spring leaks soon. They will never reach the Madeira."

"Not in those canoes, at least," she said, granting her vanished son, a mistake of flesh barely clinging to life, the fabulous toughness of the *bandeirantes*, who again and again, she knew from her schooling with the nuns, had returned from impossible journeys. For her tiny whey-faced son she tried to summon a maternal mourning, a milky flow of feeling, but only produced a stringent wry relief that he was off her hands, through no fault of her own. She was free to concentrate on the loved one before her. In the clutter of civilized life she had attracted and held him; now she enjoyed this majestic solitude in which to win him to her again, by new magic, or a new coloration of the old.

He took charge, as never before. It was as if his brain, now that he had white skin, had become a box squared off with linear possibilities—a grid of choices, alternatives, projections. Before, when they had decided to buy their stake at Serra do Buraco, or when she led him to the hotel in São Paulo and then made the decision to go with her kidnappers without futile resistance, Isabel had been Tristão's guide in the world beyond the *favela;* now he boldly planned to guide her through the wilderness back to that world. He decided they were not to leave the encampment immediately, but to bury the corpses, reroof the upright log walls of Antônio's old shelter, and wait for the manioc and beans and sweet potatoes to mature. Then, laden with *farinha* Isabel had pounded and the sun had dehydrated, and with dried meat prepared from the fruits of his hunting with an old blunderbuss the *bandeirantes* had left behind, they would set out across the *chapadões* where they once, alone together, had nearly starved.

Indians from the surrounding *selva*, observing the couple make thus a temporary home, and seeing the encampment subdued to a less menacing domesticity, filtered in from the edges, resumed fishing, lent assistance where asked, and pilfered remnants of the *bandeirantes'* treasures; but Isabel and Tristão did not seek, in the fragments of language they had mastered, to enlist any of these indigenes in their return journey. They were anxious to test themselves again against modern times, and these dwarfish, nude, and self-mutilated inhabitants of the remote past, with their runny noses and smoke-reddened eyes and the bulbous bellies and incessant flatulence induced by intestinal parasites, seemed childish schoolmates that must be left behind, to suffer and to dwindle.

xxv. *Alone Together Again*

WHEN THE BURNED ROOF was replaced with interwoven palms, Tristão and Isabel had privacy enough to re-explore their marriage. Three years had passed since the flare-up of their sexuality, in the interval between the Guaicuru raid and the rescue by the *bandeirantes*, a flare-up fanned by the fevers of starvation and the romantic imminence of death. Since then, Isabel and Tristão had done nothing to earn their name as lovers. Now, slowly—her bodily rhythms seemed slowed, and his more nervous and preoccupied—they reclaimed for cultivation the muddy riverside tract of sex. Their new skins gave them a fresh opportunity for that most parlous act of love, negotiation. Who were they, these psychic shapes each to be defined by the invasion of the other? With different skins came different glands, different smells, different hair, different self-images, different histories. There was something sardonic in her sexuality now, something jaded by the experience of black female generations.

From her dead white mother Isabel had inherited

mostly an empty flirtatiousness, and perhaps a fear of childbirth. Now a different inheritance had descended, and a strength not merely passive; black, she found in herself a store of reckless anger, and became, when darkness enclosed the rustling straw pallet she and Tristão shared, something of a bully, a rough tease. His whiteness glimmered in the shadows of the hut, whose roof admitted only a few splinters of moonlight; she played at dodging him, invisible as she was now. In the dark she presented him with unexpected portions of her body, and bit his shoulder and clawed at his back, a departure from the timid reverence with which she had handled his body before. She had known there would be a new sadism between them, but had not expected it to come from herself. He—and this fed her anger—felt often preoccupied, as he lay beside or strove above her; she was no longer the color of something he was travelling toward, but of something he had left behind. His yam was satisfying but no longer, quite, alarming; perhaps it was a new juiciness in herself that diminished, not exactly its size, but its elemental essence, its lovable brute being. His prick had shed since she first saw it in Uncle Donaciano's apartment its primordial monstrosity, its amphibious reptilian look of a reality far older than human minds. Being a white woman fucked by a black man is more delicious, she had sadly to conclude, than a black woman being fucked by a white man. The former, to a descendant of the masters of colonial Brazil, had the exaltation of blasphemy, the excitement of a political defiance; the latter transaction savored of mundane business. No wonder Brazil's slave women had swung their hips in their bell-shaped skirts, and twirled their fringed parasols, and borne their generations of mulattos like a guild of seasoned experts. Fucking was no big deal, or, rather, it was part of a bigger deal: perhaps this was a common female realization, but slave women could come to it easier than the frail, cossetted, priest-dominated little mistress captive in the big house, who never saw her husband naked and modestly accepted his organ—the fecundating instrument, often, of her death—through a hole in the nuptial counterpane.

Yet, if faintly hardened in her sexuality, Isabel found a new excitement, lying beneath Tristão's preoccupied thrusts, in trying to connect herself with a nervous network more angular than before, less rounded by perennial hopelessness. To lift herself up into this system, to be not left behind—these were Isabel's own neural ambitions, exciting her to a passion that left her fingermarks still red on his white back the next morning. She was fighting for her life, where formerly she had been fighting merely for pleasure, and for freedom from her father.

The sexual world, being the underside of the real world, is to an extent an inversion of it. An underdog, he had been "top" before; now it was she who dominated and demanded. To use the terminology in which she and Eudóxia in their girlhoods had gossiped about the nuns, she was the cock and he the hen. "You are my slave," she said.

"Yes, mistress."

"Lick me there or I will beat you." She brandished a piece of the frail spear José had cut in two with his broadsword. When Tristão had obeyed for many minutes, and she had come to her climax, she said, "I think I will beat you anyway."

He loved her more than ever—he was dizzy with his new love of her, which was confused with love of his white self. Their new relation gave at last full scope to his instinctive chivalry. He, too, had felt the something brutish in his former appeal to her. He had not been insensitive to the burden her loss of social position placed on his shoulders—the flattering wreath of martyrdom it enabled her to wear—or to the indignities of her whoredom at the mine and her concubinage at the camp. Had he not been black, would she have been so casually and serenely unfaithful? True, she could justly blame his poverty and helplessness as leaving her no choice; but had she not taken a certain relish in her degradation, because the blame was his? She had used him to become shameless, denying him the luxury of shame. She had led him through the expensive streets of Ipanema and through a subsequent maze he could never have entered without her. She had condescended to him, and it was her love therefore which had shone the brighter, with the greater heat of self-sacrifice.

Now it was he who descended, to accept a nigger wench as his mate; it was he who now tasted the thrill of sexual release when the loved one is not a social and spiritual equal but a thing of flesh, imported from afar. A thing with a psychology; it is the psychology that leads our love on—twisting it, deepening it—but the thingness, like a more massive and versatile masturbator's hand, that delivers the bliss. Her whole body seemed leaner and knobbier, its bulges and recesses more emphatic, now that she was no longer the color of clouds and crystal but that of earth, of wet smooth wood, of glistening dung. Now he could without difficulty think of Isabel as a digestive system on legs, that needed to shit and liked to run, taking a mild joy in motion and defecation much as he did. Her anus, which had slightly disgusted him before, set in its pocket of brown-tinted skin like a smear between her buttocks, a permanent stain in a silken crevice, was manifested now as a tender whorled flesh-bud hardly distinguished in its purplish tinge from the surrounding eggplant sheen. Her pubic bush, no longer lank and colorless like a wispier version of her head, was curly and oily and resiliently thick; he had only to bury his nose in it, while she kneeled straddling his face, grinning down at him between her jutting breasts, for his erection to rise like a corrugated tusk of ivory, down where her hand, reaching behind her, would playfully find it and tweak it painfully. Isabel had formerly handled him with a certain reverence; now she led him on an impudent chase, forcing him on occasion to wrestle her into submission and to experience, while she energetically writhed, cursed, and spat at his face, the criminal bliss of rape, each spurt hurting like the passage of a bullet through his urethra. There was hostility in her but he did not mind it as long as he could pin her down and fuck her with a liberated hostility of his own. Sex is a tussle our sane selves resent.

At the end of one such violent session, she amazed him by nestling her bottom against his stomach and preparing to sleep and saying, "Maybe that is the one that will make a baby." Thus she admitted, what her daylight self had never confessed, that they had not yet made a baby together.

"I hope not," he confessed in turn. "Not yet. We must escape the wilderness first."

"Once we are back in civilization, you will drop me. You will use me as your whore for a time but find another wife, a white wife."

"Never. You are my only wife."

"I think it's shitty of you, frankly," Isabel went on, "to discard me when I gave you my precious color, but that's how men are. They use you and knock you up and don't give a damn."

"Isabel, stop this talk of pregnancy. It is premature. We are not psychologically ready to be parents, we are still too much in love. I will never leave you. I love you as you are. You have all your old elegance, and something else as well. Forgive me, but I think you have become your true self. You were black all along, your whiteness was a disguise. The amusing tilt of your face and the way you arched your feet were black."

She pondered this awhile, until it seemed she was truly asleep, with throngs of his violent sperm climbing and kicking toward her looming lone egg; then he heard her say, in a deep voice on the edge of dreams, "I forgive you, Tristão, for being such a bastard."

He was keener to return to the cities than she was. His chivalry was empty without a social context. They carried the context in their heads, in their social conditioning, but he wanted the confirmation of others witnessing, of seeing his whiteness so gallantly set off, as in a tuxedo. Not that a white man and black wife would be as conspicuous and poignant in Brazil as they would be in South Africa or North America—but, still, in his envisioning mind, they would attract glances that would gauge the dizzying height of his love. Did not Portugal, here in this continental backland of brazilwood and sugar cane, make a wife of Africa but not consecrate the fact? He would be one white man who would elevate his black mistress to his own level. He would, in a sense, lift his own mother up from the *favela* and its *cachaça*-soaked poverty, out of the arms of all those fleeting stepfathers, men the muddy in-between colors of the merciless *bandeirantes*.

And Isabel, who had engineered this transposition, savored the revenge on her father, who in her immature, superstitious mind had spurned her offering of naming a child Salomão by letting the child be an idiot. Her father, elusive yet omnipresent, was God to her. She imagined herself rubbing her new color in his face as a defiance of the Big Boys, an identification with the masses more dramatic and indelible than any she and her fellow radicals had chattered about at the university. Yet, paradoxically (for the heart thrives on contrarieties, fattening itself on the energy of both love and hate), she imagined that her father would love her in her sensual new skin, and she would at last steal him from her pallid mother dead in Heaven.

Fed thus by their new conceptions of themselves, whose ramifying permutations whipped their nervous systems into a continual stir, they made so much love that the Indians, stealing cassava roots from the untended fields, would point to the house and say, "The rocks are clashing," referring to a myth whereby one of the twin sons of Maira-Monan, Arikut, the bad and reckless brother, is crushed between clashing rocks but brought to life again by his twin, Tamendonar, the good and peaceful brother.

Because her lips and breasts and the insides of her thighs were being abraded by his beard, Tristão shaved it off, with the single-edged razor blade, Gem, who, now rusted and dulled, had accompanied him these more than nine years since he had first seen Isabel. Two in the *fusca* factory, four in the mine, three as a slave here along this river without a name. Beardless again, he looked younger; his cheeks had thinned beneath the fleece.

Now that he was white, Isabel felt herself often moved by a fragility that had not existed in the black man, or that she had not been able to see, through his skin. He could be clumsy now, and hesitant, as well as brave, and loyal. This vulnerability excited her, as poor limp dull-eyed Salomão in her arms never had. There was something prim and self-repressed, now, in Tristão that it amused her to startle, flaunting before him an increased sexual aggression. Her clitoris felt longer and firmer than before, a tense shaft of cartilage tipped by a supersensitive hard pea she drove into his face or pubic bone as a man thrusts, without consideration of the other, so that his upper lip fell tinglingly asleep under the pressure, and appeared bruised and swollen afterwards. She would make herself pay for this coarse dominance by inciting him to buggery and spankings, since pain from his direction brought again into relief that inner shape of love she was always in danger of losing in the vagueness and muck of the psyche. This shape tasted like vanilla when she was a tiny girl and the cook in the kitchen would give her a lick of the stirring spoon. It smelled like coconut shreds in an infant's nostrils. This keenness of sweet sensation was always threatening to dull. Only new identities and contortions kept it honed. Perversity, like chastity, is a way of showing human dominance over this bestial drive. Reluctantly but then with some fervor, Tristão joined her in sexual theatrics, tying her wrists with lianas, placing José's broadsword between them on the pallet as they slept, bringing his old iron foot-fetter into play as he had his way with his helpless slave. He bit her shoulders and as if with fanged open jaws sucked the soft trough at the base of her throat. The delicate membranes of his glans, scarcely changed in tint from the days when he was a black man, still blood-stuffed and hot like a heart torn from a rabbit, demanded the membranes of her mouth. The contrast of the lovers' colors was less acute than that of their genitals, two exotic flowers so contrarily evolved. Up, down, aggressive, passive, dominant, submissive, hostile, tender—Tristão and Isabel oscillated luxuriously among contrarieties, and gave each other the gifts of physical exhaustion and of a drowsy oneness with the universe.

xxvi. *The Mato Grosso Again*

A T LAST the time came to dig up the manioc roots, crush them into powder, bake them into salty cakes, and depart. Fearing the Guaicuru, they tried to stay north of their former route, steering now by the rising sun. In this season it rained, briefly but intensely, in early morning and again in late afternoon, as evening approached. The downpours blinded them but soon lifted, all the surfaces of leaf and land steaming with mist and glistening like their healthy, hopeful skins.

Perhaps it was their new route, but the vast barren upland seemed to be tamer than before, when Kupehaki had led them through it. In the second week of walking, Isabel gave up her wistful, unrealistic hope of encountering Guaicuru horsemen and, with them, Azor and Cordélia, in Indian beads and painted undress but alive. In the third week, she and Tristão began to come upon farms—single low whitewashed, red-roofed *ranchos* where a single couple, a gaunt *mameluco* in baggy peon's clothes and a shy barefoot Tupi wife kept house with their chickens and pigs and ragged children and managed a few acres of tobacco and corn, cotton and soybean, fenced off with dry thornbush from the wild pigs and rich men's cattle that roamed the *chapadões*. Poor as they were, and perched on the edge of ruin by the next drought, the farmers would spare Tristão and Isabel some rice and beans and *pinga* and lend them a night's shelter of a shed, where their luxurious bed would be heaps of unhusked ears of corn, yielding under every motion of their bodies and collapsing their lovemaking into giggles, there being no purchase for the necessary friction.

As they made their way east, the farms increased, in number and prosperity, and gave rise to dusty small towns, where the couple was able to recoup their resources by finding work. It was assumed that Isabel, being a Negress, knew how to do laundry; she lugged the soiled sheets and pantaloons of the local mayor and cattle dealer and the muslin chemises of their overweight wives to the town's trickling river and beat them clean against the flat rocks with the help of a yellow lye soap that turned her fingernails punky and her fingertips as rough as sandstone. For Tristão, with his commanding stare and broad shoulders and impressive white brow, more elevated jobs appeared—he would be entrusted, some days after his idle but dignified presence had been first observed, by the local lawyer with hand-delivering a message to a client a mile away, or be enlisted by the local hardware merchant to handle the barrels and sacks and iron tools in his emporium's back room and then, on evidence of Tristão's literacy and the air of honesty and uprightness he radiated, be allowed a position among the front shelves and bins, the scales and the till. A seamstress, taking pity on Isabel's cracked and splitting hands, invited her to do stitching, where the stitches would not show, and soon where they did show, for the nuns' lessons in domestic skills had been methodical and thorough, and the seamstress wondered how this indigent black girl, this mere *moleca*, had acquired such facility and impish mannerliness. This all happened in a small town on the slopes of the Serra do Tombador, with zigzag streets whose sidewalks rose in steps, flanking a central gutter of cobblestones for carts to crawl up and sewage to run down.

Elsewhere, in towns further to the east, Tristão won employment with a blacksmith and, in yet another, as an auto mechanic, automobiles slowly replacing horse-drawn conveyances on the dusty roads of the backlands. Wherever they worked, the couple in their liveliness and grace attracted kindness, and were more than once offered opportunities to settle permanently, with pleasant enough provincial prospects, for growth was clearly the destiny of the *sertão*. For a while, reviving the muscles hardened in the gold mine, Tristão worked on a road crew laying the crushed stone of a new highway into this vast region of underdevelopment and promise. "Roads are the future of Brazil," their foreman would intone each day, like the priest of a fledgling religion meant to compensate them for their aching backs and modest wages, paid in a currency that, the more civilized the environs became, was all the faster eroded by inflation and high prices.

When they came to actual cities, they began to have city adventures. Isabel found a store selling jewelry and silver whose proprietor was able to appreciate the fine quality of Uncle Donaciano's begemmed antique cross. Other dealers had been bored by the antique holy object, but this one's eyes lit up. He was a *pardovasco*, the son of a Negro and a mulatto, dark like an Ethiopian, with slanted eyes and a receding hairline. He struck up a collusion with her, against the invisible owners of the establishment, who he claimed were Japanese agri-industrialists in far-off Rio Grande do Sul, and offered her a price—ten thousand cruzeiros—that was absurdly generous, he swore, for such a common item as a cross from the colonial era. "But I confess it—I am not merely a dispassionate student of religions, I am an ardent devotee of several. You have found out my weakness, little lady." He furthermore suggested that during the day's long lunch break, between one and four-thirty, she might join him in his room upstairs.

"How much am I worth to you?" she asked, with an easy bluntness she wouldn't have managed in her old skin.

"I will give you a delicious lunch," the jeweller promised, "and play you my records of the newest *afochê* songs from Bahia."

"I am hard up," she told him brazenly, meaning both she was short of money and sexually excited by him. Isabel did feel, after so long copulating with a white man,

and twisting herself in knots around his curious white
psychology, she owed herself a simple session with a
man nearly as black as herself. She said, "One hundred
cruzeiros. I think I must be worth as much as one hun-
dredth of that trinket. Its arms do not move; it hears
prayers but does not answer them. I will answer all your
prayers, if they are not too indecent."

He professed astonishment and indignation and eventually reduced her to eighty-five, which he would add to
the price of the purchased object, thus transferring the
cost of his tryst to the distant agri-industrialists.

His room upstairs was crowded and bright, like the
jungle Isabel had traversed with Ianopamoko; it was
clamorously full of parrot-colored religious statues, of
all the Catholic gods—Mary, the baby, crucified Jesus,
St. Sebastian with his arrows, St. Catherine with her
wheel, the Pope in white beanie who wore little glasses
and died of hiccups—plus the *orixás* and *exús* of
Candomblé, with the same little plaster heads and
painted plaster stares, and beige-skinned busts of Elvis
and Buddy Holly and Little Richard and other *ianque*
rock immortals. There were even a gilded Buddha and
a black-enamelled Kali, with her flaming red tongue
and her necklace of skulls. This *pardovasco* truly lived
for his religions, which offended Isabel. She distrusted
the masculinity of a man who was not ready to make
her his sole object of worship.

Rather than instantly fall to lovemaking, the jeweller
insisted that she listen with him to his *afochê* records,
explaining, "*Afochê* is the most African of Brazilian

musics, with close ties to Candomblé; it has been rejuvenated by Jamaican reggae and the Black Consciousness Movement throughout the Americas." He gave her
dope to smoke but it was not as cosmic in feeling as
Tejucupapo's *yagé*. Their sex, when they finally came
to it, seemed perfunctory and tame compared with what
she and Tristão had developed. This was not a man who
loved a woman to the point of self-annihilation. She
had been spoiled for any other kind. Nevertheless, she
went back to the jeweller—his name was Olympio
Cipóuna—several times, to his room full of the stubs of
votive candles, and deposited the money she wheedled
from him in a savings account, whose rate of interest
was adjusted to the rate of inflation.

The further east she and Tristão had travelled, from
wilderness fit only for Indians to unfenced cattle country
and on into farmland varied by pockets of government-
sponsored industry, the more apparent was their need for
money, for capital. They must have clothes, shoes, cruzeiros for rent and restaurants. This provincial city,
named Bunda da Fronteira, not many years before still
had board sidewalks and wooden false fronts and hitching posts, and every man carried a gun. Photographs of
old lynchings and dance halls were displayed in the windows of Main Street barbershops and on the walls of the
local historical society. Indian artifacts, especially featherwork by the Erikbatsas, were on sale everywhere, for
the German and Swedish tourists, who were hauled in by
bus; also there were parties of Canadian fishermen organized to plunder the teeming waters of the Araguaia and

Xingú rivers. Amenities were rapidly being installed, for the tourists and the local gentry. Ten-story office buildings were being constructed, with sealed windows and air-conditioning; streetlights had been installed at six intersections; faucet water was being rendered potable; and a shopping mall was taking shape on the edge of town.

Isabel, citing her experience with the seamstress in the hinterland, in the town with steep cobbled streets, found employment in a dress shop, at first in the back rooms, pinning and sewing, and then, because of her comeliness and saucy sophistication of manner, up front, in the sales force. Tristão found work as a bouncer and front-man in a discotheque that was just starting up, called Mato Grosso Elétrico. The crucial part of the job lay not in evicting the occasional cocaine overdoser who had become too frenetic or the pusher who had become too blatant, but in judging whom, in the jostling crowds that lined up each night on the sparkling cement sidewalk, to admit. It was like composing a bouquet, a fresh salad, whose variety spelled gaiety and otherworldly carnival. A few garishly costumed, bewigged transvestites were all right, but too many would frighten off the straights; a few paunchy middle-aged pleasure-seekers were desirable, to lend weight and historical perspective to the crowd of dancers, but the youthful note must be prevalent; a tarted-up girl in a spangled miniskirt and see-through blouse was fine, unless her escort had the squat, anxious, sexless look of a pimp. To make a little paradise within, anxiety and hope of profit must be left at the door. The profiteer, the open voyeur, the too-raw aspirant to social success must be excluded. Tristão scanned the crowd of eager faces in the blanching light of the Elétrico's flashing sign for the pure at heart. Some poor could be admitted, but not so many as to discomfort the comfortable, or give rise to social clashes and revolutionary gestures as the night's dancing and shedding of inhibition progressed. Revolution had been left behind in the Sixties. This was the Seventies. The bacchanal must keep a flavor of apolitical innocence. Blacks, regrettably, had often to be excluded, since they showed up in numbers much greater proportionally than their representation in the population of Bunda da Fronteira, which was relatively pale. The white and *branquelo* customers must feel part of a multiracial society but not swamped. A discotheque is not a *batuque*, a Congo jamboree. It strives with its psychedelic effects to create an ecstasy free of danger and depravity, with none of vice's sodden consequences—an aëration in which the tender shoots of mating may reach out and expand. The strobe lights, the colored lasers, the piping, uninsistently rhythmic music, the watery champagne all seek to caress the passions into courage, into a kind of plumage, rather than frighten them away. The nightly spectacle, of which Tristão with a growing skill selected the human elements, must not be a harsh spectacle, at the mercy of the most ruthlessly showy and professionally exhibitionistic. His height, his white brow, his commanding, overarching gestures indicating selections in the rear of the waiting throng, his noble reluctance to smile, either in approval or apology, made him commanding in this judgmental role, and a bit of a celebrity in after-dark Bunda da Fronteira. His employers, pock-marked mestizo gangsters personally unpresentable, valued his handsome fronting and offered to increase his salary and benefits when, after five months, he announced his determination to quit.

He and Isabel had by now accumulated enough money and clothes and city wisdom to depart, not by bus but by DC-7—a hop of less than an hour—for Brasília.

Their journey from the encampment had taken the better part of a year.

xxvii. *Brasília Again*

EIGHT YEARS had passed since Isabel had been a student here at the university and she and Tristão had lain together amid the wild banana trees and Spanish bayonet on one of the capital's vast median strips. Her father was no longer Ambassador to Afghanistan, where King Muhammad Zahir Shah had been deposed by a group of young military officers increasingly subject to Soviet influence. Islamic militance was on the rise and trouble was brewing in central Asia; Salomão was glad to leave. Now he served the Big Boys as Assistant Minister of Interior Development, with a suite of offices in the marble stretches of the Palácio do Planalto. He sounded, when he picked up the phone, older to Isabel, his old paternal force and majesty dwindled—or was it that she had been seasoned in hardship and love and had grown to adulthood? She was now twenty-nine, and had noticed a few white circlets as she tended her sizable Afro. In certain lights the backs of her hands looked ropey, and the skin beneath her chin a trifle loose. Her father did not argue or resist when she firmly told him, "Daddy, I am well, no thanks to you. I want to visit you, and for you at last to meet my *companheiro*, my dear husband."

His silence was not long, and may have been merely a diplomat's attempt to find appropriate phrasing. "My darling, nothing could please me more. I have missed you, and spent many a sleepless night churning with anxiety over your whereabouts and welfare. After the life of a miner's wife at the Serra do Buraco, of which rumors reached me halfway around the world, you disappeared from the face of the earth!"

"We never left Brazil," she said coldly.

"Your voice has changed. Was it always so . . . throaty?"

"People change, Father. Children grow up. This is my voice now. Would tomorrow at six fit into your busy schedule? Do not trouble yourself to give us dinner. Tea or cocktails will suffice—perhaps more than suffice."

If she was curt, it was partly because Tristão was lying on the hotel bed, listening. When she hung up, he said, "This is the man who kidnapped us, and sent an assassin to kill me; now I am supposed politely to meet him?"

"It's a different you now," she said. "And Daddy sounded different, too. Older. Sadder. I believe he *did* miss me, actually. He never had time, before, to be a father."

She put on as many dresses as before going to Chiquinho's house in Moóca ten years ago, at last settling for an ankle-length unbelted gown of splashy silk, in peacock colors, with voluminous split sleeves that displayed elegantly the black of her slender arms. Such a garb formerly would have made her look quite washed out.

Her father's apartment, in the white-sided, curved, glass-balconied skyscraper on the Eixo Rodoviário Norte, seemed less grand than it had when she had lived here as an impressionable college girl. The serving couple—the man tall and lugubrious and greenish, the woman chubby and brown—whom she had grown to know and depend upon for companionship during her father's frequent absences, had been replaced by a single manservant, a nimble slight freckled fellow with orange hair done up in Rastafarian dreadlocks, like a basket of tangled yarn on his head. He admitted Tristão and Isabel to the foyer with an impertinent bow. As they waited for her father to appear, Isabel realized that the apartment was in fact smaller—that it was not the same apartment. The Tibetan *thang-ka*, the Louis XV *coiffeuse* with its black Ch'ing vase, the Japanese prints and carved Dogon figures were still here, along with a lambskin rug and a massive peened copper pot that must come from Afghanistan, but more crowded together, without the lavish surrounding space that, before, had given their beauty the breathlessness of isolation. Now this gathering of objects had the hectic clamor of a party too large for its space. The long corridor down which she had dragged herself and her books to her room night after night was no longer there, and the living-room windows looked not toward Lake

Paranoá but, less scenically, toward the Rodoferroviária. Perhaps her father's career, in the days of President Kubitschek seemingly infinite in prospect, had reached, under the succession of generals, its limit, in ambassadorships increasingly peripheral and in administrative posts that not only concerned the hinterland but partook of the hinterland's neglect.

Salomão Leme entered the room. He had aged, though his tiny narrow feet still twinkled in his patent-leather at-home slippers. He had put on a maroon-lapelled smoking jacket to receive them, above pin-stripe trousers with a razor-sharp crease. The thin hair on top of his skull by now was a mere halo of fuzz on the broad, faintly corrugated pate, and his pendulous gaze had grown heavier, pulling down more pronouncedly than ever the delicate colorless skin, swarming with nerves, that surrounded his eyes.

Did she imagine it, or did a tiny muscle, below one of these gray eyes, twitch at the sight of her, after eight years? If so, his determined gaze brushed aside the irritant of surprise, his slippers continued to glide swiftly across the lambskin carpet, and the lips with which he grazed first one cheek and then the other were cool. "My beautiful child," he said, and softly gripped her shoulders the better to stare at her defiantly uptilted face.

"Father, this is my husband, or fiancé, or something, Tristão Raposo." Just seeing her father again had made her feel giddy and girlish, certain of indulgence.

"Enchanted," her father said, taking the younger

man's muscular pale white hand in his own, pudgier hand.

"As am I, sir," said Tristão, not answering with even the hint of a smile the older man's tentative beginnings of one, which exposed—touchingly, to Isabel—her father's small round teeth, even smaller than she remembered, and yellowed by age. These men taking each other's measure was giving Isabel butterflies in the stomach.

"From your accent, you are a Carioca," her father told Tristão.

"Born and bred, sir. My family lived on the slopes of the Morro do Babilônia. The house was not much, but we enjoyed a splendid view of the sea."

The diplomat said, "I no longer know Rio well, though my brother cannot be pried from the place, like a hermit crab in a discarded shell. My life in Rio ended, practically speaking, when the capital was moved to Brasília."

"A brave move, that did our nation proud," said Tristão, somewhat stiffly ignoring the older man's subtle indication that he could sit down, in one of the several cushioned chairs available.

"And yet, I wonder," said Salomão, seating himself in the wide-armed beige corduroy-covered one that was, Isabel knew, only his second favorite. Her father's favorite was the red plush wing chair, worn to a salmon color on its arms and seat, which Tristão now did perch upon, with too obvious a wariness. She placed herself between them, on the long white sofa, her knees coming up to the level of the low table whose inlay contained a chessboard. A slim vase, a clean ashtray, a crystal paperweight suggested that an endgame was in progress. "The move has left our beautiful Rio," her father sighed, "very much what the English call a 'grass widow,' and has heightened the people's sense of government as something distant and fantastic, that has little to do with them."

"In time," Tristão offered in consolation, "Brazil's development will engulf the new capital, and Brasília be in the thick of things. Men of the future will wonder, indeed, why it is situated so far to the east. In travelling through the Mato Grosso recently, Isabel and I were struck by how rapidly development is proceeding. All the idle luxuries of the modern age, including tourist buses, arriving on top of an innocent desolation."

"It is a dreadful headache," the senior gentleman agreed, slapping his patent-leather-shod feet down on the white wool carpet in emphasis, "and as it happens, *my* headache, for I have recently become, as perhaps Isabel has informed you, Assistant Minister of Interior Development, the 'Assistant' being a mere euphemism—the *soi-disant* Minister is an unreconstituted general whose sole authentic passion is spying on the Argentines and Paraguayans to make sure they have no rocket or supersonic jet fighter in their arsenals that we do not also have. He is quite paranoid about it, and imagines that Castro is getting all sorts of wonderful Russian goodies which our alignment with the Western imperialists is denying him! Please—what can I offer you to drink?"

The manservant had glided in, with almost a dance step, wagging his woolly orange locks. Isabel asked him for a glass of white wine, not Chilean or Australian but not necessarily French either, and her father, expansively gesturing with his short arms, for a gimlet, very dry, with two onions, and Tristão, puritanically, for a *vitamina*. Isabel fought off the fluttering fear that he was keeping his head clear for a fight, and that the hand that kept drifting into his side coat pocket was fingering his razor.

"Oh Daddy," she gushed in her nervousness, "*don't* let them develop the interior any more; it's *horrible* what it's doing to the Indians!"

Her father turned on her his large—for such a small man—face, with its looming forehead and heavy, watery gaze, and said in a voice not so gentle as to veil totally the tone of rebuke, "We have a Bureau of Indian Affairs, Isabel, FUNAI, which receives a generous budget and more than its share of publicity. Indians, Indians, everywhere the government seeks to take a step, there they are, underfoot. Vast lands are set aside—along the Amazon, the Xingú, in the Pantanal—for them to frolic and loaf and conduct their nasty little raids on each other's women in. But, seriously—and I appeal to Mr. Raposo in this—how can the interests of one hundred thousand throwbacks to the dawn of mankind be allowed to hamper the progress of a nation of over one hundred million! Treasure the Indians, yes!

Repent of past atrocities, yes! But is one ignorant, disease-ridden Indian truly worth a thousand civilized men and women? I ask you, sir."

"Of course not," Tristão answered. "But he is worth *one* civilized man or woman, yes? He is a Brazilian, as are we all."

Isabel's father blinked, realizing that an arrow of wisdom, a polite sally, had passed through him, as he took his second sip of very dry gimlet. He smiled, with a kind of blankness Isabel had never before seen in him. "Exactly so."

"Daddy," Isabel intervened. "We lived among Indians for a while, and they couldn't have been nicer. Except for a few exceptions," she added, remembering the Guaicuru who stole away two of her children. She was beginning to feel pregnant again, she suspected by the promiscuously religious *pardovasco*.

"Yes, dear, no doubt." The polished political functionary brushed his daughter's assertion aside. He asked Tristão, "And what took you so far afield, Mr. Raposo? Might you share with me the title of your profession?"

"Knight errant, you could say," Tristão offered, unsmiling, after a pause. "I have been involved in a number of fields—mining, automobile manufacture, boat manufacture, retailing, even, most recently, the music-and-entertainment industry, in a managerial capacity. I am not myself musical, or creative in any palpable way. I have always lived by my wits, and a certain dispassionate ruthlessness."

"Tristão!" Isabel protested, thrilled by her lover's daring honesty.

"Mining, automobile manufacture," her father repeated, as if to give the phrases more weight. The sequence meant something to him, it rang a bell, which would have troubled him but for the alcohol smoothly working in his veins, and his wish that everything concerned with this encounter go well. He was too old, too tired to want unpleasantness. He had explored the limits of power. He had seen fanatics enough in Afghanistan, in Ireland. "My daughter," he confided, "has a taste for adventurers. In the university a few steps from where we sit, she was involved with a boy so revolutionary that only his wealthy father's intervention and voluntary payment of a surtax upon his estates saved the young man from official discipline. And in Rio once, during the Christmas holiday, she . . . But I am embarrassing her. Perhaps I must blame myself. Her hot blood is inherited from me. In my dull way, Mr. Raposo, disguised in the drab motley of the negotiator and the administrator, I, too, have adventured—the trophies of my travels are all about us. Her uncle, my brother, with whom she lived for a number of years, as I am sure she has told you, is quite otherwise—a staid businessman who can hardly bear to venture from Ipanema as far as Leblon. His office, his club, his flat, his mistress's flat . . . that is his round, day after day. When I beg him to visit me here, he says he is frightened of airplanes, and the altitude of Brasília thins his blood and affects his inner ear! Thins his blood! He has become an old woman.

Still, like the spider motionless in the center of his web, Donaciano has many contacts. If you were looking for one more field to conquer, my young friend, and were willing to settle with Isabel in São Paulo, where all our nation's serious business is now being done, it is possible that he and I together might arrange a position that would utilize some of your expertise. What is your view of workers' strikes?"

Tristão glanced toward Isabel for guidance and, seeing little there, just the wine of love sparkling in her gray-blue eyes, told him, "When I was a worker, I did not strike. I could not in truth tell who was a head of the *sindicato* and who was a plant boss. I only knew that my back hurt, and theirs did not."

"Exactly! Evolution, not revolution, don't you think? Change for the better, of course, for all classes, but at a pace that does not destroy the old matrix, yes?"

"Yes. Preserve the matrix."

"What the young call 'the system,' in quotes, like tongs picking up something distasteful. But what is the system but what has evolved, what has emerged from the struggles of men, each man seeking his own self-interest, and by maximizing his own self-interest thus maximizing the glory of the nation?" And he told a long story about himself as a young man, when his wife— God rest her breathtakingly beautiful soul—was still alive, and Isabel was an infant, and how they came to Brasília when it was just a wilderness, an ancient dream sustained by a few dedicated men. . . .

Isabel let her attention wander, since she had heard

the story before, or stories like it. She stood up, the stem of the wineglass like a silver wand in her hand, and the cigarette in her other hand a wand of air, of spirit and sensation. She moved to the windows and looked out upon the cubes of Brasília glowing in the velvet night that had descended. The glowing parallelepipeds, the arrowing expressways, the parabolic monuments to the national history of strife and struggle, all seemed projections of her own inner life, her ability to conceptualize and to love, which was itself a concept. These two men at her back loved her, and when she heard her father's story finally reach its point and Tristão bring forth an appreciative laugh, she turned triumphantly, her abdomen buzzing with its butterflies, to face their double blast of adoration.

But they were ignoring her, excluding her. Tristão was telling, in courteous turn, a story of his own, about the difficulties of discriminating, when he was the bouncer and the doorman for the Mato Grosso Elétrico, between women and transvestites, and his fear that by mistake he would exclude all the real women, who did not look as much like women as the men in drag. And then there had been a dwarf transvestite, and the whole political question of how many dwarfs a night should one admit, or, rather, how many could one exclude, since on the one hand the short people of Bunda da Fronteira formed one of the community's most prickly and vociferous special-interest groups, and on the other hand the normal-sized discotheque customers complained of tripping over them on the dance floor.

Their laughter and talk, male laughter and male talk, tumbled on as their wills playfully wrestled; the whimsical servant brought her a second glass of wine, her father a second gimlet, Tristão a second *vitamina*. The wine began to press on her bladder; the city lights and the nostalgia of being back in Brasília and the strangeness of hearing her father and lover laugh together pressed on her corneas, forming tears. She moved across the living room, catching a glimpse of herself in a piece of mirror tall and slender like one of the sides of the two skyscrapers that housed the Congresso Nacional. She held herself, in her voluminous garb, with her slender neck very straight, as if she were carrying a pot on her head. Shadowy troughs in the shimmering cloth appeared to reverse the colors on the glossy ridges. She was satisfied that she looked, on the verge of thirty, magnificent.

The two men were aware of her, as the magnet that had brought them together. As soon as she was out of earshot in the bathroom Tristão said to Salomão, in a low deliberate voice, "I have described myself as single-minded—that single-mindedness, I want to assure you, is consecrated to your daughter's welfare and happiness."

The older, shorter man blinked, and nodded in gratitude for the affirmation. "As you heard me say, she has had strange tastes in male companionship. Like so many warmhearted young women who have always enjoyed comfort, she lacks understanding of practical limits, of the parameters of the Brazilian matrix."

"She is perhaps wiser now than the college girl you last knew. Tell me, if I may ask—"

"Yes, my dear fellow?" his host said, since Tristão had hesitated.

"Do you see—how can I say?—any physical difference in her?"

Salomão blinked but said nothing.

Tristão pursued awkwardly, "Is her complexion, to be specific, as you remember it? Though I scolded her, she did not always, in our travels, wear a hat in the sun."

The diplomat lifted the heels of his slippers a fraction, broadened his shoulders, and let a twitch of his features forecast the momentousness of what he was about to assert. He spoke as carefully as if the words were memorized, or in a foreign language he had but lately learned. "To a father, a daughter is always perfection. I find Isabel as enchanting as I did when I first saw her, in her sainted mother's arms. Do not worry overmuch about protecting her from the sun; she takes a tan well. Her mother was an Andrade Guimarães, and it was said that the Andrade Guimarãeses, back in Portugal, had acquired a drop of Moorish blood." He held the other man's eyes with his own. "Do you not join me in finding my daughter perfection?"

This man, Tristão noticed, had a meaty upper lip, like Isabel's, and like hers ridged in the middle, but slightly off-center in his case, making his mouth look scarred and quizzical. Tristão said firmly, "Sir, I do. I also

271

loved Isabel at first sight, and each day since that glimpse she has given fresh cause for my love to increase. She is not merely beautiful but brave, and not only brave but resourceful. I have found my fate and the purpose of my life, in loving her. She is perfection."

Salomão heard a grim undertone as the young husband pronounced these insistences, but ascribed it to the well-known melancholy of the Portuguese race; no less an authority than Gilberto Freyre assures us that, had not the early colonizers imported Africans to cheer up their settlements, the whole Brazilian enterprise might have withered of sheer gloom. And yet the Africans themselves suffered such homesick sorrow in the New World that a word was coined for it, *banzo*, a kind of black *saudade*.

Isabel returned from the gleaming grotto of the bathroom, her femininity renewed by gushes of liquids and sprinklings of perfume. She extended a still-moist hand to each man—her father, her lover. "I see no ring," her father said, holding her gift for examination. "Have you children no use for the rites of our spiritual mother the Church?"

"There was a ring," she told him. "A very precious ring, which I traded away, in a moment I beg both of you not to find foolish. It was a beautiful ring that Tristão had given me; it had letters that spelled DAR. We never knew what they might have stood for."

"If I may hazard a guess," her father ventured, "the ring came from one of the most sacred and arcane institutions of the *ianques*—an association of venerated daughters of the soldiers who fought in their uncouth revolution. It would be an epic achievement to wangle one. But I have still some few friends in Washington, as long as Henry Kissinger serves the present President—I will try, I will try."

The fussy, whimsical, mock-modest repetition signalled, for Tristão and Isabel smilingly to appreciate, that he would succeed. Thus Salomão bestowed upon the couple his long-withheld blessing.

xxviii. *São Paulo Again*

Yes, they lived happily then, in São Paulo, first in an apartment in Higienópolis, and then in a house in the Jardim América district, off the Rua Groenlândia, for a dozen years in all. The Leme brothers succeeded in obtaining for Tristão a position in middle management, not at the *fusca* plant where he had tightened engine-mounting bolts opposite gap-toothed Oscar—for *fuscas* were no longer made—but at a textile mill in São Bernardo, one of the so-called ABCD cities, industrial satellites of São Paulo.

The mill was a single vast room where giant looms kept up a clatter which pressed on Tristão's ears with a million small concussions; each noise was smaller than the clashes of metal on metal in the *fusca* factory, but there were many more of them. At first, he tried to understand the intricacies—the warp, the weft, the batten and its beating-in, the ways in which twill differed from plain weave, or tabby, and how variations in lifting the threads of the warp with the heddles produced satin and damask, warp-pile velvet and weft-pile corduroy, and the truly dizzying operation whereby many spinning cones of thread, drawn by a mechanical drawboy controlled by punched cards, could be woven to make elaborately figured fabrics.

The shuttle, that carried the weft threads back and forth under the lifted warps that formed the shed, was the basic awkwardness, he perceived, for at the heart of the weaving there must be this moment of suspension when the shuttle flies, or its flying is imitated by rapiers, by dummy-shuttles, and even by jets of air or water that propel the thread from one edge, called a selvage, of the cloth to the other, making a "pick." Just so, at the heart of our lives lies a supernatural leap, an oscillating unlikelihood. Miraculously, the looms clanked and clattered, repeating the shedding, the picking, and the beating-in with a merciless speed that yet did not snap threads: there was no resistance in the material universe to an inhuman acceleration. The human attendants of the machines, indeed, looked grotesquely lackadaisical and soft, like wet clay dropped here and there, idle spectators who would suddenly spring into action at the depletion of a bright-colored cone or glistening heavy shuttle. The workers, mostly women, wore kerchiefs to keep their long hair from becoming entangled with the machines, which in a flicker of mindless operation would pull their scalps loose from their skulls. Some of these women had Indian blood; others had come with the Japanese immigration, or the Italian before it, or among those varied Middle Eastern peoples lumped as *turcos*, Turks.

And then there was another giant room of the factory, in which the altogether different operation of knitting was carried on by machines built on quite different principles, needles being the fundamental unit, ingeniously bent needles of two types: spring beard and latch, the latch having a tiny pivot closing the needle's loop and permitting the stitch to be cast off. The needles in a variety of gauges ranging from the size of a pencil to that of a mouse whisker were arrayed in bars or circles, cylinders or plates, controlled by moving cams that imitated the motion of knitting over and over and over, gnashing like piranhas, producing sheets or tubes of knitted fabric as coarse as ski sweaters or as seductively filmy as pantyhose. Tristão's attempt at understanding the details of manufacture gave him terrible, million-toothed dreams and lasted but a few weeks; then he perceived that his role was to understand merely his relation to the men above him in the management chain, and those below him, and to fit himself into the organizational motions. Together, like a dim-witted animal that nevertheless knows enough to move toward food, the factory and its employees lumbered toward market; meanwhile, the government heavily rode the animal's back and inflation shackled its feet. Some of the managers interfaced with the market—the fashion experts, the advertising men, the wholesalers, the retailers' representatives—and others with the government, as it extracted its taxes, fine-tuned its price controls, imposed its safety and pollution regulations, accepted its bribes. Still others interfaced with the engineers and the machinery, which needed to be repaired, re-evaluated, and replaced with ever newer, more computerized and robotic equipment. Tristão, as it evolved, interfaced with the workers and their unions.

He had a certain social blankness, with his high solemn brow and unexpectedly dark eyes—the irises melting sorrowfully into the pupils—and a cautious dignity that fit him to the position. Though he was white, *claro*—almost unnaturally so, as if his skin had never seen the sun, or had been bleached by fiat—he lacked the upper-class Paulista accent that the workers and their leaders instinctively hated. He had none of the prissy, languid arrogance of the *filhos do poder*; he seemed, actually, to be the son of no one, and he attended earnestly and carefully to the workers' complaints and the labor unions' schemes for rectification of inequities and elimination of bottlenecks as if striving to puzzle through a maze where he lacked the guidance of prejudice. The whole legitimate modern world seemed something of a puzzle to him, that he must work through step by step. He was patient. He never condescended. Though he grasped, as if once one of them, the harsh monotony of work on the factory floor, he did not attempt, in the fascist manner ascendant during the military rule, to usurp the leadership of the rank and file. He kept on his silvery-gray suit and snow-white collar, visibly a company man, yet rose in prestige with the workers as—beginning with the sit-down strike of a bus factory in 1978 that spread to seventy-eight thousand metalworkers—waves of strikes and defiances effected a revolution in wage increases, safety regulations, health benefits, and employee rights. Mass assemblies thundered their votes in soccer stadiums; union offices moved out from under the wing of government and corporate collusion into the Cathedral of São Bernardo, at the invitation of the newly reform-minded Church. The ultimate bastion against Communism is a bourgeoisfied worker class, and Tristão, whose own bourgeoisfication had about it something skin-deep, served as a kind of enzyme in the process. His neutrality of bearing and accent was like that of an actor on television, which was reassuring to workers who, at even the most abject level of poverty, lived more and more within television's soap operas, newscasts, and quiz shows.

His textile factory emerged from the strikes of 1980 with worker-management relations intact; it had become clear that the old class wars, which had driven capitalism like an engine overheated to the point of explosion, must give way, on a globe dominated by Japanese and German methodology, to arrangements of mutual dependency and satisfaction between government, industry, and the populace. Tancredo Neves' brilliant defeat, in 1985, of the military rulers in the electoral college, and then his stunning death the night before his inauguration, passed in Tristão's clattering, shuttling world with scarcely a dropped stitch. As the years wore on, Tristão ever more patiently (and, it must be confessed,

absent-mindedly) sat listening to the voice of the work
ers with the healing tact and non-committal silence of a
Freudian psychiatrist, whose patient, never cured, is
nevertheless enabled to limp forward under the load of
daily woe. Tristão prospered in his job. He took up the
status-appropriate activities—tennis, jogging, squash,
wind-surfing—and excelled in all, with his limber grace
and latent ferocity. He even seduced a few of his
middle-management colleagues' wives, when it became
clear that this, too, was a game.

Yet he never really felt at home in São Paulo. Except
in his daily commute to the industrial belt, and the
routes to certain favored restaurants and their beach
house in Ubatuba, he was forever getting lost, finding
himself going around on the same viaduct, or circling
the same neighborhood, or one that looked exactly like
it. He could not shake the impression, received on his
first visit nearly twenty years before, that the city had
no limits, no shape, compared with Rio, where the
beaches and the breadloaf mountains pinch the streets to
a series of dainty waists, and a horizon of untamed
nature—bare mountaintop, sun-battered sea—is always
in view. When he and Isabel, as their status befit-
ted, travelled to Paris and Rome, New York and Tokyo,
Buenos Aires and Mexico City, it all seemed to him,
aside from the unmistakable difference between the
Eiffel Tower and the Colosseum, more São Paulo, more
cement-gray people-sprawl, eating up the planet. He
thought back nostalgically upon the emptiness of the
Mato Grosso, when he and Isabel had first traversed it,

with its faint woody tang of some spiritual heartwood, and the flocks of flamingos rising in billows beneath the eastward-drifting outpouring of blue-bottomed clouds, and the upside-down silhouettes of the *pinheiros* beckoning them, from a far rosy cliff, to that night's campsite. He thought of how in their worst extremity her pale body alone had sustained him, with the food of love.

Isabel, patterning herself after spotty girlish memories of her mother and her dashing aunt Luna, went through the motions of being a young housewife of the middle class. To be of the middle class in Brazil is to enjoy what, in countries where wealth is more equitably distributed, would be an aristocratic life-style. Servants are cheaper than appliances, and Isabel had from the start a combination maid and cook, and then employed, when they moved from the Higienópolis apartment to the house off the Rua Groenlândia, a woman to take care of the children. There were three—Bartolomeu, the offspring of the religious *pardovasco*, with Ethiopian eyes and a skin but one shade lighter than her own, and three years later the twins, Aluísio and Afrodísia, nonidentical, but born of the same gush of sperm late at night, between bouts of the lambada at the Som de Cristal, in a broom closet on the way to the ladies' room, out of a man she hardly knew, a business contact of Tristão's at the textile plant, a supplier of polyester thread, and saturnine enough, though racially mostly white, with his tennis tan and brassy big predatory features, to appeal to her. For a few minutes she thought he was a *bandeirante* and she was back in the Mato Grosso. After this indiscretion reaped its alarming double harvest—neither non-identical twin showing a glimmer of Tristão's natural dignity or a wisp of his straight fair hair—Isabel began to practice birth control, by sleeping with no one but her husband.

She had long since realized that a price for the intensity of their love was sterility. Their spiritual ardor burned away the natural consequences of physical union. Whether he with other women might have become a father—or indeed was, and that somewhere in some jungle or other a little brown Tristão was padding, with bright frog-eyes, through the sensitive early years of his life—interested her rather abstractly, as belonging to some other story. In the story which was hers, in the life given to her to live, and which was now rushing on, it seemed to her, at a terrifying pace, she found herself touched by a certain pity for Tristão, a sense of him as her victim, as if it had been she, not he, who had made the approach on Copacabana Beach. She had worn a pale two-piece suit, daring for the times, that made her look naked from a distance. Certainly it was she who had conspired with a magician to turn him white, so he could be accepted by her father and give her a comfortable life. *You are in no danger from me,* he had assured her on the beach, though he radiated menace, and a desperate freedom. But had he been in danger from her? The very docility with which he put on his gray suit each morning and drove his gray, second-hand Mercedes-Benz out through the expanding maze of the city to the plant in São Bernardo afflicted her with guilt, so that she sometimes asked him, abruptly of an evening, when they had returned from a dinner party or an opera:

"Do you miss it, the freedom and excitement of the old days, before you met me?"

Pausing in removing his pleated shirt, placing the cufflinks and tieclip in the small bureau drawer where such things were kept, he gave the question his usual heartbreaking solemn attention. "It was the life of a street dog," he said. "I would have been killed, by the police or another street dog, within a few years. With you in my life, there was hope, and a goal. I did not even mind the backbreaking years in the mine, when I had you to return to. Remember, how I would sit outside as darkness came and chip the rocks and pan for the pieces of gold, while you inside made our meal, or cleaned up afterwards, and settled our children into bed? I have never been happier, Isabel."

"Oh, don't, Tristão!" she cried, tears having started to her eyes, erupting as violently as semen. "Don't make me better than I am! I have made you into an artificial man! Your work now—honestly, isn't it meaningless and dreadful? Don't you hate me, honestly?"

His voice remained soft, withheld a bit from passion, perhaps delicately to punish her. "No, my work is very interesting. It deals with men—men and women, of course I mean, though women with corporate power are still rare—who must be brought into a singleness of purpose, to make a future world. We are seeing the end of slaves and masters in Brazil, and I, who have little competence, can help here, having been both. As to hating you, it would cancel my life to hate you. The Amazon would flow backward to the Andes were I to hate you. You are my love-slave, my blue-eyed *negrinha*."

And he stepped closer, there in their bedroom with its cushions and curtains and framed photographs of themselves on vacation and their children in school uniforms, and stood where she was sitting on her satin-covered dressing-table stool so she could see the bulge his yam was making behind his fly, and sense its warmth, and touch its hardness with her fingertips, and then with her lips, through the tuxedo's black cloth. They rarely made love any more, like a rich couple that rarely resorts to visiting their safe-deposit box; but when they did, their treasure was still there, and never quite the same, as if the box had been shaken in their absence.

Her life was constantly busy, and yet its content could hardly be described. She gave orders to the help, and gave affection to the children when they were presented to her, in their school uniforms or pajamas. She planned Tristão's evening meals, and saw that the lazy, sluttish maids—one after another, all *nordestinas*—did not outrageously neglect the housekeeping, or screw the garden boy in the potting shed. Isabel shopped for clothes, at Fiorucci and Huis Clos, and planned the trips she and Tristão would take to foreign cities. She, too, played tennis, though it was the chatty, catty luncheons with her female companions afterwards that were the

283

point of the sport—around umbrellaed outdoor tables, in sweated-up whites, with cotton cardigans draped around their shoulders becomingly, showing off their bare arms.

But it was no longer fashionable to be idle rich in the style of Uncle Donaciano. Men, even rich men, worked, and women younger than Isabel worked, too. Work had become chic. For her, it was a little late. Her education had been frittered away in titillating talk of revolution; the Mato Grosso had been her graduate school, teaching survival in a vanished world. A sweet silence surrounded her past; her new friends never asked her where she had gone to school, or what her life previous to marrying Tristão had been. They assumed that she had slept her way up from the slums into the upper-middle class. Her blue eyes heightened her social charm, but were not strictly needed. The Portuguese, lacking the northern European's superstitious fear of blackness, never disowned Africa; the Brazilian disowns only the immense black poverty, and the criminality it breeds. Isabel, so lovely in her manners, so piquant in her vivacity, reassured everyone that their society was producing such ebony ornaments. She became active in charity affairs, and was often photographed in the papers, a darker set of halftone specks among the lighter. Everyone loved her—loved them both, for their essential monogamy in a world where everything stable is slipping, everything sacred is mocked, and appetite erodes everything from within, hollowing out entire corporations and companies that, like capybara corpses whose guts have been invisibly consumed by rapacious vermin, collapse with a puff of ill-smelling smoke. Inflation, resurging, approached one thousand percent; the Big Boys had sold Brazil's future to the international banks, and had spent the money on themselves.

In these years there were for Tristão and Isabel promotions at work, renovations at home, little crises in health, an automobile accident or two, vacations, and the steady rise of Bartolomeu, Aluísio, and Afrodísia in the fashionable Catholic schools they attended. And there was a funeral: Isabel's father died, of arteriosclerosis and myocarditis induced by overwork and the cumulative strain of all the derangements of the body incidental to his years abroad. For some years, he had not been well, in his body or his mind. His hiring a Rastafarian fool for a servant had been one of the first signs of deterioration. All the information in his top-heavy brain, the languages and protocols and subtleties of past intrigue, became scrambled toward the end. Among his effects, surprisingly, they found the gold nugget that Tristão had gouged from the Serra do Buraco and that had been last seen in the care of the coöperative bank; it had found its way into the care of the Assistant Minister of Interior Development. With it there was a confused note: *Devote half the proceeds to the education of my son or if it is too late for that of my grandson Pacheco*. Pacheco? The name rang a faint bell for Tristão, but he could not quite place it. Further, they needed all the money they could inherit. Salomão's death made them less additionally rich than they had expected. Money, in the form of numbers occasionally trimmed by governmental redecimalization to counter the insatiable inflation, came and went in their bank account, and was never quite enough, or as much as their friends appeared to have. There were dental appointments, teas, dinner parties, confirmations, graduations, school soccer matches, and children's recitals to attend. The banality, the brightly masked tedium, of bourgeois life—taletellers remain balked by it. Though this chapter covers the greatest stretch of time, let it be no longer than it is!

xxix. *The Apartment Again*

AN ODD THING had happened to Uncle Donaciano. Divorce had become legal in 1977, and a decade later he had, after all those years of unacknowledged cohabitation, divorced Aunt Luna and married his housekeeper and cook, Maria. Within a year she had left him, no one could imagine why. He seemed fated to romantic failure. Isabel felt sorry for him, and her visits to her bachelor uncle, and to Rio, become more frequent.

On this fateful occasion, Isabel persuaded Tristão to come with her, in the several days of vacation that the textile plant allowed after Christmas. They considered bringing along the children but agreed that Rio under its holiday sun offered pre-teens too much opportunity for mischief. Crime, vice, homelessness, and public nudity were rampant. Their children had grown to become spoiled, sheltered Paulistanos, and their sulky and rebellious presence in the apartment would be difficult for their childless, aging host.

Uncle Donaciano welcomed them warmly, gratefully—he had aged, at the blow to his pride from his second wife. His hair, slicked back to an occipital point such as can be seen on the head-crests of some tropical birds, was streaked with gray now—striped, really, with an odd regularity that seemed achieved by a mechanical vanity—and his hands shook with the effect of too many sunset gins. His charm had withered to something like a maiden aunt's, a matter of doddery hesitations and an automatic, bemused, rather pleading habit of deference.

In his apartment, the two crystal candlesticks Isabel and Tristão had stolen so long ago had been replaced with a pair nearly identical, and the huge chandelier still hung like a vast holy spider, with curved brass S's for legs, from the center of a domed rose of frosted glass. To Tristão, the space still had the radiant stillness of a church, but the furnishings, the fringed pillows and cloisonné vases and gold-stamped backs of never-opened books, no longer seemed fabulous but faintly shabby and dated, belonging to a bygone era of luxurious decoration. He and his São Paulo friends went in now for a rougher, squarer look, of tans and off-whites in coarse weaves, of low lamps that make circular pools of dull light—the look, in fact, of a modern office, though softer, and without quite so much gleam of plastic-encased computer gadgetry. Compared with such modular chambers, these rooms seemed to compose a latticed harem, cushioned to receive diaphanously clad female bodies that were, disappointingly, not there.

"I think, concerning Maria," the old gentleman tried

to explain, when the raspy red Argentine dinner wine and garlicky, ducky richness of *pato ao tucupi* had worked to loosen their tongues and create social ease, "she preferred the clear though modest wages of the servant to the larger but vaguer rewards of a wife. I urged her to spend money upon herself—her clothes, her hairdo, manicures, health spas—but she took each suggestion as a veiled implication that I found her messy, underdressed, common, and rather fat—which, in truth, I did. Nevertheless, she could have ignored my suggestions, taken them or left them, much as she took or left me before we wed. But in becoming her husband, I became somehow aggravating, as if I was now a part of herself over which she had no control, like a cancer. My smoking, upon which she had never let drop a single critical word, that time suddenly became a source of worry and pain to her, and a matter of constant nagging. She became, in truth, a nag on many matters, when she had been before so soothingly phlegmatic. The girls I hired to replace her simply could not please her; they were dishonest, sluttish, careless, designing, empty-headed—the litany was endless, none could satisfy her, I fired them one a week, it seemed. And yet, in the intervals, when Maria herself took over the duties that had been hers, she complained that her becoming my wife had made no difference, except that she no longer got paid. Even the sex between us— forgive me, Isabel, for such details, but you are an old married woman by now—became grudging and stilted on her part, where she had readily yielded before, to the most peremptory demand. It was as if, alas, the brute authority of an employer aroused her in a way the more complicated figure of a husband could not. Her note to me, on her disappearance, simply read, in her barely literate but beautifully formed hand, 'This asks of me too much.' "

"Tristão and I find," Isabel volunteered, challenged by his reference to her being an old married woman, "that it sometimes helps our sex if we pretend we have never met before, and just happen to be in the same room."

Her uncle looked flustered and embarrassed by this detail. Teasingly, she continued to instruct him: "Women, too, resent the tyranny of sex, and the necessity to make lasting social attachments to what was meant by nature, perhaps, to be a passing fit. Women and men occupy two different realms—their mating is like the moment when a bird seizes a fish."

"I understand," Tristão said, more practically, "you used to beat Maria."

"Very rarely," the embarrassed former dandy hastened to claim. "Once or twice, possibly, in the fury of my younger days. The women I used to be entangled with were infuriating flirts, and I would bring my frustrations home to my one constant and faithful mistress."

"It could be," Tristão offered, "barbaric as this seems, that she took your failure to beat her, once she became your wife, as a sign of lack of affection, and the perverse behavior you describe was an attempt to provoke you into using your fists. The poor grow such thick skins, the loving touch has to be heavy." He was thinking, Isabel lovingly perceived, of his own mother in saying this, as a way of justifying her rough treatment of him.

Before Uncle Donaciano could change the subject, Isabel took the opportunity to ask, "Aunt Luna—why did she leave you, do you think?"

A silence fell upon her uncle, making his face look more fragile than ever, and shadowy, as it had those evenings in her childhood when he would come into her room to read her a story and seal with a kiss his wish that her dreams be sweet. In the silence, Maria's present replacement languidly brought in their dessert, *fruta-do-conde* with honeydew sherbet, in long-stemmed tulip glasses. "I have never understood that," Uncle Donaciano at last confessed. "Your aunt's defection is the failure of my life. She was past her youthful bloom, and has not found happiness away from me, my informants in Paris tell me. A few flings with married men who could not quite bear to leave their wives, and then some younger men who take advantage of her money, and now there is nothing for her, not even the Church, for she had no faith."

In the long pause, Tristão, to be polite, said, in his serious, businesslike voice, "Faith is necessary. Otherwise, there are too many decisions, and each one seems too important."

But Uncle Donaciano continued to gaze at Isabel; his face, refined and fatigued, seemed pitted with shadows of undeclared yearning, as on those nights when he would tuck her in. He continued, "There were *two* romantic failures of my life. The second was that your mother never treated me with a particle more than the proper courtesy a woman owed her brother-in-law."

"Perhaps the one failure explains the other," Isabel pointed out. "Aunt Luna sensed your love of my mother."

But no, here, at this so obvious gate of truth, the old man balked, and he shook his head obstinately. "No. She never knew. I scarcely knew myself."

"Oh, *do* tell me about my mother!" Isabel cried, with a vivacity that irritated Tristão. He saw in her too much red wine, and a giddiness at being away from her children for a night or two, and a girlish wish to flatter her uncle by travelling with him back into the past. She held her mouth open as if to display to her uncle her arched, velvety tongue. "Am I like her?"

Steadily, sadly, Donaciano gazed at his niece, with her majestic sheaf of frizzy hair and her gold-hoop earrings and her slender black arms—an iridescent brown, the color of burnt sugar—glittering halfway to her elbows with bangles. Her dress was an armless and unbelted jade-green sheath that concealed and flattered her body. She had gained weight, but no more than five pounds. "You are her essence, crossed with the Leme determination," he stated. "She was the kind of woman who was fit only to lie about in a harem. The Andrade Guimarãeses had Moorish blood, it was said. She could do nothing—not cook an egg, not write a letter, not organize a party. She could do nothing to help your father's career. She could not even, the second time, manage the labor of childbirth. Even when she was alive, Isabel, she left your mothering up to the servants, and to Luna. When my wife was around you, she was very affectionate. In your decisiveness and nervous temper, you take after Luna; but in your voluptuous essence, you are the ineffable Cordélia."

With an impulsiveness she was sure her husband would find lovable, Isabel reached out across the corner of the dining table—to be shared by both men, she had been seated at the head—and seized Tristão's pale hand in her fingers, which by candlelight seemed as dark, below their pale nails, as the tarry sweet *cafezinhos* that had been served in little upright cups. "Hear that, Tristão? We are alike in having bad mothers!"

"My mother was not bad. She did her best, given the limits of her oppressed condition," he said sullenly.

She would not be denied a reconnection with him. She felt him sliding away, but would not have it. "See! We share that, too. We loved them! We loved our bad mothers!"

Uncle Donaciano, his thin mustache eclipsed by the rim of his lifted coffee cup, glanced from one to the other of his young guests, sensing their tiny struggle, here in this setting more congenial to one than the other. He said peaceably, "We are all children of the Earth, and she is a bad mother, it could be said. It is our triumph to love her, to love existence."

They sat up late, Isabel and her uncle reminiscing about her mother, about the days when Rio was like a glass of Venetian crystal, about the trips to Petrópolis to escape the summer heat. Petrópolis! The splendid imperial gardens where Dom Pedro himself once strolled with the Empress Teresa Christine and their headstrong daughter, the famous Isabel, who defiantly danced with the mulatto engineer André Rebouças and as Princess Regent decreed the end of slavery. Ah, the city's canals and bridges, squares and parks, virtually European in their finish and charm; the Gothic cathedral and the precise copy of London's Crystal Palace; the mountain vistas from the restaurant, including a threadlike waterfall! Eagerly Isabel remembered with her uncle's help those enchanted days of family holiday, when her father sat beside her at the snowy tablecloth and gaunt, amusing Aunt Luna showed her which forks to use. She had been a precious girl in starched voile ruffles, surrounded by bowing waiters and distant music and a glittering, flowery, watery matrix: Brazil, a Europe without strain, without guilt. Ah, the day the tent blew down in the hotel garden; the day Senhora Wanderley's white poodle bit the barbecue cook; the day Marlene Dietrich and an entourage of local Krauts dined at La Belle Meunière!

Tristão, listening, grew restless; he had little to contribute. Their world had not been his world. In São Paulo, he had created a past, and among their friends could reminisce to the depth of twelve years. But now, except when Uncle Donaciano turned and made a deliberate effort to include him in a general topic ("And what do you in industry think will come of the newest price freeze?" "Are you younger men as alarmed as I at the prospect of free elections for President?"), Tristão had little to do but puff on a Cuban cigar and slump deeper into his creaking leather armchair and stretch out his legs, trying to suppress their tremors of muscular agitation. In his enforced idleness he studied Isabel, dewy-faced, lost in her dream of childhood, imagining an idyll for herself. She had taken off her shoes and bared her feet, her elegant two-tone Negro feet, and tucked them up beneath her on the curvaceous crimson sofa. Tristão felt the warmth between her and her uncle as oppressive, as subtly noxious, like the cigar smoke. This had been her world, an enchanted world. *What had she wanted of me?* he smokily wondered. Nothing but his yam. The yam of a stranger. To do nature's dirty work.

At last their host, his striped hair standing up in loose feathers, doddered toward bed, and the couple made their way to their own bedroom, on the duplex's second floor, beyond her old girlhood room, which Maria during her brief tenure as wife had turned into storage space. Their windows were splashed to the top with Rio's champagne lights. Tristão said, "My love, would you mind if I took a walk? I am a bit sick on the cigar. I am not used to cigars, or to so much dinner conversation."

"We bored you, I know, darling. Forgive us. My uncle will not be with us forever, and it amuses him to think of the old days. He is afraid of the future. He is sure that, if there is a popular election, the Communists will win. The Communists or some idiotic television personality. He is a poor frightened old man." Sensing that in some way she had offended Tristão, Isabel moved across the bedroom to him; her green sheath dress was off, and her white underwear made two violent interruptions of her skin. "He is the only person I know now," she told him, in a throaty seductive voice, "who remembers me as I was, when I was ... innocent."

"He knows," Tristão told her. "He knows that I in my gray suit am the same black trash he forbade his niece to go with twenty-two years ago. He knows, but can't do anything about it."

"He doesn't want to do anything about it," Isabel told Tristão, caressing his face, trying to rub the crease of anger from his tall forehead with her thumb. "He sees I am happy, and that is all he wants." Tristão's fine straight oak-colored hair was thinning back, making his brow even higher. Tenderly she stroked his bared temples.

Her insistent attempt to soothe him irritated him, and he snapped his head to shake off her hand. Her hand bore on its third finger the substitute DAR ring her father had succeeded in obtaining from Washington, as he had promised; but it was not as good, as well-engraved and antique as the ring he had stolen from the blue-haired gringa in Cinelândia, and this, too, irritated him. "Not just your uncle was infatuated with the past. You, too, were overjoyed to remember what was, all that luxury built on misery. You sank into it, out of my reach."

"But I have returned, Tristão," she said. "I am within your reach." Steadily watching his offended face—as if, unwatched, he might strike her—she bent over to slip off her underpants, one leg at a time. Her expression was that of a spying black girl, with widened eye whites, who is frightened yet about to laugh, if she receives the smallest permission. But for her pale eyes she looked, with her watchful monkey face, her bushy hair, like one of the ragged playmates he had known back in the *favela*, the one he had liked most, Esmeralda. He gave a small smile of permission, and Isabel laughed, and straightened her body from its careful crouch. Her triangle of glistening black hair showed that her skin was merely brown, pale by contrast. Her navel was like the dimple in the underside of a brown bowl, with two thick handles—her hips, curved outward like great roasted cashews. When he put his hand on her rump here, his hand was, he saw, another shade of brown, tanned from tennis and wind-surfing. The hair on its back had a coppery tinge.

"I enjoyed watching you and your uncle," he told her, in a voice fallen wearily into its manly timbre. "There is true affection between you, based on blood and shared memories. I am not in the least angry. I am melancholy, being so close to my old home. . . ."

"Tristão. There is nothing here. The *favela* was razed to make a botanical garden and a tourist outlook."

They had gone, once when in Ipanema, to the shop of Apollonio de Todi, but the crystal candlestick, as far as the imperfect records showed, had never been hocked for redemption. *Keep my gift, if you prefer, and light a candle against our return some dark night.*

"And if you did find them," she added cautiously, "they would not know you."

"Yes," he sighed. "How sensible you are, Isabel, when it comes to my past and not your own. But you must let me have a little walk around the block. My calves are cramping, my head is stuffy. I will be back in a matter of minutes. Compose yourself for sleep, my dearest. I will take a key, and if you are not still awake, I will slip into your dreams. I will be naked."

She came closer and on tiptoe pushed her warm lips up into his. "Go out. But be careful," she said, seriously.

He was surprised. Careful in his own city? How old had he become? She was forty, he forty-one. Looking back at her, as she slipped off her brassiere and jokingly posed for him beside their wide white bed in the jaunty posture of a naked *boîte* dancer, he remembered her asking once, *You still like me?* The sight of her sucked at him powerfully, but he went out the door.

xxx. *The Beach Again*

T HE AIR IN THE TROPICS suggests, during the day, that nothing can be accomplished, that decay and lassitude are man's lot. But at night the air feels full of excitement and potential action. Some humid perfumed promise waits in it to be realized.

The old Japanese behind the desk of green marble nodded deferentially as the gentleman passed in his silvery-gray suit. Tristão pushed open the transparent door, and salt air like the kiss of a spirit greeted his nostrils. He walked toward the distant music from the nightclubs and strip joints along Copacabana Beach. The shops of Ipanema were shuttered; the doormen of the apartment buildings stood behind their transparent doors like visitors to an aquarium through whose murky waters Tristão swam. A few restaurants were lit up for business, and the automatic tellers of the banks glowed sleeplessly, but there was little foot traffic to go with the swish of automobiles, though it was not quite midnight. On the Copacabana side of the fort, there was more light, more activity, at the mouths of the great hotels, where tourists came and went in taxis yellow and green like parakeets and store windows illumined from underneath the gems and minerals—tourmaline and amethyst, topaz and rubellite—culled from the mountains of the Minas Gerais.

At outdoor tables a mixture of the poor and rich, the bought and the buyers, waited for the night's transaction, while chattering over their sweet intense coffees as if life and time demanded no reckoning. Along these tables he and Euclides used to cruise, skimming tips from the saucers, and looking for a dangling purse whose leather straps might be slashed in a second. Up the shadowy side streets off Avenida Atlântica, the drunken tourists, stumbling downstairs warm with a sense of well-being after half an hour with a mulatta whore, were as easy to tumble and shear as stunned sheep.

Now he himself, striding along in his gray suit unaccompanied, caused young women wearing costumes of a toylike frivolity and skimpiness to float forward as if magnetized, and a man or two as well, in jeans as tight as paint and with a face painted almost as carefully and ornately as that of an Indian. Tristão strode undeviatingly on the tessellated sidewalk of wavy black-and-white strips; the night air, its kiss and shiver of excitement, the snatches of samba and forró and hilarity drifting entwined with the fragrances of coffee and beer and cheap perfume, was all he wanted, to clear his head of the stale smoke of Isabel's past, the smoldering truth that there was more of her than he ever could possess. And the realization, which had helped to depress him back in the apartment, that his attempt to possess her had twisted his life into a shape there was no changing, ever—a guilty shape, somehow, stained with murder and desertion.

He wanted his head to be cleared of such muddled, useless thoughts. Tristão, too, craved the old innocence. He had crossed the *avenida* and stepped from the sidewalk into the sand. He sat on a bench, removed his black laced shoes and silk ribbed socks, and hid them in a patch of beach-pea near the bench. How marvellous it was that these small clumps of beach-pea and sea-grape grew here, in 1988 as in 1966, despite all the feet that had passed this way.

To his bare soles the sand felt tepid on top and cool beneath a thin skin of sun-warmed grains. On the stretches of illuminated beach several soccer games were being played by the spindly, agitated silhouettes of abandoned children. Tristão moved down toward the shadows where the sea, cresting and collapsing, made lines of foam. The sea's incessant rhythmic noise, its moist breathing while it slept, overlaid the tinnier sounds of traffic and music, without quite drowning them out.

The Southern Cross, like an imperfect kite, small and fragile and lacking a center star, hung low in the moonless sky. Overhead, where the night glow of Copacabana permitted them to prick through, other stars upheld their random rigid patterns, their ancient phosphorescence. In the small waves collapsing at Tristão's feet, a less steady phosphorescence winked and slid under, as the beach blotted the wave. These lights were like spirits, they *were* spirits, it seemed to Tristão, alive as was he. He walked along through the wavering ghost of sliding foam, feeling the saturated sand suck at his bare feet, sinking deeper or less deep, the odd tongue of water licking his ankles—all sensations from childhood, when this beach and the view from the shack were the only luxuries of his life.

Then, in a place where the lights of the bustling beachfront were especially distant, so that to his expanded pupils the wavering foam had an intimate brilliance of its own, a human shadow was in front of him, and two more were behind. A medium-sized knife reflected starlight on its flat side. "Your watch," a boy's fragile, panicky voice said, in English, adding, to be safe, *"Ihr Armbanduhr."*

"Don't be a *pentelho*," Tristão told the sudden presence. "I am one of you."

His deep and easy Carioca accent made his assailant falter, but not change attack. "Your watch, your wallet, credit cards, cuff links, everything, quickly," the boy said, adding as if to keep his childish voice from rising out of control, "You *filho da puta!*"

"You mean to insult me, but you speak simply the truth," Tristão told him. "Go home to your own whorish mamas, and I will not hurt you." His adult voice trembled, as the adrenaline of combat rushed to his chest. He felt the point of a second knife between his shoulder blades, and the hand of a third boy, quick and silent as a gecko on the wall, crept into his coat's breast pocket

302

and lifted out the billfold. This impudent delicacy, as if one of the children he had never had were playing with Papa's clothes, both tickled and enraged Tristão. A car on the distant avenue turned around, and by the flick of its headlights he saw the face of the shadow before him—the glinting face, glazed by a betranced nervous tension, of a young black male. Tristão even could read the boy's dark T-shirt, which in white letters proclaimed BLACK HOLE, a new nightclub somewhere. "You want my watch? Here is my watch." Holding his hands high, like a *xangô* dancer, Tristão stripped off the flexible band, let them see that it was a Rolex, the heavy wrist-band alternating gold and platinum, and flipped it into the sea, the firmament of phosphorescence.

"*Porra!*" exclaimed the boy in front of him, in simple wonder.

The knife at Tristão's back had felt dull, like a stick or a knuckle, but it slipped through his coat and skin as easily as a razor, painlessly in the first instant, then with a burning that rapidly swelled, into an insult too severe to bear. He reached toward his belt for his razor, but there was no razor, Gem had been his friend in another life, and he laughed, wanting to explain this and so much else to the boys, who could have been his sons, but who, frenzied with the terror and magnitude of what they were doing, but all striking to express their solidarity, slashed and stabbed at the crouching, toppling white man, as a lesson to all such white men who think they still can own the world. There were sounds, here where the sea noisily sighed, as victim and murderers grunted with effort, and metal struck bone.

Tristão's body fell into a surge of foam, which rapidly receded, tumbling him over once and no more. The boys, frantically thinking to hide his body in the sea, attempted to kick and drag him into the next wave, but, still alive, he grabbed the ankle of one in a grip as powerful as a torque wrench, and the child, only twelve, screamed as if seized by a ghost. Then he was released. He and his friends fled, their bare feet making frantic spurts of sand, and scattered, each melting down a different corridor of darkness across the hustling Avenida Atlântica.

Tristão, feeling the warm, pulsing saltwater replace his outflowing blood, fainted and died. His body slopped back and forth between the wrack and a sandbar five meters away, which refused to let him be carried toward the horizon, but held him, there where the desultory breakers hit with enough force to make spray in the moonlight; the foaming water kept fondly slinging him, in his gray suit blackened by the wet, up to the line of wrack, and tumbling him back again.

Isabel, who had sunk rapidly into sleep beneath the weight of the red wine, woke from a dream in which her children, the dead or disappeared three mingled with the pampered three back in São Paulo, had been besieging her, needing something—breakfast, clean clothes to wear to school, money for cassette tapes—that she was too paralyzed to provide. She hung in the midst of their strained faces feeling a gathering dread. In her dream they were all the same age, as high as her waist, though some had never reached that height, and others had grown beyond it. The unbearable pressure of their demands snapped her body's peace; she awoke, and her dread attached to the vacancy beside her in the bed, where Tristão had promised to be, naked. The space, explored first by a tentative, flirtatious foot and then by a groping, panicked hand, was cool and unwrinkled.

She rose and wrapped a long white chenille robe, which had belonged to Aunt Luna and still hung in the guest bathroom, around her own nakedness and searched the apartment. She walked the balcony and pushed open the doors and looked down to see if her husband was curled on the sofa. The clocks said five-fifteen. She telephoned the desk downstairs; the sleepy Japanese said the gentleman had gone out a little before midnight but had not returned. She knocked at her uncle's door. He was impossible to rouse; he took pills and wore earplugs and an eye mask. Isabel went in and reached into his bed's warmth and shook him awake. At first, he was disposed to dismiss Tristão's absence as a male peccadillo, to be cleared up by a sheepish morning return and a cleansing marital brawl, but her tears and wailing, with an unanswerable force of premonition behind them, led him at last to call the police.

The police of Rio are overworked, and paid in money whose worth constantly erodes. As with police the world over, proximity to corruption has corrupted them; the endless poor exasperate them; in the *favelas* they have surrendered the enforcement of order to the drug dealers. They are overwhelmed by our propensity for sin and disorder, by the falling away of religious restraints. And yet there was a man on duty, who after a weary time away from the phone returned to say that no one answering Tristão's description existed on their records of the night. He, too, was inclined to take lightly a case of a wandering husband, but consented, upon being repeatedly reassured of Uncle Donaciano's importance and high connections, to send an officer. Isabel could not wait. Pausing only to put on tan sandals, naked beneath her robe, she strode as if with a sleepwalker's blind determination the transverse blocks to Copacabana, while her uncle, who had thrown on suit trousers and a white shirt without a tie, pantingly tried to keep up with her and to talk reason and hope.

But there was a stony beseeching hollowness within Isabel that knew how to satisfy itself; she must move forward until this terrible mortar within her found its pestle.

The nocturnal scurry of the *boîtes* was breaking up, the revellers emerging into the open with slackened faces and flimsy spangled costumes and ears ringing with spent ecstasies. A few taxis were moving, their headlights looking increasingly dim and unnecessary. A few early runners were already out, in jogging suits against the morning chill. Night's indistinct clouds now had clear blue shapes—rounded castles, a line of horse heads cut off at the shoulders—against a sky not yet

rose but a paling gray-brown beyond the humped islands, the sword-sharp horizon.

Yes, he would have walked here, this sand where
their youthful footprints were lost among millions of
others, and hid his shoes where she now found them,
hidden in a tuft of beach-pea. He would have walked
along the sea's waving skirts like a boy, thinking of
himself as he had been, before she had imposed a miracle upon him. From afar she saw, like a clump of kelp,
a dark interruption in the pale highway of sea foam and
tilted soaked beach reflecting, with a glaze of saturation
that came and went like breath's mist, the brightening
sky. She did not halt, nor did she run toward the
kelplike interruption, but took off her sandals and strode
in what she imagined as Tristão's deep, spongy steps,
though they had been utterly erased.

He was face down, his flawless teeth bared in a little
polite snarl, his hand curled near his chin in the childish
way he had when he slept. His eyes, half-open, with his
irises lifted out of sight beneath his lids, had the lustre
of shell fragments that are washed up on shore. His bare
feet, as the water tirelessly broke and swirled around
them, had dug their toes into the sand, his ankles locked
at right angles in death. *Fidelity,* his stiff body said,
clinging there to the beach.

Uncle Donaciano caught up to her, and a chubby,
very young policeman was with him. A crowd collected
in the dawn light: dancers and waiters and taxi drivers
and pleasure girls done for the night, bankers and bou-
tique owners and housewives beginning their day with

a run along Copacabana. A forest of thin brown legs had sprouted. A wrinkled old vendor, his unshaven bristle white against the burnt hide of his face, had already manned his sidewalk stand and was selling coconut milk and Coca-Cola and yesterday's cold *empadinhas* to those with appetites. One black boy, with buglike eyes, brought Tristão's emptied billfold, from where it had been dropped along the curb, and looked to the policeman, and then to Isabel, and lastly to Uncle Donaciano for his reward. Receiving a pastel sheaf of cruzeiros, he scampered away, sand flying like wings at his heels. The murderers had superstitiously left in the billfold a photograph of teen-aged Isabel and Tristão with their heads together in a booth on Corcovado, and a St. Christopher medal thin as a razor blade. Had she given it to him, in her girlish piety, those ardent furtive first weeks? In the air there were questions, expressions of interest and sorrow, and a general expectation, focused on Isabel; the crowd waited to hear her wail and keen, giving memorable expression to her grief. Yet the feelings inside her were of a severe formality, like pieces of antique carving, worn and chipped but still testifying to an established symmetry.

She remembered a story she had once read, in the early days at the Serra do Buraco, before she became involved with the manicurists and had borne Azor and Cordélia. To fill her lonely days in the miner's shack she perused the pieces of narrative, crumpled and greasy, in which the tools and supplies came packed to the mountain, mostly concerning the amorous adventures and scandals of the famous. One of them told of a woman, long ago, who, her lover dead, lay down beside him and willed herself to die, and did. She did die, to show her love.

The body of Tristão had been dragged higher on the sand, to wait for the ambulance. Sand grains adhered to the corneas of his open eyes, and sugared his grimacing lips. She lay down beside him and kissed his eyes, his lips. A bitter seaweedy taste already flavored his skin. The crowd sensed the grand thing she was attempting, and grew reverentially hushed. Only her uncle marred the hush, crying out, "For God's sake, Isabel!" in sheer embarrassment at this vulgar display of Brazilian romanticism.

She inched her body higher and opened her robe so Tristão's marble face rested against her warm bosom, and curled one arm around him in his dank, drying suit, and asked her heart to stop. She waited to ride her lover's body like that of a dolphin into the submarine realm of death. She knew what a man about to fuck feels, his soul stretched to enter a voluptuous darkness.

But the rising sun continued to redden her shut lids, and the chemicals within her continued their fathomless commerce, and the crowd grew bored. There would be no miracle today. Eyes still shut, Isabel could hear people resuming conversations and drifting off; a distant ambulance, like an evil clown with its self-important, popping bleat, pierced the hum of humankind to come for Tristão, the piece of litter he had become. The spirit is strong, but blind matter is stronger. Having absorbed this desolating truth, the dark-eyed widow staggered to her feet, tightened her robe about her nakedness, and let her uncle lead her home.

Afterword

Two great books have gone into the making of this small one: *Rebellion in the Backlands* [*Os Sertões*], by Euclides da Cunha (translated by Samuel Putnam), and *Tristes Tropiques*, by Claude Lévi-Strauss (translated by John Russell). *Through the Brazilian Wilderness*, by Theodore Roosevelt, is perhaps not a great book, but I found it entertaining and informative. Also useful were *Red Gold*, by John Hemming; *The Masters and the Slaves*, by Gilberto Freyre (translated by Samuel Putnam); *Brazil*, by Elizabeth Bishop and the editors of *Life*; and two guidebooks to the country, in the Real Guide and Lonely Planet series, by many youthful, venturesome contributors. Joseph Bédier's *The Romance of Tristan and Iseult* (translated by Hilaire Belloc and Paul Rosenfeld) gave me my tone and basic situation. And I took courage and local color from the truly Brazilian fiction of Joachim Machado de Assis, Graciliano Ramos, Clarice Lispector, Rubem Fonseca, Ana Miranda, Jorge Amado, and Nélida Piñon. Thanks to Luiz Schwarcz and his colleagues at Companhia Das Letras in São Paulo, many errors and implausibilities were corrected; if many remain, the fault is mine.

J.U.

JOHN UPDIKE